# Slash of Crimson
# &
# Other Tales

# Slash of Crimson
# &
# Other Tales

*Carl R. Moore*

Cover art: Aaron Drown Design

Cover art in this book copyright © 2017 Aaron Drown Design & Seventh Star Press, LLC.

Editor: Margie Colton

Published by Seventh Star Press, LLC.

ISBN Number: 978-1-941706-59-6

Seventh Star Press
www.seventhstarpress.com
info@seventhstarpress.com

Publisher's Note:
*Slash of Crimson and Other Tales* is a work of fiction. All names, characters, and places are the product of the author's imagination, used in fictitious manner. Any resemblances to actual persons, places, locales, events, etc. are purely coincidental.

Printed in the United States of America

**First Edition**

# Acknowledgments

I wish to take a moment here to express my heartfelt gratitude to some amazing people—first, I am lucky beyond words to have the love and support of my wife Sarah and daughters Madeline and Isabel. Without you, I am not. This particular book must next thank Jerry Benns and Margaret L. Colton, without whom the book itself would not be. I thank Jerry for envisioning a longer collection with an expanded version of the title novella, along with the inclusion of the short stories. I thank Margie for her sharp mind, sharp pen, and the brimming cup of imagination, wit, and knowledge she brought to her tasks as editor. She taught me a great deal and I will ever appreciate and admire her work and her friendship. Thanks also to some talented writers I have met since *Slash of Crimson*'s initial incarnation who have offered great insight into the craft. These include Sydney Leigh, Daniel Knauf, Maddie Von Stark, Jeff Burk, and many others encountered during my sparse but inspiring attendance at conferences over the years. I also wish to thank my present publisher, *Seventh Star Press*, particularly Stephen Zimmer, Holly Marie Phillippe, and Eric Jude, as well as artist Aaron Drown of *Aaron Drown Design* for his exquisite cover. It is an honor to be working with you all. As always, there are also many other close friends and associates to whom I owe thanks, these include Armand Rosamilia, Harrison Fisher, Robert L. Fleck, Ben Eads, as well as Fran, Sean, Lew, Rich, Julien, Aaron, Becky, Gyllian, Erika, Celina, Tammi, Liz, Zac, and so many friends and family, new and old. Thank you all.

"Though all men shall be offended because of thee, yet will I never be offended."

—Matthew 26:33,
*King James Version*

# Slash of Crimson

# 1

His kayak cut across the dark water, whitecaps exploding around him like volatile stars. The early morning gale was getting stronger and Drew felt his muscles start to burn. Not far to his right he glimpsed the jagged rocks of a small island, and he leaned into his stroke and made for it.

As he pushed closer he realized the island was little more than a heap of granite, soil, and frail pines. Not much larger than a buoy, but at least someplace he could wait out the wind. He moved into a gap between the waves and saw a shadow gliding beneath the boat. Its shape was sleek, like a shark's, except not quite right because it had two dorsal fins. Whatever it was, he couldn't let it distract him as he tried to get ashore.

But as he fought on, six-foot waves hammered the tiny craft until it finally capsized. He tried to catch hold of the tether as he rolled over, but the waves pushed it out of reach. For a moment he struggled amid the whitecaps, grabbing at the granite boulders while the undercurrent raked him across their surface and tore open his wetsuit. *My chest is bleeding*, he thought, just before his skull smashed against a rock and his mind went blank.

_*_

When he awoke he was choking out a spume of salt water, clinging to a branch of one of the emaciated pines.

"So, you're alive," said a voice. "Which means we have a covenant."

Drew hunched over, coughed out the rest of the water then turned to face the source of the voice.

There, couched on a tuft of withered grass, sat a naked woman with fins sprouting from her back. Her torso rippled with corded muscles and her breasts rose and fell with her uneven breath. Her skin was covered with patchy discolorations, some places mottled maroon, others ashen gray. Along the edges of her fins some of the tissue looked charcoal black. Her hair was the color of russet seaweed, and though it cascaded down her body, it hid neither her dark nipples, nor the singed flesh between her legs.

Despite pain and dizziness, Drew found himself returning her gaze. She put a slender finger to her mouth, and its curved nail edged along her lower lip as if she were lost in thought.

"Are you some kind of mermaid?" he asked.

"No," she said, her expression unchanged, an expression he realized was one of appraisal.

*Well,* he thought, *I hit my head pretty hard. If I'm going to start a conversation with a hallucination, I might as well finish it.* "Then what are you?" he asked.

Her crimson lips spread into a grin. "I'm an Atlantean," she said.

Something about the way the glowing embers of her eyes held his gaze implied she told the truth. And yet he also wanted to turn away from her, his desire as uncomfortable as her beauty. *If I stare any longer, I'll never look away again*, he thought. He forced himself to scan the island's tiny shoreline, where he noticed his kayak bobbing in a narrow cove.

"But we have a covenant," she said again, her voice soft as sea foam, full of fluid invitation.

Drew didn't answer, instead he took a dive between the granite boulders, grabbed hold of his kayak, and pulled himself inside. The wind let up as he began to paddle, and he made as fast as he could for the beach.

## 2

When he got back to his apartment he was still dizzy from the rocking of the waves. Like a come-down from his teen acid-tripping days, he felt like he couldn't trust his own eyes. *I'm an Atlantean,* she had said. *Yeah right*, he thought. Damn that plastic mescaline his friends used to bring up from the city in Advil bottles. Two bucks a hit in Central Park, turn it over for ten up in Maine and voilà, a senior class full of big dreamers. The ones who were thinking of state college found themselves instead slinging burgers and fries while they melted their brains out of their eyeballs. The ones bright enough for the Ivy League tripped through their first semester and spent their second channeling the spirit of David Bowie in the funny farm.

Drew had gone far not to end up like either sort, but here he was facing a ten-hour shift painting houses with a wounded head if he was lucky, and insane and drug-addled if he wasn't. His father would have called him weak to skip, back in the marines if you got drunk you still had to jog up the hill, goddamnit. But he didn't believe it was so simple. Fuck up and lose his job and he wouldn't be able to pay rent, and government food cards didn't buy guitar strings.

No, sleep or the hospital were his choices, and he didn't feel like lying about his name to get out of the bill. Instead he called in sick and hiked across the hilltop slum to the bodega for some beer and aspirin. On the way back he took the long way to collect his thoughts. The apparition he'd seen that morning was just that, he told himself, nothing real. Whether it was drugs, the blow to the head or both, his mind had simply gone into as much shock as his body.

He turned the corner off the Eastern Prom just before the old men could hit him up for change. It seemed their staggering shadows had multiplied lately, and even from a distance he detected their sweat-boozy stench.

As he rounded the second corner by the abandoned church he took in the familiar sight of his dilapidated block—the meth dealer waiting on his sagging porch for a sale, more ragged pan handlers at the far corner prodding students as they passed, and Reverend Brinsdale, the preacher from the born-again ministry over in the old police armory with his gaggle of youths handing out pamphlets. It was in an attempt to counterbalance this scene that he'd started kayaking every morning in the first place.

He arrived at his building and climbed the stairs to his own sagging porch determined that he wasn't going to let what happened stop him. He might have dropped out of community college, but he was going to make his own way. He would stick with the kayaking, stick with the job and the band, hallucinatory sea hags be damned.

~*~

Two days went by full of sleep, aspirin, and beer. He'd been consistent enough at work that the foreman bought his flu story. On the third day he felt his routine coming back into focus, while the strange woman on the rock seemed to return to the fog from which she had appeared.

That morning on the way back from another run to the bodega, he saw Brinsdale and his proselytes were still at it. The little troop had even moved a block closer to his building. Usually Drew just walked past those fools in their trench coats, and ignored their chatter. But this time there was something strange about the way they kept their eyes on him. The shorter kid with the black buzzcut glared at him, head tilted, pupils fixed. The kid beside him, the taller one with red curls spilling over his shoulder, smiled viciously.

"Care to hear the good news?" he asked. He pressed the flaps of his coat against his body as he spoke, as if he were concealing something.

Drew crossed the street to avoid them, but the square-shouldered figure of Brinsdale himself followed him across and down to the corner.

"Have you ever considered joining us on Sundays?" he asked.

Drew shook his head.

"You should try it sometime," he said.

"Gotta go home. Gotta work tomorrow," Drew said.

Brinsdale nodded, a frown spreading into his jowly cheeks. "You might consider repenting, son. It's not getting any better in this town. I mean, where do you think you're going? What do you think is your ultimate destination?"

Drew didn't answer, was already hurrying on, hands in his pockets pressed into fists. Where was he going, indeed. Not to Brinsdale's rent-a-church basement. Not among his little flock.

And yet the preacher had a point, the city often did feel like it was falling apart. Where *did* he think he was going? Who knew, maybe Atlantis.

# 3

That afternoon he got up from his beery nap and started doing some push-ups. He was close to fifty reps and beginning to feel refreshed enough to play guitar when his roommate Buzzy appeared in the doorway.

"Hey, Drew, there's some weird chick at the door," he said.

"Well, that's what you get for answering it. She a pan-handler?"

"No, I don't know man. I don't know what she is. She's weird lookin'. Anyway, she asked for you."

"You mean she knows my name?"

"Nah, she said the guy with the kayak. You're the only guy in the building with a kayak."

"All right," said Drew. "I'll go talk to her."

~*~

When he reached the door he found she had already stepped inside. A shiver ran from his head to his stomach. It was her, though this time she wore a thin summer dress that clung to the curves of her body. It was her, though over the dress an oddly cut leather jacket had replaced her fins.

"I'm Sondra," she said. "You're Drew?"

Drew nodded as he forced himself to steady his nerves. He figured Buzzy must have told her his name, and despite his initial shock, found her presence carried an almost intoxicating familiarity. A part of him didn't mind at all that she knew who he was. Her eyes still seemed to glow, as they had on the island, but were also friendlier, more settled somehow. He found himself happy she was there, though beneath the sheer fabric of the dress her skin looked no less mottled, no less soaked with sweat and brine.

"Will you help me, Drew?" she asked.

Drew nodded, and when she pushed past him and walked into his bedroom, he followed.

~*~

"I need you to help me," she said.

"How?" he asked.

"Kiss me."

She stood in front of his window that looked out on the bay. The sky had become overcast and the whitecaps were rolling. He stepped toward her and she embraced him, crushing their bodies together. Their mouths opened, and their tongues and lips began to dance as he felt her damp hair fall across his neck.

Her whole body wore a watery sheen, in places scalding to the touch. Several times his hand wandered and he had to pull it away. But he couldn't pull his lips from hers, and when she paused for a breath, he remained captured by the glittering embers of her eyes.

"You do that so well," she murmured.

"Let me do it again," he said.

"You must," she said. "Every kiss makes you a little sharper, every caress a little stronger, and by them all I'm preparing you to go there," she said, pointing out the window at the waves.

They began kissing again and Drew felt something, like he was energized by a kind of electricity. He began to see the cracks and bruises in her flesh differently, wounds borne by someone strong and courageous.

5

"You will help us," she murmured as he moved down her neck. "We only wished to live freely; instead we were met with catastrophe, all of us, save a few, trapped in catastrophe."

Drew's desire amplified. He tried to take off her jacket, slip his hand under her dress, but the fit was too tight. Finally, he lifted her arm and kissed her bruised wrist. Sondra began whimpering, pressing harder like she might give in. That's when he realized she was holding something, a strange, soggy, leather-bound book. He took it from her and put it on his night table, then guided her away from the window and over to the bed. Keeping his lips on hers he began bringing her down, but she put her hand against his chest, stopping him. He leaned back and saw that her leather jacket was gone, but not because she had removed it—no, she had only pulled a pair of dorsal fins off her chest and opened them wide behind her back. The film-like dress that had clung to her skin flattened and spread into near-translucent scales. They only partially covered her body, along her back and sides, and were sharper and larger than those of any fish he'd ever seen.

"That's enough for tonight," she said. "Too much may damage you. I need you strong, not damaged."

"But what do you need me strong for?"

She blinked her long lashes. "To help my people," she said. "To help us unspring a trap of our own making. Please do this for us Drew, and remember we have a covenant. Remember, I saved you."

"Yes," he said, lying back on the pillow as she crawled into the bed and rested her head on his chest. For a moment, as he drowsed, he watched the moon rise and the fog roll in over the bay. "Yes," he murmured. "You saved me. Of course I'll help."

~*~

When he awoke the fog had thickened and his room was lit only by the blurry glow of the streetlights. He sat up on the edge of the bed and found himself reaching for the book resting on the nightstand. Its leather cover was still soaking wet, and as he opened it, he smelled the salty sea and something else he couldn't quite place.

All thoughts were erased when he saw an image spread across the opening pages. It was a drawing of a city that rose before him like a diorama, though the lines lit up with a resolution clearer than anything he'd seen come off

6

a 3-D screen. The scene depicted a maze of crystalline buildings and streets hewn out of dark stone. Thousands of figures teemed within them, most tall and streamlined like Sondra, with the strange dorsal fins on their shoulders, rising up out of bejeweled robes.

But before he could look closely at the faces of the men and women, the picture began to shake. The crystalline spires fell into the streets like daggers, and stalactites rained down out of the cavernous sky. *It's a city inside a cave*, he realized, then turned away as the debris maimed the bodies of those whose faces he'd not yet seen. He heard the screams of children, of mothers, the mounting catastrophe bursting in his brain until he slammed the cover shut with a soggy splash.

# 4

In the morning he awoke alone in his bedroom, the overcast sky outside his window graying out the sun. He got up, threw on his jeans, and went into the kitchen to make some coffee. His roommate Buzzy was sitting at the table staring at a black stain burned into the wood, like its surface had been licked by a jet of flame.

Buzzy didn't seem fazed by this. He just sat and stared at the burn mark while he ate his cereal, like he was reading the morning paper. Unlike the other kids Drew had known, Buzz had never needed acid to fry his brain. His mother had taken care of that by signing him up for paid pre-clinical trials for antidepressants. He once told Drew his dad talked to him through the radio back in Flynn Houses, the projects where he grew up. He said his dad could make the speaker into a TV sometimes and show him where he took the girls who rode in his cab.

When you'd seen shows like that, burn marks on the kitchen table were nothing to panic about.

"Dude, you're finally up," said Buzzy.

"It's Saturday," said Drew. "I slept in."

"Dude, it's Sunday. You slept through half the weekend." Buzzy paused, sucked on the little flask that earned him his nickname. "And you missed band practice, man."

"It's Sunday? Shit, I guess we must have stayed in bed."

"Yeah right. Look dude, your new girlfriend's hot in a gothy kind a way, but that chick's trouble. I mean, I think she burned the table." Buzzy pointed at the three-foot, charcoal black streak. "She a meth-head or somethin'?"

"No," said Drew. "And she's not my girlfriend."

"I hope not. She's like, a vampire mermaid or some shit."

"She's not a mermaid, she's Atlantean," said Drew.

"Oh man, it's worse than I thought," said Buzzy, taking a swig. "Look dude, before you decide to go native with Chicken O' The Sea, I think you should look in the bathroom."

Drew crossed the hallway to the bathroom where he found the floor flooded with fish bones and blood. Burn marks trailed down the wall from the mirror to the sink. Someone had filled the bathtub halfway with water, then plugged it up with a small octopus. From the way its tentacles wavered in the still water, he wasn't sure it was dead.

Buzzy appeared beside him. "Your girlfriend, you clean it up."

"Not my girlfriend," muttered Drew.

"Right. Your mermaid-with-benefits."

"She's not a mermaid!"

"Look, whatever man. She's not bad under the scabs." Buzzy reached into the hall closet and pulled out their mop and crusty bucket. "Anyway, don't miss practice next time, we got gigs comin' up."

"Yeah man, I know," said Drew. "I promise I'll be there."

"Sure, whatever, it ain't me you gotta worry about."

"Yeah, I know," repeated Drew, because it wasn't their slightly deranged drummer who cracked the whip in their outfit. It was their lead singer Garvy, the one who started referring to their band as an *outfit* in the first place, like rock musicians were a branch of special forces.

~*~

He told Buzzy he'd deal with the bathroom later, threw on his jacket and made his way over to Garvy's apartment. Drew called him ahead like the singer liked, and found him waiting on the porch, smoking a cigarette.

"I was in the middle of a workout," said Garvy, glancing down at his own biceps.

*Damn, singers*, thought Drew as he was led inside and up the stairs. Garvy offered him a beer and wooden chair to sit on. The room smelled like sweat, and there was little to see besides the PA system, weight bench, and TV.

Drew knew that Desiree, their bass player and Garvy's girlfriend, practically lived at his apartment. But as he looked around, the only sign of her 'feminine touch' was the presence of her Fender bass and an empty bottle of Colt .45.

"Told the old lady to go to the bar so we could talk man to man," said Garvy.

*Yeah right*, thought Drew. As if Desiree ever needed any encouragement to go to the bar, let alone followed anything resembling an *order* from El Capitan of their *outfit*. Still, control was Garvy's thing, even if it was only pseudo-control of things like girlfriends and bands. He stared at Drew, mouth straight beneath his long Mohawk, as if whatever he might say, it was going to have to be taken very seriously. There were times when Drew wondered if the singer had it in for him because he and Desiree had sort of dated some years back. And yet Garvy was always smacking him in the shoulder, complimenting him for being 'hard,' one of the few real 'hard' metal guitarists in town.

One of those smacks came now.

"So, out with it man. What's the deal?"

"The deal is I'm sorry I missed practice. Just wanted to come over and tell you in person because I know we got stuff coming up."

Garvy brushed a hand over his bristly black hair. "Well we both know that's not all right. But we both know that's not like you, either. So don't worry about it. Just come next time." The singer smiled and gave him another thump, a little harder this time.

"Well, cool man, thanks. See, there's this girl that's been comin' around..."

Garvy chuckled. "So I heard. Look, say no more. Just don't blow off rehearsal."

Drew nodded and finished his beer, feeling like he'd just completed some kind of fucked-up job interview. What Garvy really thought went without saying—that people who blew off practice weren't serious enough, and that people who weren't serious enough got replaced.

Still, Drew chalked up his tolerance of the band situation to being happy that Sondra was around now. Her presence might relieve some of the tension that lingered between him and Garvy over Desiree.

As the singer followed him back out to have another cigarette, Drew glimpsed the photograph of his mother where it was perched on a wooden shelf. Looking awkward in the ill-fitting pantsuit and plastic hairband she wore to her bank job, Drew knew Ms. Heisen's appearance was deceiving. Garvy always said her one mistake had been his deadbeat dad and she had worked hard ever since. A managing loan officer at a bank, she'd driven her son's aggression not through deprivation, but a life of needling precision. What he couldn't live up to academically, he'd tried to make up for in the way he approached his own passions. It was from her that Garvy's 'hard' thing had come, be it with music, workouts, or money.

The fact that Drew didn't just play guitar well, but came from a military family and was making his own way, qualified him as also being 'hard' in Garvy's mind. It was a title not easily earned and gave someone hero potential in Garvy-world. And yet it was a potential that could never be fully attained. That belonged to the woman in the photo, the one who Garvey said wore that same dumpy pantsuit to the bank the day she told the gunman she was opening the safe, please don't hurt anybody, then turned around and put two shotgun shells in his stomach.

When they got downstairs, Garvy shook Drew's hand. "Hey, don't worry about it," he said. "You're still the hardest, or maybe next best thing, heh."

"Yeah sure," said Drew. "Next to you."

Garvy winked, and Drew thought he would follow it up with 'just kidding.'

Instead the singer took a final drag on his cigarette and went back inside.

## 5

By Friday Drew felt like he had his routine back and it didn't hurt to have a paycheck to boot. On his way home he picked up a six-pack at a deli along the bottom of the hill, then decided to cut through the back lot to his apartment building. Slipping through a couple rusty fences was preferable to lugging the beer up Congress Street and dealing with the proselytes up on Ridgehall.

Cradling the plastic bag under his arm, he cut through a gap in the first fence and entered an old parking lot covered with smashed glass. Tall clumps of yellowish weeds poked through cracked pavement until it gave way to a jungle of high grass.

"Hey, Drew man, wait up, it's me."

Drew turned to see Lyle, one of the old bums who collected bottles along the Eastern Prom. Usually Lyle hit him up for a dollar and moved on, but lately hadn't bothered, since Drew never gave him anything.

"Sorry man, I don't have any money."

Lyle shook his head. "No man, I'm alright right now."

"Okay, well, have a good one," said Drew. He took another step toward the grass, then suddenly felt Lyle's hand on his shoulder. He batted it off and turned around.

"No wait, take it easy man," said Lyle. "Look, you know, um Drew, would you like to have a beer with me? I've never, uh, repaid you for your kindness."

"I've never given you anything," said Drew.

"Oh yeah, right," said Lyle, scratching at his gray stubble. "Well, that's alright. Hey, you know that shack by the old firehouse, just over there? I gotta couple of sandwiches and beers in there. My buddy was supposed to play cards, but he ain't around. You wanna come by?"

Drew looked at him askance. The guy was making thin excuses. If he'd gotten desperate enough to try to jump somebody, why would he pick someone young and in shape? Not that the streets hadn't given a kind of rat-like leanness to Lyle's physique, but it still seemed risky. No, guys like Lyle operated in a cowardly, opportunistic way. He had to have backup waiting somewhere, and he had to lure Drew further into the lot to keep the assault unseen. *Well, so much for taking the shortcut,* he thought.

That's when Lyle's hand shot out at him. It snatched the chain hooking Drew's wallet to his belt. Drew slammed his fist into Lyle's chin, and saw blood squirt between his lips. But the bum absorbed the punch and let it buy him time to pop the chain off Drew's belt and sprint into the weeds.

"You fucker," yelled Drew as he dashed after him.

Sure enough, Lyle ran for the old shack behind the firehouse. He pushed through a single door between two boarded-up windows and disappeared into the shadows. Drew charged in after him, and the second he crossed the threshold, the door shut behind him. It took a moment for his eyes to adjust to the dimness of the shack's single room. Lit only by cracks of light seeping through the boards, the structure consisted of four relatively solid walls, a set of rusty sinks, and a dirt floor.

"Okay man, I did it, just give me the money," said Lyle.

Drew slid to the side and moved his back close to the wall. Lyle was talking to somebody else in the room, somebody who was keeping to the shadows in the far corner.

"Your money's here," said a voice. "Come and take it."

As his eyes continued to adjust, Drew made out the contours of a dark figure with a man's build. Something seemed wrong with him, like he was hunched over, though still very tall. The bum seemed hesitant to approach, but when the tall man flashed a fan of cash, he overcame his fear.

"That's it, Lyle, come for your reward. Come and take thy wages."

It was a strange thing to say, but Drew had no time to think about it— once Lyle stepped within reach, the man dropped the cash and grabbed hold of his neck. With his free hand he plunged a thick-bladed knife into the bum's chest and slashed sideways. There was no scream, only the crackle of deflating lungs and the gurgle of blood pumping out of the wound.

The man turned to Drew. "It'll go easy for you, too," he said, "if you hold still."

Instead Drew made a quick dive to the right. He felt the wall vibrate as his assailant leapt after him and impacted the rotted planks. The blow loosened some of the shack's rusty nails, and a board fell away to let in a ray of waning sunlight. Now Drew could make out a tall, balding man. He was muscular and wore a vest and blue jeans. Something seemed wrong with his face, the jaw seemed too large, like it was stuffed with something.

When he leapt again it seemed impossible, like even legs that long shouldn't jump so far. And the guy was going crazy—he let out a high-pitched shriek, spitting on Drew as he clawed, bit, and slashed. It was all Drew could do to make a grab at the hand with the blade. He managed to take hold of the wrist and squeeze, but not before the crazy fucker put a tooth into his pectoral, a single tooth from his deformed mouth.

Drew twisted his torso and slammed his attacker against the wall until his jaws let go. Keeping hold of his wrist, he bent the man's arm until the blade dropped between them. That's when Drew realized it wasn't a knife. It was too long and thick, and had spikes jutting at diagonals from a steel crossbar, like a dagger. "Who the hell are you?" Drew demanded.

But the man just snarled and spit a piece of flesh from his mouth. Drew glimpsed the hooked tooth that had bitten him. It looked like a beak pushing its way out of his lips. Above it hovered eyes that glittered with flecks of blue light. Like the faint reflections of gems in the window of a run-down pawn shop, they had a cloudy yet mesmerizing lure.

Apparently beak-man thought this hypnotic power would keep Drew still while he lunged again. And by the angle of his head, it looked like he aimed to rip out his throat. But he had failed to daze Drew enough to keep him from snatching the dagger. Just before the attack hit home, Drew feinted left and let beak-man impale himself on his own blade.

# 6

Night had fallen by the time Drew made his way home, stunned and exhausted. The wound on his chest bled into his clothes as he walked back up the hill. It was deep enough to need stitches, but there was that emergency room issue again. He'd just have to wash it out with some peroxide and drink half a bottle of vodka.

He hadn't actually killed anybody, he told himself. They weren't really dead. The messed-up dude would make it, and it would be his problem to call 911 and deal with the cops.

Yet as Drew emerged from the liquor store and twisted the cap off the bottle, it was as if he heard the wheeze of deflating lungs. The thought stressed him enough to think about getting some pills from the dealers further up the hill. He also knew he had another option. *I could go see Sondra*, he thought. *I need to see Sondra.*

~*~

She was waiting for him when he got home. Buzzy was out and they had the place to themselves. This time she had her fins wrapped around her in a manner resembling a devotee's robe.

"Drink this," she said, offering him a cup of warm, fishy soup. It had bones in it, and eyes, and she said she had chewed them to saturate them with a healing tincture.

Her body felt warm beside him as they stretched out on the bed and she fed him sips of the soup. As he swallowed he inhaled a musk that smelled like a sweet rain, and it felt good to have her there, nourishing. Only when he had finished the soup and she was kissing his chest did he realize he'd forgotten the peroxide. "Shhh," she said. "Let me." Her kisses felt like a balm on his wound, and he lost consciousness as the pain faded away.

~*~

The next afternoon he emerged to find Buzzy sitting at the kitchen table with an actual newspaper to go with his flask. "Couple of bums killed each other yesterday," he said.

Drew shuddered. He felt an impulse to snatch the paper away from his roommate. Instead he said, "No shit, where?"

"Behind the old firehouse, in that crack shack. Guess it's true what they say about the dangers of drugs, eh? We oughta go down there sometime with our phones and video that shit. Ever seen those bum battles online? That shit's so funny, and these guys like, killed each other. Imagine seeing that? That'd be so funny."

"Yeah," said Drew. "Hilarious."

Drew decided maybe it was better to leave Buzzy to finish his flask on his own. He headed outside, but even though it was his day off, it was too early for beer. He felt strange from the night before—not bad, his wounds weren't nearly as sore as they should have been—but he felt a little odd in mind and muscle. He decided to hike along the old railroad tracks, and soon found himself approaching the Old Port.

As he emerged among the fishermen's wharves he heard a familiar voice: "Hey, Drew, where ya been?"

He looked up and saw a pair of girls sitting at a table outside *Brendan's Brew Pub*. One had long, dyed-black hair spilling over a leather jacket unzipped to reveal a bit of cleavage. The other was a slender, pink-haired crescent of a thing in a threadbare blouse. Both wore torn jeans that seemed to have trouble containing colorful swirls of tattoos.

"Desiree, Taffy, what's up?"

"What's up is where you been?" repeated dark-haired Desiree.

"Sorry, I couldn't make it to practice the other day."

"Hey no big thing," she said. "Buzzy told us you were busy." The two of them giggled over their beers, though Drew thought he heard a hint of jealousy in Desiree's tone. He never understood that, a girl could move on to someone else, be dating the singer of your band, and still act like she had jealousy rights.

And yet for a moment, despite his understanding with Garvy, Drew found himself sort of liking it.

"Well, hey, I'll definitely be there tonight," he said. He dug into his pockets then and pulled out a thick wad of wrinkled bills he'd somehow forgotten he had. "Here, have a round on me," he said, tossing a twenty on the table. "I'll see you later."

"No wait," said Desiree. "Stay for just one."

Drew found himself grabbing a chair and sitting down at the end of their table—not that he couldn't have just slid alongside either one of them on their benches. Taffy even gave him an inviting flash of her tongue ring, an easygoing flirt meant in an oh so platonic, we-both-know-I-already-have-a-boyfriend-so-it's-okay kind of way. After all, for her it was all about looking cool anyway. Beneath the torn clothing, her skin had a perfect tanned and powdered look courtesy of the nearest mall. Drew knew boyfriend Rodge paid for it all and took it in stride that the high price of her angry-metal look belied its authenticity.

Desiree was different though, with eyes sad and wicked any time she and Drew happened to be together, especially when Garvy wasn't around.

"So tell us about your new girl," she said.

"Yeah," said Taffy, "is she hot?"

"Hot and wet," Drew answered as the waitress brought their beers.

Taffy giggled, said, "Ewwww," but Desiree just took a deep swallow of her beer.

"No, well, seriously," said Drew. "She's just sorta been hanging out at my place, she's kinda different. I dunno, it's no big deal."

"I dunno," parroted Taffy, "it's no big deal."

This time Desiree laughed. She lit a cigarette and rolled her eyes. "Well, we know you don't do the groupie thing. I mean, how long's it been for you, a year? We were starting to wonder."

*Yeah*, thought Drew, *you were starting to wonder why I wasn't trying to get you back from Garvy.* The worst thing was that he had wondered that sometimes himself.

Drew pounded his beer as if it were last call instead of two in the afternoon. "Look, I really gotta go," he said.

"Wait, what's the hurry?" asked Taffy. "Come on, I'll get the next round."

"Sorry," he said. "Gotta hit the shed, be ready for tonight."

"The maestro has spoken," said Desiree, already down to the bottom of her own beer.

"Hey don't get too sloshed," said Drew. "We're still in the same band, right?"

Desiree chuckled. "Suddenly so serious. Don't worry, it'll sound fine."

Drew left it there, figuring it was better to let her be for now. He turned around and headed back up the railroad tracks toward the East End. As he walked he tried to ask himself where he'd gotten the extra cash he'd thrown on the table, but he already knew. It had come from Lyle, and the thing in the shack. He'd taken it from them. Part of him wanted to just throw the whole wad of it into the tide pools and let the ocean take it. But no, he would bring it home. Sondra was waiting for him, and he would bring it home.

## 7

As he climbed the hill he tried to tell himself things would be all right with the band. Even with the weird shit that was happening, they were still getting along, and still getting better. But despite her steel-toed boots and leather clad exterior, he worried about Desiree and old stuff coming back to haunt them.

They had grown up together up the highway in Cairns, a small town where the river met the woods. It was a place where the tide couldn't go any further north, but from which the crooked pines and cedars stretched their dark mass far past the Canadian border.

When he'd first met her in high school, she was gawky, pretty, and a little touchy-feely. He remembered how she'd just come up and hugged him while he sat against his locker plucking his guitar. Back then she had long, crimped, red hair accented by rose-colored lipstick. She hadn't dyed anything black yet, but a shadow already lurked behind her eyes.

"It's Drew," she'd say with a giggle.

In those days her smiles never stuck around for long. The only exception was when they would make out sometimes on the way home from school, rolling in the weeds along one of the various shortcuts through the woods. Their outsider status among the rest of their class helped them see their time together for exactly what it was—a sweet and sweaty affection that earned them neither ridicule nor status. It felt good just as it was, and for a while she would take on a look of genuine joy; then the shadow would return and she would suddenly get up and disappear into the trees without saying goodbye.

He didn't ask about her bruises, didn't know if it was his place to. He wondered if she even thought of him as being close enough to confide in, as being anything like a boyfriend. When he finally asked if he could be, she shrugged and said, "If you want."

After a while he began teaching her some bass—a purpose which brought him to her house after school one day, where he ran into her father. A tall blonde trucker who the other kids said was really into church. He didn't say anything to Drew or shake his extended hand.

When she snuck out the next weekend, she said he'd yelled at her a lot and Drew couldn't come over anymore. But he didn't hit her that night because she was meeting Paul, a family friend who attended a Christian college. "My dad says he only lets me be in a room with him because we're betrothed. By the way, he asked me if you're an Indian. Are you?"

*No, nor am I 'betrothed'*, he thought. *Was that a word anymore?* If the guy was in college, he was way too old for her. And yet the guy's presence in her life seemed like another extension of her father's hand. Blows to the body, blows to the heart, and blows to the brain. It was after that Drew would walk by churches and imagine every plank in their construction having the potential to be broken across a face.

Desiree was fourteen at the time, and they were freshmen. Her father's plan mostly worked—the few times he saw her after that she was a little distant. They kissed again at a party she snuck out to that spring, but he spent the rest of the night holding her while she cried, telling her everything was okay, and no, there was nothing wrong with her.

Drew thought about asking his own parents if he should do something about it, maybe call somebody. He remembered the day he got the courage up and walked into the living room of their little farmhouse where his father was watching the news. "Dad, I wanted to ask you something, I…"

"Shhhh! I just want to hear this Middle East thing," he said. Drew waited while the old man drained a can of beer to a montage of gunfire, weeping civilians, and mic-clutching newscasters. When the commercial came on he turned around. "So what did you want?"

"Um, just wondering where Mom is."

"She's upstairs, taking a nap."

"Right, well, I guess I'll come back later."

Drew changed high schools after that, then made it through one year of college at the state school in Cairns. The next time he saw Desiree was when he moved to Portland, where he noticed the spider web tattoos all over her arms. "Except the elbows," she said. "What a fuckin' cliché. I figure let the needle crawl everywhere else, though."

Her red hair was dyed black by then, and she was working the counter at a tattoo parlor on Congress Street. She'd even enrolled part time as a music major at the local university. "We should start a band," she'd said.

"We should," he'd agreed. He couldn't add then that he wouldn't realize how he felt about her until he'd fallen for someone else. A someone who'd pulled him from a swamped kayak and drowned him in a mix of lust and gratitude. Was Sondra like rain that blurred his eyes, or acid poured on bonds of youth in need of breaking? He couldn't free his thoughts from either of them as he continued up Munjoy Hill. The sooner he had his hands on a guitar the better, it had to be that or go back to the bar, to still his churning brain.

# 8

When he got back to the apartment he headed straight to his room, plugged in, and sat on his bed and practiced. Sometime after sunset Sondra crawled through his window. She was stark naked, all fins and flesh and carrying a trash bag which she heaved over her shoulder and dropped on the floor. For a moment she stood catching her breath, bare breasts heaving over her scarred ribs.

"I heard you playing on my way in," she said, as if standing naked beside a trash bag in a puddle of salt water were perfectly normal. "It sounded low and melodic, unusual."

"I like the low strings," he said, fighting the urge to pull her body against his. It was like that's what she wanted this time, she'd gone from steam to sparks in a single night. She was completely open, ready for something and daring him to do it.

But it still felt like something wasn't quite right, something he didn't understand. And it was messed up the way she had just come into his apartment, like she owned the place.

"Look," he said. "I think there are some things we need to talk about."

"If you insist," she said, wrapping her fins around her body in the shape of a mini dress. She proceeded to dump out the contents of the trash bag, flooding his floor with a dozen small tuna.

"I mean about you and me, about the apartment."

"Yeah, Buzzy didn't like where I stored the last catch," she said. She strode out of his room to the kitchen, returned with a steak knife and began cleaning the fish.

"All right, whatever," he said. "I gotta practice anyway." He picked up the guitar and began slamming out a dissonant riff.

Sondra stopped cutting and stood up. She came to the bed, pushed away his guitar and took hold of his wrists. She pulled his body against hers, so close he could see his reflection in her smoldering eyes. "We have to go further tonight," she said. "Each time we go a little further and you get a little stronger. That's how you fought off our enemy's attack. And when you're strong enough, you will help save the survivors."

"Yeah, right. I'll be the savior of Atlantis."

"No, Atlantis has been destroyed. We're the survivors. You'll be saving the survivors."

She kissed him, wriggling against his chest so he could feel her skin's burning wetness. They dropped to the floor, sliding among the dead fish and kissing thirstily. Turning herself over, she pushed up her thighs, unwrapped her fins, and enveloped him. That's how their bodies merged for the first time, splayed amid a tangle of scales and blood. Was it his, hers, or theirs? The wound on his chest reopened and bled, but pain was subordinate to desire. He took in their reflection in the window, his legs entwined with hers as their speed increased and their bodies rocked, splashed, and churned against each other.

~*~

He awoke later to the sound of sizzling. He threw on his jeans and went into the kitchen where he found Sondra standing at the stove. She was frying steak after steak of the tuna and shoveling it all onto a platter on the table. A stack of plates stood next to it as well as a crate of 22-ounce beers. "Hey, look who made it for dinner," she said.

"What time is it?" he asked.

"I dunno, around eleven maybe?"

"Eleven? Are you crazy? I missed rehearsal again, they're gonna kill me."

"I doubt they could kill you," Sondra said, tossing a sizzling chunk of tuna on the platter.

He noticed more burn marks on the table then, and saw others on the counters and cabinets. "You should be more careful when you cook," he said.

"Where I come from we have a certain technique," she said.

He gave her a savage glare, but she just smiled. "I mean, look, we have a few twelve-packs of beer here, and enough food for everybody. Relax, they'll be all right, trust me."

Just then the apartment door opened and Buzzy trooped in with Garvy and Desiree. They tossed their leather jackets on the ratty old chair by the back door and Buzzy went straight to the table for one of the large bottles of beer. "'sup Drew, feelin' better?"

"Look guys, I'm sorry," Drew said. "It won't happen again."

"S'okay man, Sondra told us you had a headache. Said next time she'd drag you there herself, which I believe, since she rules your life now."

Drew chafed at Buzzy's words, but let them go since it was obvious she'd sated him in other ways—he was already on his second bottle of beer, smoking and chuckling with Desiree while Garvy loaded a plate with fried fish and cranked their demo through the stereo. "I love the guitar here, so fuckin' *low*," he said. "Man Drew, you gotta be there next time."

"I gotta be there every time," Drew said, waiting for the singer's inevitable tirade.

But instead he said, "S'okay. Shit happens."

Drew began to exhale a sigh of relief when the singer punched him in the upper arm. Meant to look like a play punch, it impacted hard, guaranteeing a bruise that said, *nothing's okay, you screwed up again!* Drew grit his teeth, said, "Thanks for understanding."

At this Sondra gave a husky chuckle and swaggered over to the table. She handed Garvy a beer and added the last of the tuna steaks to the platter. She popped a few more beers for the others, then led Drew by the hand back to the bedroom.

"Come to me," she said as she moved to the far side of the room that overlooked the bay.

He went to her, and she lifted the fins that made up her dress. She threw her arms around him, scratching the small of his back with her slivery nails. Again their bodies merged amid the rays of the cloud-strewn moon. In that light her bloody wounds appeared like gashes of darkness which he devoured with his tongue. She took him even deeper inside her this time, their bodies slamming in a rough rhythm until they both cried out.

~*~

Afterward he couldn't sleep. He felt incredibly energized, alternated between door jamb pull-ups and scales on his guitar until somebody in the next bedroom pounded on the wall. He thought over crawling into bed with Sondra again, but started as he glanced toward the doorway.

Desiree was standing there, wrapped in a spare blanket. Her long black hair was still wet from the shower and the skin of her neck shone pale and smooth down to the edge of her tattoos and rise of her breasts.

"Um, wrong bedroom," said Drew.

"No, I meant to come here," she said.

As she spoke Drew glimpsed Sondra sitting behind him on the bed. She was leaning against the pillow, knees pulled up and arms wrapped around them. Her eyes glowed coal red, the color bleeding a little light onto the surface of her skin. Huddled though she was, the position served to display rather than hide the opening between her thighs.

"Garvy's in the other room," said Drew.

At the mention of her boyfriend's name, Desiree seemed confused. She had taken a step inside, and now brushed her hair back and blinked her eyes. "Yeah, right," she said. "Anyway, he's kinda drunk, and we were gonna crash, so he pounded on the wall then told me to come ask you to keep it down."

She pushed past him and knelt on the bed in front of Sondra. Though she had been speaking to Drew, her gaze was locked on the Atlantean's glowing eyes. They began kissing, first nibbles, then thirsty pushes. Drew felt a fin reach out and nudge him forward, its surface already sizzling with flashes of sweat.

He watched as Desiree, the lanky young girl from his band, stood and let the blanket fall away. He was used to only seeing her wrapped in thick leather, strumming the heavy strings of her bass. Now she was naked and lowering herself onto the mattress, feeding her body to Sondra like her bare flesh was nourishment to the stranger's salty lips. Drew felt the fin nudge him closer again. He joined in the kissing, taking one of Desiree's tattooed breasts and tracing its barbed-wire pattern with his tongue. Their bodies became a blur, and for a dark, delirious sliver of the night, their desires combined into a single ravenous will.

# 9

Drew lay awake in the hazy glow of the streetlight while the two women slept on either side of him. The night's foggy stillness needled at him, as if mocking the fury of their passion from just hours before. He thought of going to the couch, telling Garvy he'd gotten drunk too, and hadn't realized what he was doing. But he doubted the singer would have much appreciation for honesty in this particular case, and instead got up and went to the book sitting on his nightstand. He opened it, curious what lay beyond the first page.

Again the city sprang up before him. The miniature model stood in flames this time, cracks of lava forming at the top of the cave. Faces were choking in the smoke, skin melting beneath a rain of scalding stone, until a hand reached around and closed the cover.

Sondra's voice sounded bitter behind him— "Seen enough?" she asked.

"But I don't understand," he said. "The last time I looked it was an earthquake."

"Don't earthquakes and volcanoes go together?"

"I guess, maybe sometimes. I don't know." He shook his head, watched her naked form as it moved through the moonlight. She had her dorsal fins spread wide behind her shoulders, and it occurred to him he never realized how large they were.

"Come, I'll show you," she said, beckoning with a wave of her overlong nails. "Besides, it probably wouldn't hurt to get out of the apartment." She nodded to Desiree sleeping naked on the bed.

*She was right*, he thought. *Just go with her, clear out until sunrise.* And the book, he'd understand her if he understood the book. He went to her, embraced her as if they would kiss. Sondra took hold of his arms, locked them against her. She turned, threw open the window and dove out. His mind went dizzy like when his skull had impacted the rock, and at some point as they were falling, it felt like they were flying.

They moved out across the bay until the lights of land vanished and they hurtled over an endless void of midnight waves. Madness blasted his brain as the wind blasted his body. Hurtling too fast to speak or even scream, he could only cling to her as she took a sudden dive and plunged into the depths. The harder he pressed against her, the better he could breathe and resist the pressure of the water.

Through the tangle of her hair he peered into darkness cut here and there by strange lights. He glimpsed skeletal fish with golden organs lit up along their spines. Beyond these he saw larger creatures with transparent heads, fang-crowded maws and lantern-like filaments hanging between their eyes.

As they dove even deeper, he noticed an immense shadow, the contours of an underwater mountain. Sondra slipped through a crevasse in its side, a fissure that flashed with lava, its light continually extinguished as it poured forth.

Making a winding right, they turned into a cave that looked hewn by a giant worm. The crushing current sucked them deeper, and despite his newfound strength he was barely able to cling to consciousness. He felt like he was overheating, being boiled alive. When they finally surfaced he floundered on a rock ledge, spewing water from his mouth and crying, "Fire! I'm on fire!"

Sondra crouched beside him, brushed his soaking hair from his face and kissed his quivering lips.

The pain began to subside, and when he'd calmed down and regained his breath, she spoke: "Remember, I saved your life. We have a covenant."

Drew didn't answer, only stood and looked around the cavern. Strange stones glowed with phosphorescent mosses—ambers, reds, purples, and blacks. One by one their misshapen surfaces gave way to a cut passage. Sondra was already walking down it, steam rising from the trail of water she left behind her. Drew followed, feeling a crazed desire come over him, he wanted her more than even *she* knew, wanted her no matter what she was hiding from him.

On the walls beside him he noticed strings of letters. They looked a little like the kind he'd seen in pictures of rune stones, uneven and weaving in and out of each other like tangled serpents. It was as if they were making their way inside a giant book, being devoured and digested by it. There seemed something in the writing not meant for him to understand. Yet at the same time he felt mocked for his lack of knowledge. Resisting the feeling of being infinitesimally small, Drew turned away and tried to focus on the passage ahead.

For a long time it sloped downward, then abruptly they were going up, at last reaching a chamber that would have been circular had not the walls partially caved in.

In the areas left undamaged stood figures cut out of the rock. *Like coffins standing on end*, thought Drew; but they weren't exactly coffins, he realized, recalling a documentary he'd seen online—they were sarcophagi—that's when a figure's shape protrudes from the top.

The figures wore robes like those he'd seen in the crumbling city. They were long and strangely angled with ridged shoulders and daggered sleeves. Most looked over seven feet tall, some more than twice that, and wore odd, spectacular crowns shaped like fiery stars. They had glowering expressions on their faces, at once aristocratic and desperate. Everything about them had an intoxicating sharpness. He suspected the sight of them alone would have drowned him in fear and confusion had he not experienced an increased strength of mind as well as body.

Sondra crossed the room and knelt at the feet of one of the tallest figures. It was a dignified looking male, though his face wore a bemused snarl beneath his goatee. In one hand he held a scepter, in the other a sword. His form-fitting robe contoured thickly muscled arms of a size disproportionate to the rest of his body.

"This is Darjen," she said. "He is my brother." She paused to brush away the tears flowing from her eyes. "Ours is a tragic story. If you help us, I will tell you everything. For now, I brought you here only to prove that our need is real, and to show you the task I ask of you."

"Because we understood how fragile our kingdom was. Though we had adapted to life deep below the ocean, though we had harnessed the power of the submarine volcanoes, we knew a time was coming when an overwhelming… force… would be unleashed upon us."

"And so we built these catacombs. Think of them as safe rooms, of a sort. They're small cavities carved into the rock and imbued with certain protections against the most extreme conditions."

"When the catastrophe struck we fled, as many as possible, to these chambers. Unfortunately, even these were not one hundred percent immune to the eruption. The force of its… assault… was so severe many of them collapsed. What's worse, those who remained were subject to a terrible malfunction. These doors which you probably think look like coffin lids, well, they were designed to only be opened from the inside. Anyone attempting to open them from without would receive a high-voltage shock, not to mention fail to pry them open. They were designed to keep us safe and to keep out any threats." Sondra's gaze listed low with her last word, as if *threats* were an understatement.

"Unfortunately, the eruption disturbed their electromagnetic field," she continued. "Now instead of only being open to an Atlantean, they are open to anyone *but* an Atlantean. That's where you come in."

"But why would you need protection in the first place? No human being could ever come here without your help."

"Probably not," said Sondra. "But Atlanteans are very old, and we have learned to be cautious."

Drew stared up at the gargantuan figure with his sword and scepter. Some of the spikes on his crown looked thicker than others, and the jewels trimming his robe had the oddest shapes, like diamonds collapsing into

24

themselves. As he watched they became vaguely octagonal, and then seemingly became many diamonds at once, as if showing the shape's potential positions through time.

"And so when I have made you strong enough," she said, "if only temporarily, you will lift the lid to my brother's niche and reunite us. Do this, and you will have fulfilled your covenant, and you will have the gratitude of all Atlanteans."

He opened his mouth to answer, but she kissed him, long and languorously. She pushed him down to his knees and rested his head against her belly until he was dizzy and clasping her legs. Before he knew it they moved. She dragged him to the pool in the grotto, spread her fins and then carried them back through the ocean's abyss.

_*_

By the time they returned it was evening again. He felt at once tortured and numbed. He knew Sondra had tried to prepare him for what happened, and he could feel some part of him had been steeled for it. But another part of him felt his life coming back into focus accompanied by a kind of nausea scratching at his gut. Worrying about the fact he hadn't gone to rehearsal ate at his nerves with its absurdity. Yet Garvy's constant threats still felt serious enough to bother him. The music still mattered, and the thought of picking up his guitar had a kind of strength in its own way akin to what Sondra imbued within him.

It also didn't hurt that no one was around when they arrived. Buzzy was lying in bed hungover, and said Garvy and Desiree had taken off that afternoon. Drew decided to follow his example and head to his own room where Sondra didn't follow for once, allowing oblivion to consume him.

# 10

The Reverend stepped out from behind a tree—had to be a big old oak to have hidden a guy the size of a linebacker, if on the short side.

"You're Garvy? I'm Reverend John Brinsdale."

Garvy opted not to shake his hand. It had been a crazy night, and his mind had been on Desiree, how she hadn't wanted to come back to his apartment with him. Besides, there was something weird about the guy. He had a priest's collar, but said he was a reverend. He wore a black jacket trimmed at the waist in front, with two long points trailing down the back, like some kind of eighteen hundreds tuxedo. Two of his minions slid in from the side. They had matching gray trench coats, like they were the goddamn rhythm section.

"Have you heard the good news?" asked Brinsdale. "If you join us this Sunday, we shall hear it together."

"Sorry, I'm already in a band," said Garvy.

"Please, we just want to talk."

"Move over, Gramps," he said, knocking shoulders with the Reverend as he stepped forward.

But Brinsdale didn't budge. "Just a moment of your time," he said, stepping sideways and blocking Garvy's path. "Come, let us sit down."

The Reverend pointed to an old picnic table tucked into a shaded grove. Garvy had walked through Deering Oaks Park thousands of times, and hadn't noticed that particular table. He didn't like the way they surrounded him and started steering him in that direction. Brinsdale stayed in front, while the two lackeys swung in behind, like they were carrying him in a current. It was one thing to run into these guys out in the open, another to let them coerce him to a secluded corner. Everyone knew the stories about prostitutes luring old men into the bushes where friends lay in wait to pummel them, rob them, and leave them for dead.

He sat down at the table, a lackey on either side and the Reverend across. The table's paint had long ago chipped away and left the wood bare. An infestation of miniscule red ants chewed a lacerated line across its surface. Garvy was afraid if he leaned, he'd break through, and he didn't want the damn things crawling on him anyway.

"I don't have time for this shit," he said. "To be honest, I don't know why I'm talking to you."

"It's because you have some sense," said Brinsdale. "You sensed us. You know something is very wrong in your life, something that has recently begun to reveal itself."

Garvy shuddered. He'd been working out more than ever, his arms felt strong, his mind focused. He'd been singing and writing songs, too, and felt at the top of his game. Only thing odd had been Desiree's mood. Still, it was weird how as soon as Brinsdale had said something was wrong, he'd immediately thought of Drew's new girlfriend, just her in that damn vomitous kitchen full of beer and dead fish.

"Look, there ain't nothin' wrong, and I ain't giving you any money."

"We're not interested in bread alone," said Brinsdale. He reached out, took Garvy's hand.

"Whoa, whoa, no way, dude, not my thing."

"You don't know what I'm asking," said Brinsdale. He squeezed Garvy's palm. Admittedly the old dude was strong, but Garvy believed there was nothing the lot of them could do that he couldn't handle. If it's one thing his mother had taught him, it was to look danger hard in the face. If her old pear-shaped ass could take down two felons with two shells when she was forty-nine, he could demolish a gaggle of park-preaching choir boys.

Brinsdale let go. "And yet you know nothing of strength," he said.

"Excuse me?"

"You were thinking just now of your mother. You admire her, and rightly so. But what are you really doing with your life, Garvy Heisen? You are the most talented member of your band, yet nobody cares. Certainly not the drunken fools who half-listen to your set at the bars, certainly not the chubby, underage groupies, or the far off and utterly uninterested record labels."

"How the hell did you know what I was thinking?"

"It has been revealed to us through our faith in Him. We are here to advise you to rethink your life, young Garvy. The world is changing. A new way approaches. Those who would know strength must choose the right allies, a source of power for their spirits."

"I don't believe in religious shit," said Garvy.

"There is only one true religion," said the Reverend.

"Yeah, that's quite the fashion statement, but I gotta get outta here." Garvy rose, but the tall lackey with the long red hair put his hand on his shoulder and pushed him down.

"I beseech you," said the Reverend. "Stay a while longer."

Garvy glared at him. He would elbow the redhead, throw a right hook at the Reverend. He wouldn't bother with the small guy, who'd run off when he saw the big boys bleeding.

That's when Brinsdale reached in the pocket of his jacket, took out a thin roll of hundred dollar bills, and fanned them across the table. "Six hundred dollars," he said. "You mentioned you had no money for us? It is we who have money for you, if you would venture a wager."

"Heh. Isn't gambling a sin?"

"Sins can be forgiven."

"Yell, well the ante looks a little steep."

"Not to worry, we accept collateral. Indeed, we believe you'll learn something from our contest. Our challenge is that you arm-wrestle Brother Bryce. If you put him down, the money is yours."

Garvy looked at Bryce, the smaller of the lackeys. He had muscle definition, but both his biceps together didn't match the circumference of Garvy's forearm. It was a joke. "You're kidding, right?"

"We are dead serious," said Brinsdale. "We know you are a hard man, in your prime, no less. That is why we are here. We think you deserve more than you've received. We wish to teach you, that in submission, there is power—in surrender, a vast kingdom."

"What's that supposed to mean?"

"It means that if you lose, you will become our affiliate. You will attend our church, and you will help us with a certain young lady who has of late made herself a companion of your bandmate."

"You mean that crazy Sondra chick?" asked Garvy. "She ain't that young, and she's nuts. She says she's a friggin' mermaid."

The red haired kid chuckled. "You mean Atlantean."

Brinsdale waved his hand. "Stay thy tongue, Zechariah," he said. "Garvy, do you accept our wager? If you win, the money is yours. If you do not, we will accept you into our service."

Garvy wasn't sure what the hell Brinsdale was talking about, but Bryce had already moved around to the other side of the table and planted his elbow on the wood. Garvy clasped his hand. *Get it over with*, he thought, *and get the money.*

He pressed downward, easily bringing his opponent within an inch of the table's surface. The kid frowned, face flushed as he strained to resist. For a moment Garvy saw him as some high school loser in a cafeteria, giving up his lunch money. He almost let up a little to give him some game, then glimpsed the hundreds. *Screw that*, he thought, slamming his fist down.

But the kid curled his hand upward, kept it just barely in the air. Garvy squeezed in earnest, but the kid pushed back.

"What's the matter?" asked Zechariah. "We expect no mercy. You should expect none from us."

Garvy noticed the red head was holding something, a sledgehammer and a four-inch nail. He was about to ask, when he felt a pain in his forearm. Bryce brought his arm up from the table to the halfway mark, held their fists steady between their faces. Garvy saw his lips curl into a grin. "The Lord gives me strength," he murmured.

That's when Brinsdale swept the hundreds back into his pocket. "It appears you are having some difficulty," he said.

Garvy felt a crushing pain in his hand as Bryce squeezed his fingers. Zechariah chuckled again. "Hey Bryce, what time is it?" he asked.

Bryce slammed Garvy's fist onto the picnic table, digging his knuckles into a spatter of smashed ants and splinters. He glanced at his wrist and shrugged. "Guess I forgot my watch," he said.

Garvy tried to leap up, but Bryce kept his hand pinned. Zechariah stood and raised the hammer. Garvy threw a left hook, bashing Bryce in the forehead. The kid took the wound but didn't flinch. Before he could swing again, Zechariah pierced his palm with the nail and began to hammer. Garvy screamed and pushed back, but Bryce was too strong. Zechariah pounded the nail through, blood squirting across the gray wood. As he screamed and twisted, Reverend Brinsdale leaned down and murmured into his ear: "Remember this," he said. "We will treat you well. We will make you stronger. But remember, while we do, that if you disobey us, we will complete your crucifixion."

~*~

Garvy awoke in the church basement. He had been stretched on a couch along the wall, his hand washed and bandaged. He saw a dozen rows of folding chairs lined up in front of a podium. One had been taken off the end. Reverend Brinsdale had pulled it beside the couch and was sitting in it.

"Coffee?" he offered.

Garvy took the mug in his good hand. "Are you gonna let me leave?" he asked.

"You may come and go as you please," said the Reverend. "But before you do, allow me a courtesy."

"Don't think I want any more of your courtesy," he said.

"Please," said the Reverend. "Allow me to unwrap your hand."

Garvy took a gulp of the coffee and put it down while Brinsdale removed the bandages. He knew it wasn't the caffeine making him shake when he saw the bloody puncture in his palm.

"We humans are imperfect creatures," said the Reverend. "Prone to error, ever attempting to recover our lost grace." He moved his palm over

Garvy's, held him hand over hand. "You will persuade you bandmates to move
in a new direction. It is not the music you make that concerns us, so much as
the company you keep. We will try this method first, for we are truly gentle,
truly forgiving of human imperfection."

The Reverend removed his hand and Garvy saw there was now merely a
scar where before there had been a bloody hole. The pain subsided, and he could
clench his fist.

"See? You are stronger already," said Brinsdale. "We will make you
stronger still. Your friend Drew is not the only one who can change, and his new
companion is not alone in the ability to imbue power. This is the message you
must take to them, and this is the grace we are offering. We hope you succeed in
this method, for if you do not, as we have shown you, there are ways to impose
our will. Either way, you will serve us now, you will help us achieve our goals,
one way or another."

# 11

The next morning Drew awoke relatively level-headed. He made it
through the work day and picked up a message that they were having a make-up
rehearsal at the space that night. Drew took his guitar, hiked down Munjoy Hill
then swung around to Fore Street. His fingers itched to play, and the cockiness
of a good night's sleep had him revved up to set his solos on fire with piercing
aggression. Where was this coming from? He knew the answer to the question,
could feel the strength Sondra was instilling stirring within. And yet there was
foreboding of knowing her gift's true purpose, even if a side effect was charging
up his band's sound.

The sound of footsteps interrupted his thoughts. It was Brinsdale's crew
coming down the sidewalk behind him. They came in very close, and he could
tell by their shadows the tall one with the vicious grin was right behind him.
Drew was about to turn and confront them, but they just stepped to the side
and walked past him.

"Don't you guys have anything better to do?" Drew asked.

They stopped, the shorter kid with the buzz-cut looking up at his
partner. "What's he talking about?" he asked.

"I don't know," said the taller one. He tapped his phone and glanced at
the clock. "You know, I'm afraid we don't have time to talk tonight," he said,

then reached into his jacket and took out a handful of pamphlets. "But if you like, you could share some of these with your bandmates."

Drew thought he saw something flash under the trench coat, something metallic.

Before he could say anything, the pair of them turned right onto India Street and vanished into an alley.

*Creepy bastards*, Drew thought as he made his way past the Old Port. He hung left and walked along the weedy harbors that led to the warehouse where they rented their studio. He did wonder why Brinsdale would go so far as to have him followed. It was one thing when the panhandlers got aggressive, but the proselytizers? If it happened again he'd have to have a talk with the preacher.

When he reached the studio, Rodge and Taffy were just arriving, waving from their truck as they pulled into the lot. Taffy bounced out of the front seat in her shorts and torn t-shirt. She'd rounded out her attire with a bellybutton ring and burnt black tips on the spikes of her pink hair. The whole ensemble on so slight a body looked more like an inappropriate children's Halloween costume than an adult's sense of style.

She ran up and gave Drew a hug and peck on the cheek, "I'm so glad you're back," she said.

Her six-foot-seven boyfriend seemed to concur, following up her kiss with a warm handshake. "Long time no see," said Rodge.

Like Drew, Rodge's look was a little downplayed compared with some of the other band members—plain leather jacket, just a few tattoos, and brown hair barely touching his collar. Some said it was because he still had a bit of his country upbringing in him. All anyone knew was that Rodge didn't work and always had a van or an SUV less than two years old. A few guessed he had some kind of trust fund and that was the only reason Taffy was with him. Others said no, it was only a little money he got when he sold a piece of land and they were just having fun until it ran out.

Either way, Rodge and Taffy seemed to be perpetually happy. Whether there were ten or two hundred at a gig, they were always smiling and in a good mood. Their near-Hollywood good looks were enough to make them among the hippest of the Portland music scene, even though neither played an instrument. Though it went without saying that Rodge would follow the band wherever it went, the couple showed no signs of wanting to leave the city, even if they did have the means to do it.

Occasionally hangers-on, college dropouts, and the more burned-out segment of the local rock scene would spread rumors about Taffy. They'd say she'd only moved back from California because she'd been in rehab or was done with porn or was "doin' what Taffy needs to do," as if anything she did had anything to do with them.

It was one of the few times Drew had ever seen Rodge's face turn grim, when some snot-sleeved jean-jacket dude with a skull tat put his hand on Taffy's thigh. Rodge got barely a month's probation for the simple assault charge, presumably making a deal for restitution.

"Of course it was worth it," he muttered when Drew fronted the money for the bail and picked him up. They were the only words he ever heard about it. Either way, snot-sleeve was on liquids until he was well enough to catch a Greyhound south.

That night it was great to have the sound man and full band all together. Drew's solos came off fluid and accurate, and Garvy's voice had an edge, even if he was a little quiet between songs and off smoking by himself. They agreed they only needed one more session before their gig that weekend, and left in good spirits.

"All thanks to your scaly friend there," said Buzzy through his shit-eating grin.

"What's she got to do with it?"

"Nothin' besides free food, free beer, and you know, a little extra attention when you need it."

Buzzy gave Drew a puzzling wink. Puzzling because he wasn't sure if the 'you' referred to Drew himself, or just anybody who happened to be looking for said "extra attention", anybody like him.

~*~

For the rest of the week Drew let it go. Sondra only came around a few times, keeping him strong, but always a little hungry for more. On Friday night they loaded up Rodge's van and played their gig at *Lionni's Basement*. Sondra showed up early while they were setting up, as if she were a part of the crew. She wore her fins wrapped in the leather jack pattern, and even threw on a pair of jeans.

When they first started playing she hung out by the soundboard, then a few songs in, she and Taffy moved out onto the cracked slab of concrete that passed for a dance floor. They made a mesmerizing pair as they swayed along the edge of the stage, in and out of the drunken crowd. Sondra even started kissing the little thorny-haired girl and tearing at the front of her t-shirt. Taffy laughed and tugged at her hips like she was daring her to go further. Drew thought about cutting the encore before things got carried away. It was all fun and toplessness until somebody called the cops.

But Sondra seemed to be keeping things just on the edge, and Drew found his ear responding to the dancers' movements. His fingers fell like lightning from his mind's storm. The amps echoed and thundered. A waitress and some college girls wandered in from the bar and began wrestling their way into the black-booted throng. Rather than ease up, the moshers intensified their brawl, the newcomers giving a lascivious twist to their sweat-and-throttle ritual. The tempo increased as the crowd writhed. Bodies blurred and wailed as Buzzy laid down an assault of a beat like his rhythm could break skulls the way voices broke glass. Desiree kept up a wicked grind all the while, her bassline the blade on the drumbeat's ax. Even Garvy got into it, more present than he'd been at rehearsal, a crushing violence bristling beneath his throaty growl.

The set went into a second hour before it let up, extended versions of the songs bleeding from one encore into another. Even after the rumble of the final chords, Sondra didn't let up. She used the confusion of the exhausted and thirsty crowd making their way to the bar to move her attentions from Taffy back to Desiree. Rodge looked relieved but Taffy gave a full-on tabloid pout at the loss of her playmate. *You're paranoid*, thought Drew as they were packing up their gear. *Get over it, you finally had a good gig for a change.*

Sondra stayed at the bar where she kept buying Desiree rounds of tequila. They took turns doing belt-buckle shots and slurping the spillage off each other's bare bellies. It was the sort of thing a lot of boyfriends fantasized about, but even as Garvy watched, he didn't laugh. He just sipped his beer and stared.

"Oh come on, you gotta try it," Sondra told him. She grabbed him by his t-shirt, pushed him to his knees and stuffed a shot glass in the front of her jeans. "Don't worry, she won't be jealous."

Her grin became fiendish as she leaned down, pursed her full, black lipstick-smeared lips and whispered something in Garvy's ear. Whatever it was, it finally made him laugh a little. When she stood again, he drank the shot off her belly and ordered another. Sometime around midnight, they disappeared into Lionni's crumbled brick cavern of a bathroom.

By the time they came out, Drew and Desiree had already made their own trip to the van, screwed on the carpet between the amps, and come back. They were sipping their post-last-call vodka while Rodge and Taff talked and smoked. Desiree hadn't bothered fixing her t-shirt or anything underneath, and from the second Sondra and Garvy emerged from the men's room, Drew noticed the singer stared at him. His long Mohawk was matted down and caked with a little blood, no doubt from where Sondra had clawed him. Strangely unable to feel jealous, Drew was only glad Sondra had returned. His heart craved access to her presence and her body, and sought to preserve this even if the price was giving up any thoughts of exclusivity for either of them.

And yet when Garvy sat down, he appeared to have a whole other bone to pick, and his raw blue eyes packed his thousand-mile stare into the five feet between his barstool and Drew's.

Drew wasn't sure what it meant—whether it was 'we're even' or 'we're never gonna be friends again'. It reminded him of all of his 'we're the hard ones' bullshit. Except Drew always chalked that stuff up to lead-singer style vanity, part of his persona but not serious, like a Harley hat on someone who didn't really ride a motorcycle. But this seemed different, like it had something underneath, some sickening purpose.

Garvy gave a sudden chuckle, threw his cigarette down where it added another burn to the bar.

"You know," he said, "you can always see Heaven and Hell in a man's eyes."

"What's that supposed to mean?" Drew asked.

The others grew quiet as Garvy stood and lifted his freshly poured shot. He pointed with it, spilling vodka as he spoke: "It means when I look at you I see a little hick lost in the city, late on his rent and going nowhere. Hell."

"Come on man, leave him alone," said Rodge. "It's getting late."

"What?" Garvy snapped. "To behold the best kept secret of the northeast? The hottest guitarist since the Internet invented tablature, Drew Aldrin? Hey, we're not a bad band, but Drew's the only one who could roll down to New York and blow up on his own—true descendent of Dimebag Daryl. Real country boy made good. Heaven."

Rodge attempted his trademark easy smile, like it would make things okay. He coaxed Garvy back to the barstool, saying he'd get him a glass of water, nodded to Desiree like she was supposed to be a good girlfriend and try to calm the man down. But she just looked away as if no thought were more repulsive.

Drew figured the real problem was the bartender kept pouring rounds of shots. Usually A.J. hated it when bands tried to hang late, saying he wanted to get home. But usually A.J. didn't have the attention of sultry-eyed redheads like Sondra, who'd moved down to the corner of the bar and started asking who made his rings, "oh, he made them himself? A metal smith? Wow…"

"You know, Rodge," said Garvy, slurping down his shot, "you kinda look like Hell yourself. I mean speaking of country boys made good, how about trust fund boys gone bad? Always walking around smiling and mellow until someone messes with the missus, then it's time to show you're a real tough guy. Like she's not with you for the money, no, you throw down for her, and no she wasn't flirting with that other dude because he's the real thing and you're a talentless bore. Tell me, exactly how long are you guys gonna play humping-gothic-hipsters before you let out your inner ranch house?"

The uppercut shut Garvy's mouth. Rodge held back from the second, his long arm hovering beneath the singer's chin as if the fist expected an apology.

Garvy only coughed, chuckled, and spat blood back into his shot glass. "Hell," he said.

Desiree put down her cigarette, threw her hands up, "Guys, hey enough, seriously."

Drew thought she sounded sincere this time. Even if it was possible she was getting sick of being Garvy's girl, she seemed to care something for him.

But Rodge's fist looked a little less convinced, as did Taffy's frowning face. The ranch house thing had pissed her off. The free swagger she'd had on the dance floor left her in that moment, and among the shadows of her sagging thorny locks, Drew thought he saw the silhouette of a housewife's perm, complete with tight, disapproving lips.

"Ha," spat Garvy. "Don't worry guys, I was just joshin' with ya. You guys are some of the coolest shits I know. I can see how you relate to each other. I mean, people are always seeing you for your looks and your money and stuff, but all the two of you want is something real. Shit Rodge, most kids with your resources squander it and never work at anything. You actually learned how to use the sound gear you bought. You're a real member of the band man, we'd do anything for you. Things keep going good, I'll more than put you in the album credits, I'll put you in the damn reality show. Shit, why not the movie? How'd ya like that Taff? You guys'll be just perfect, we'll have a scene just perfect for you, ha ha, just wait, it'll be Heaven. That's what it'll be for all of us. Follow me, and it'll be Heaven."

Rodge didn't wait for the end of Garvy's babble. Instead he used the mention of the sound system as an excuse to check the stage one more time for said expensive gear. Taffy slid down the bar, as if she hadn't been listening either, but by the way she stood dazed while Rodge searched for his flanger it was obvious she was still pissed.

Sondra finished taking down the bartender's email, "oh yeah, she'd love to see his studio, oh yeah, sometime that week," then moved down and put her arm around Taffy.

This seemed to perk the girl up and make her smile again between drags on her cigarette. "Hey Mr. Lead Singer man," said Taffy. "What kind of pseudo-poetic bullshit do you see in this one? Is she a good girl?" Here she giggled and slid her hand down along Sondra's thigh. "Or very, very bad?"

Garvy straightened himself, waived his cigarette. His sudden lucidity, as if stone cold sober, gave Drew a chill. "Her? I hear she's from Atlantis, so who knows? Can't see anything in the eyes of someone like that."

For a moment Sondra and Garvy glared at each other. Garvy's eyes flicked to an aluminum baseball bat behind the bar on which A.J. had painted *The Bouncer*. It was supposed to be half a joke.

Sondra curled her lip, eyes fiery with challenge. Drew considered reaching across and snatching the bat just to remove the temptation, when Garvy turned away and shrugged.

"Come on," he said to Desiree. "Let's go make sure the van's locked so we can leave it here. You know, so nobody gets killed. Driving home, I mean."

# 12

A few nights later at rehearsal Garvy acted like he'd just been drunk and couldn't remember anything. Nobody questioned this but Drew did notice Rodge didn't have much to say to him. As long as nobody was quitting over it, he figured it was alright.

After rehearsal Drew walked across the street with Garvy to the convenience store. They bought some cigarettes and six packs and were on their way back to the van when Drew noticed the group of trench coats gathered around the pylons under the bridge.

"I can't believe those assholes have been coming down here," he said.

Garvy looked up, squinted into the shadows beneath the bridge, then waved.

A couple of them waved back.

"What, you know those guys?" Drew asked.

"Not very well. They just, you know, they gave me some advice on some stuff. Anyway, let's load up so we can drink these beers."

Drew nodded and helped him load the van. He wanted to ask him again about Brinsdale's crew, but he didn't want to remind him they were nearby and end up having to hear about their pamphlets again. Better to leave Garvy alone on that one and let him snap out of it on his own.

~*~

Over the next couple weeks, the gigs kept coming in. Lionni even paid them on time and asked them to open for *Core Kill*, a new band on the High Scythe label. What was weird was how even though he was happy about it, it was like he didn't care, just wanted to get back to the apartment to be with Sondra.

After each gig he'd bring her his cut of the cash they made. She'd fan it out, count it, and stash it in his top drawer. He noticed there were other clips of cash in there, too, like the whole band was using her for a bank. *But no, it couldn't be that,* he told himself. It was safe there because he and Buzzy and Sondra all lived there.

Sometimes Desiree came over, too. She'd lose herself in the bed with the two of them, bathe herself in their bodies. Afterward she'd smoke a couple cigarettes and casually down a third of a bottle of Jack Daniels. Drew would offer her a cab home, but she'd say no, could she crash there?

"Again? How come you never wanna go home?" he finally asked her.

"It's Garvy. He just keeps showing up and acting weird. Like, he keeps telling me he's so into the band and you guys are so cool, and as long as you follow the band's new direction, you can do what you want."

"New direction?"

"Yeah, but he's weird about it, I mean, he said, 'Oh I know what you guys do, I like it too, I like drinkin' and screwin' 'cause we're all sinners, right?' I mean, I don't know, it's kinda freaky."

Drew said all right and let her stay over again. It was hard to make himself worry about Garvy when the band was going well, and what little other time he had, he spent with Sondra. Still, the singer's attitude was getting annoying. Things *had* changed, he worried about stuff he didn't use to worry about, had to comment every time someone popped a beer. Drew tried to chalk it up to some weird mix of anxiety and ambition, his way of getting used to their recent success.

One night when he got back in the bedroom with Sondra, he asked, "So what's the deal with you and Garvy?"

"What do you mean? There is no deal."

"You have a deal with me, I thought you might have a deal with him."

"You and I have a covenant. Your friend I just screwed at the bar. I was hoping a little fun might help him get over himself while I'm making you strong."

"But wouldn't that make him strong, too?"

"We used protection, Drew. I don't impart strength to everyone I sleep with. I mean, look at your friend Desiree."

"What about her?"

"She is no fool, and knows more about our common enemy than many. I would share my gifts with her, but her indecision threatens her fate. Independence can be a virtue, but also a fault. She remains wary about my true nature."

"True nature? You sound like a fortune teller. What the hell's that supposed to mean?"

"All will be revealed in time."

Drew sighed. "Okay, well, Dez can do what she wants. But I don't think being with Garvy helped at all. It might have made him worse."

"He is getting worse either way," said Sondra. "But the band is doing better. You're actually making money, which is something we're going to need."

"What, is Atlantis in foreclosure?"

Sondra chuckled. "Atlantis is demolished, remember? It's *Atlanteans* we're trying to save."

Drew let it be for the moment. Things were weird, but she was right. They were doing better than before, and there was a part of him wanting to just go along with it and not look deeper.

He even noticed on Monday mornings he didn't care about getting up extra early for work. He gulped his coffee, played his guitar, then headed out. He rode his bike across the bridge to South Portland where the crew was painting an old Victorian owned by a couple of lawyers. He started getting into the work, slamming the heavy ladders just right, angling his brush with precision. When he pedaled home later he didn't have that blasted feel, wasn't compelled to spend any of the little roll of twenties they paid him. Instead he stashed them in his dresser with the others, refolded them so the bills were flat, so they fit a little better when he added more on top.

He began hitting the studio early for rehearsal and found the others were already there, too. The sounds of their set echoed out of the broken windows. Garvy sounded a little hoarse, a little garbled on the vocals, but Drew, Buzzy, and Desiree played more accurately than ever. His solos flowed fast over the thundering drums, triplets flashing like lightning between the fills. They got rid of their old garage band name, *The Broodbloodz* and changed it to *Madshores* in honor of the erratic autumn nor'easters that swept off the ocean across the rotted docks.

And he liked that Sondra waited until after practice to come around and find him again. Buzzy was cool with her now and they all went around to Lionni's for a couple of beers before closing. One Friday Rodge announced he had gotten them two more well-paying gigs, one at a slightly corny eighteen-plus goth club and another at an amusement park a few towns away.

"Great, we can blow our gas money to play for the Walmart crowd in a half-empty barn," said Garvy.

At this all conversation ceased. Until then, they had been sitting around a slanted card table in the back of the bar, talking up their new prospects. But Garvy was the only one who didn't seem excited. He sat opposite Desiree, and instead of setting down his beer glass, slammed it next to her hand, splashing hour-old swill over her fingers.

Rodge cleared his throat. "The amusement park's giving us a thousand bucks, plus a piece of the door."

"Oh, big money," said Garvy. "I gotta wonder how carnies out in Dingleville are gonna pay that. Either it's bullshit, or it's coming from somewhere else."

"What's that supposed to mean?" asked Rodge.

"Oh I dunno, ask your mutual fund manager, big guy. Maybe you're just keeping us around to entertain black-lipstick Barbie."

Rodge scowled and Taffy put a hand over lips that had been steadily black since the night she danced with Sondra.

Garvy laughed, bumped the table with his knee, nearly knocking it over. But all at once he was straight faced again, glaring at Rodge. "Problem is, it's not just where the money's coming from. It's where it's going, as in, not in the band's pocket. As in, someone's skimming."

"What the hell's wrong with you man? You sound crazy," said Rodge.

"Seriously," said Garvy, leaning in close. "Don't you guys get it? It's this hag here. She's doing something to us, and it ain't good. Shit, if we were selling weed I'd say she was a cop or something. Course she's too skank-ass for that, but mark my words, hag-lady's trouble."

As he spoke he pointed his thumb at Sondra. She only raised her eyebrows and sipped her beer.

"What?" said Garvy. "You think we're really gonna get somewhere? You think she's not gonna fuck us over?" He turned to Sondra: "Listen up hag-lady, 'cause I ain't afraid to say it to your face—you're a liar and you're fucked up. I don't care if the rest are too stupid to see it, just keep the fuck away from me."

Before Sondra could answer, Desiree stood up. "Garvy, you're an asshole," she said. "It's completely fucking over. I felt bad before, but not now. And I can't play music with you either. Shit, I can't even be in the same room with you." She yanked up her glass, like she was about to throw her beer in his face, but managed to hold back.

Garvy stood, faced her with eyes that had gone from blue to milky-gray. He looked around the table, sweating profusely, jaw shaking. "You all think you know what you're doing, think you're so fucking hard and in charge, but you don't know shit. So let me save you the trouble. I'm outta here. I quit." He paused, eyes flickering like he'd just thought of something. "And if any of you have any brains, you know where to find me. You know you should come with *me* instead of that... that... instead of *her*. It's not just about the band, you know. You have to submit—you have to submit to something. You were all born flawed just like me, and flaws can only be fixed one way. Don't you get it? One way, one way to get it all fixed."

Garvy backed up from the table. He zipped his leather jacket up to his neck, threw his hands all over himself, tightening his belt, tugging at the straps of his boots, making everything tight like his clothes were some kind of armor. "And I expected more from *you* Desiree. After what we shared, how could you do this to me? You fucked it up, we both did and it's all our fault, and we both have to own up to it. We have to state our accountability, Goddamnit, we *both* do."

By now a few regulars at the bar had taken notice. A.J. picked up *The Bouncer* and nodded to the burly man at the door of the same title. But before they made it to the table, Garvy turned and pounded his head against the cement wall. "Fine. Fuck it. It's over," he said, blood running through his smashed mohawk down over his neck. "I'm outta here, and it's over!"

Though his arms were nearly a foot in diameter, the bouncer had some trouble getting Garvy in a chokehold. "I'm outta here," he was crying. "And don't forget it's our fault, don't forget we're gonna own up, we're all gonna own up!"

The bouncer finally managed to twist him around, but he couldn't keep a grip on the thrashing singer. For a second it looked like Garvy was going to rush back at him. But instead he scuttled over to the stairs, ran up the steps and out the door. He left a damp trail that smelled like piss in his wake.

"Damn Desiree," said Buzzy. "*After what we shared?* What exactly did you do with that asshole?"

Desiree didn't answer, instead she disappeared into the Ladies Room with Taffy.

~*~

On the way home Drew found himself oddly animated. He told Sondra it was probably better that Garvy was out, a relief really. He'd never been relaxed around him, and he had never been over the fact that Desiree and Drew had been together. Drew didn't want to deal with baggage at rehearsals, and it was better now he didn't have to.

Through the whole speech, Sondra remained silent. It made Drew more emphatic about how what happened was Garvy's fault, especially the way he'd been treating Desiree.

"But what are you going to do about me?" was all Sondra said when they reached Drew's room. Instead of answering, he wrestled her to the bed. She resisted at first with flashes of strength that almost stopped him—but his hunger made him push until he had her, and she had him, and they broke his bed frame with their slamming and rutting.

# 13

When he awoke the next afternoon, Drew noticed an acrid odor permeating the air like a haze. He went into the kitchen where he found Buzzy leaning against the sink, munching on something that looked like solidified tar.

In front of him on the table lay the strangest pair of fish he'd ever seen, if he could even call them fish. Their barbed tails hung at nearly right angles from their heads, and the heads themselves looked like oblong helmets pressed over human skulls.

"What's the matter?" asked Buzzy. "Never seen a gulper eel before?"

"Where did these come from?" asked Drew.

"Oh come on, man, you would know better than me, man. Course these are really death's head gulper eels. Pretty cool, huh? She says they come from way down, says eat 'em, they'll put hair on yer chest."

Buzzy swigged his 22-ounce beer and grinned, leathery bits of eel flapping in his teeth. "So anyway, I've come a long way with your girl. I mean, I *really* like her now."

Drew stared at his roommate, his wiry drummer's arms hanging at his sides and turned inward like a pair of muscular, bowed legs. At first he thought the dude's hands were caked with paint, but then he realized it was dead skin, crusty and shifted over the bones, like it was falling off.

"What?" Buzzy asked.

"Your hands, they're, well, never mind. Look, I'm glad you're cool with my girl staying here now, it's just…"

"Ah," Buzzy chuckled, blasting him with eel breath. "So you *do* think of her as your girl. Pretty funny. Well I been doin' some thinkin' of my own, Drew. Since the gigs have been going well, I was thinkin' maybe she oughta move in here like, permanently. Seems like Desiree likes her, too. She knows how to party, that girl. Knows how to get things goin'. We could all be so much more than a band." Buzzy raised his right hand as he said this and Drew saw that his middle and index fingers looked like a pair of candles melted together.

"Look man, you're gonna just have to spit it out, because I don't think I understand," said Drew

Chunks of wet eel splashed Drew's face as Buzzy tapped his chest with his mutilated fingers: "You're not the only one she's been with, Drew. She likes me, now, too. She likes all of us. She's making all of us stronger because she needs us. For Atlantis."

Drew hit his roommate with a sharp jab to the chin, spun him by his wrist, and slammed him against the wall. "You stay away from her."

Buzzy winced from his twisted arm. He should have been crying with pain but it was like the dude had extra cartilage, some weird stringy crap under his skin. Still, Drew felt exhilarated with his own strength. He held Buzzy with a grip like a vise, felt like he could have broken his arm—broken his *spine*—in half easily.

"All right, all right get off me man! She started early with you, you're ahead, you're still her favorite all right? She loves you best, all right?"

Drew let him go. Buzzy shook his head as he turned away and sauntered down the hallway. Drew felt a chill as he watched his roommate walk. His legs were bowed like his arms, and his melted fingers and thumbs were snapping against one another.

~*~

After that Buzzy calmed down for a while. He focused on his music and paid attention to getting his beats tight with Desiree's basslines. A few weeks went by and their gigs were coming up. Drew suggested they get in some extra rehearsals. On his way to the first of these he took his shortcut that wound around behind the fish market.

As he walked along the wharves, he passed the rusted hulls of neglected lobster boats and aluminum three-seaters with dented motors. It was cheaper to moor a boat there in the old industrial harbor, where MacDonald's wrappers and Styrofoam cups congealed in the water, and smashed beer bottles and cigarette butts lay scattered along the rocky shore.

As he got closer to the studios, the wharves became abandoned altogether. Feral cats peered out of thickets of rotted pilings, lean and filthy from a steady diet of fish guts and splinters. Their incandescent eyes reflected the oily, green-black water.

"You off to play with that band, then?"

Garvy's voice startled him. He turned and saw his ex-bandmate scrabbling out from behind a collapsed wharf. He was hauling a covered plastic bucket across the stones. It looked like in a mere month he'd managed to put even more muscle weight on, mostly in the arms and shoulders, and he said 'that band' like he'd never had anything to do with them.

"Um, yeah man," said Drew. "We have rehearsal. How's are things goin' with you?"

Garvy stood in front of him panting. He'd cut off his long Mohawk and gotten a flat-top buzz-cut, military style. He still had stubble on his face and his t-shirt was caked with something putrid and pinkish-brown. The stuff was on his hands too, and he was wiping them on his dirty jeans as he spoke. "Oh you know, it's goin' good, man, real good. Not that *I'm* any good, but who is?"

He cocked his head and stared at Drew like he was supposed to answer.

"Okay man, well, uh, see you later," said Drew. As he started to step around his old friend he caught a whiff of a terrible stench. Even among the rot of the old wharves, even after the stuff Sondra had been bringing home, this was something different, something horrible. He peeked down at the bucket, saw the lid was a little open with a damp tuft of fur poking out.

"Um, hey man," said Drew. "What's in the bucket?"

"Oh, this bucket?" said Garvy. "Just some stuff, cat stuff, you know."

Drew took a step back. He saw a dozen green-black eyes among the crooked pylons, as if they were gathering behind Garvy.

"You're hunting the wharf cats?"

"Oh no, not the live ones. Heh heh, wouldn't do such a thing. We're supposed to be *kind* to animals, I mean Noah *saved* the animals. I'm just picking up the dead ones. You know, to take home." Garvy nodded in the direction of his apartment.

"But why?" Drew asked.

"Why?" Garvy smiled. "You're asking me why? Because he hath raised up a horn of salvation, Drew. *Book of Luke*, man. He hath rolled the stone from the tomb for righteous men and minion beasts. *Book of Ooranos*."

"What the fuck is the *Book of Ooranos*?" Drew asked.

Garvy didn't answer, just walked down the grimy gravel drive toward his apartment. "My eyes have seen the glory of the coming of the Lord," he rasped in his rock'n'roll voice. The bucket bumped his leg and dripped pinkish-brown slop.

# 14

"For the Lord knew his subjects, and ravished them. He left them not for dead, for they would serve in both soul and body. The soul can be likened to the heart of a stallion that hath been infested by a lengthy worm. It doth move blood through two bodies, nourishing Him first, itself surviving on the remainder. It comes to possess great sadness thereby, and pain of the flesh."

Reverend Brinsdale pointed at the page he was quoting, and Garvy shifted on the folding chair. The lights above him were bright, but the basement room was damp and stuffy. He tried to make sense of the words, but he was sleep deprived and his eyes strained from being forced to study early every morning. His new education had him feeling more addled than accomplished. He looked up at Brinsdale wanting an answer, anything to get through the lesson and back to his apartment. "But I don't understand," he said. "I thought those who served Him would be rewarded?"

"They shall, for the servant's burden is increased by His enemies. The Lord will strengthen the faithful in order to defeat them. Turn your wrath toward His enemies, and you will receive many gifts."

"She is His enemy then, and my old friends are too?"

"They have fallen to irretrievable depths, young Garvy. *The Book of Ooranos* is clear: 'Soldiers of Jarwhal, ye shall punish the fallen, their very existence blights your honor.'"

Garvy turned the page and found the second line Brinsdale had quoted in the final stanza of *The Warrior's Psalm*.

"I tried to do it differently," said Garvy, "I parleyed with the harlot, and she tried to seduce me."

Brinsdale gave a sympathetic nod. "I am not surprised," he said. "I thought perhaps as you had been one of them, they may have listened, but they are too deep in her spell. Take heart, do what you must, and you may yet be redeemed. Rejoice, for your initial failure becomes an opportunity."

"I will, I'll do anything. Just let me go, let me go home and prepare."

"But of course. You have completed your training. This morning has been our last session. Continue your preparations, and you shall soon have a visitor. Watch for him when the sun sets, at the time of the evening breeze. He shall come to you, and imbue power. You shall have great power over life and death, and bring your enemies to know great pain and acceptance."

*⁓\*⁓*

Three days later, as Garvey stood heaving from his workout, moaning sounded from the other side of the wall, a woman's sobs. He turned up the inspirational video playing on his television and forced himself through another round of sit-ups and chin-ups. The little tramp in the other room dared beg for her life, but what did she know about eternal suffering? She hadn't even learned to submit.

Garvy chuckled and pet the kitten that slinked onto his weight bench. Its mother's corpse lay on the floor a few feet away. He put the bowl of milk beside her shriveled teats, hoping to comfort her litter. By evening her eyes would re-open anyway, and his growing power would be confirmed.

"Is it about time we pay a visit to Desiree?" he cooed to the kitten as he stroked its ear. "Poor lost Desiree," he sang as he took hold of the kitten's neck. It blinked its green eyes, a tremble running through its body as he lifted it and brought it over to the floor beside its mother. He pressed it firmly against the hardwood planks, tightened his grip as he leaned in close and looked into its eyes. "Are you ready?" he asked.

The kitten squirmed in his grip.

"Ready or not," he said. "Drink your milk. Grow up big and strong for Uncle Garvy. Grow up big and strong, like your mommy."

He let go of the kitten and patted the dead cat's bloated nipples. The kitten scuttled back under the radiator. "Suit yourself," he said. "But drink up while you can. Uncle Garvy's gotta run some errands. I'll be back soon," he said, "and so will she." He gave the corpse another pat and headed out the door.

~*~

"Hey, Dez, how's it goin'?"

Garvy was leaning on the hood of the taxi cab, at the corner of Cumberland and High. Desiree switched directions when she saw him. He didn't rush as he climbed back inside and drove around the block. The dead man in the trunk was starting to really stink. He rolled down both front windows as he turned onto State to cut Desiree off just as she was stepping into the crosswalk.

"Jeez, Dez, it's like you're avoiding me."

"You think?" she answered. For a moment she stood poised, knapsack in hand like she'd club him with it. Garvy shook his head, put the car in park and stepped out.

Desiree was already walking fast back to her apartment. He caught up to her, took hold of her arm.

"Let go," she said, punching his chest.

"Dez, relax, I just want to talk. Listen, I get it."

"Yeah? You coulda fooled me."

"No, I do. Look, I just wanna help you get your stuff. I got this cab over here, from a friend of my mom's. You can come get your amp from my place, and your clothes and stuff. I'll drive you, like as a way to say 'I'm sorry', okay? We're broken up now, I get it."

Desiree's stance relaxed. She wasn't exactly tearing up, but for a moment she looked at him like she had when they were just friends who were having fun with a band. Friends who had become more, but still just had fun. "All right," she said, brushing back her hair. "I'll come get my stuff. But that's it, all right?"

Garvy smirked. Her sympathy was another bow to nostalgia. *Foolish fallen soul,* he thought. *You want to believe your own bullshit, when you should know better.* "Yeah, of course," he said. "This is an 'I'm sorry', I promise."

# 15

Drew and Buzzy were the only ones to show up to practice that night. They went over the set once, trying to call Rodge and the others between songs. Afterward they grabbed some beer and Drew went home early. Around midnight, his phone rang.

"Drew, it's Desiree."

"Dez, we missed you. Everything all right?"

Something in her voice sounded off, and Drew felt a gnawing beneath his ribs.

"No, Drew, listen," she said. "There's a problem, it's Garvy."

Drew was silent. He already knew Garvy was aware Desiree had been at his place a lot since he'd quit the band. She'd been staying in Drew's room almost every other night—sometimes when Sondra was there, sometimes even when she wasn't. Drew couldn't get the jokes Garvy had made about it out of his head, the stuff he'd said when he'd first come to the rehearsal space to get his gear: *Yeah, you're all making money now, so why not act like whores?* or *Hey, you showed me yours, so I showed you mine—girlfriend, that is, ha ha.*

Drew had seen friends lose it before, like the kids on synthetic mescaline up in Cairns Mental Health Institute. But there was something different about Garvy's ramblings. There was something underneath, something *cruel.*

"Drew, are you there?" asked Desiree.

"Yeah, I'm here," he said. "Look, I know Garvy's got some hang-ups."

Desiree let out a ripple of sobs. "No, Drew, listen, he freaked out tonight. He convinced me to come over then he locked me in his apartment. He locked me in Drew, and I'm in this room, it's really bad, I... I have to go."

Before she hung up her voice had lowered to a hiss. Drew shivered

47

because he knew he had waited too long. He had always listened to that son of a bitch Garvy, letting him dominate the band, and that was bad enough. Now Sondra had come, and brought along the vendettas against her—the thing in the shack with Lyle, now all the weird shit Garvy had said about her.

He considered asking Sondra what she thought their ex-singer was doing, but didn't necessarily want her telling him what he was supposed to do about it. He went into the kitchen and found her standing at the counter, filleting a mackerel. "Hungry?" she asked. She turned and leaned back against the stove, giving him a wry grin.

"No, not now," he said. He stood at the table with his cell phone, trying to call back Desiree, but there was no answer. "I gotta go see Garvy," he said, heading back to the living room and putting on his steel-toed boots.

Sondra followed him to the doorway. "Want me to come along, or do you think you can handle it?" she asked.

"No, we don't need you," said Drew. "I know you helped us, I know you helped the band, but I think I'd better just go talk to him."

"Are you going to bring a weapon?"

Drew looked at her as she offered the fish knife strung with cartilage and blood.

"That? The cops would bust me just for the smell," he said.

"As you like," said Sondra, heading into the bathroom and coming out with more fish.

~*~

Drew pulled his bike out of the foyer. He bolted down Munjoy Hill and across the Old Port. When he got to Garvy's apartment building, he noticed Rodge's van was parked in front of the gray wooden porch. The door hung open, but Rodge was nowhere to be seen. When he moved in closer he saw a large woman in a flower print dress sitting on the steps eating convenience store chocolate cupcakes.

"You lookin' fah Gahvy?" she asked.

"Yeah, actually, I am," said Drew.

"Well I don't rec'mend buggin' 'im aftah dahk. I just dropped off mah cat 'n' I'm outta heah soon's I catch my breath." She gave him a chocolate-smeared smile, then stood up with the help of a walker.

"Look, I really need to see him," said Drew.

"That's what you think. All piss 'n' vinegah, jus' like them othah fellas. No reason come 'round heah less you got somethin' for 'im." The woman shook a head full of greasy curls and spat chocolate as she waddled down the steps and off toward the bridge.

Drew turned to toward the alley and saw Rodge and Buzzy emerging from the fog.

"Found him at Lionni's," said Rodge. "Thought I could boost him in the second floor window but it's locked up."

"Did you try knocking on the door?"

"Fucker wouldn't answer," said Buzzy. The drummer opened his leather trench coat. From an inside pocket protruded the handle of a hatchet and one of the steel dowels he'd once tried to make num-chucks out of. "Here," he said, handing Drew the dowel. "Just in case."

Drew led them back around to the front, found the downstairs security door open. They walked up to the second floor, pounded on the old oak door with the rusted knocker. "Garvy, it's Drew," he said. "I got Rodge and Buzzy with me. Open the door, Garvy, or we'll beat the fucker in."

The door opened. Garvy stood before them wearing a puffy black winter coat. It was torn in places, strands of stuffing poking out. Brown stains smeared the fibers, some of them obviously blood. "So you guys came to repent?"

"We came to pick up Taffy," said Rodge. "And Desiree."

"We know they're over here," said Buzzy.

"Oh yeah, they're here," said Garvy. He coughed and Drew blinked. Something had moved under the winter jacket.

"Can we just come in for a minute?" Drew asked. He could feel pins and needles under his skin. The apartment wasn't very big. If they were there, wouldn't they have said something by now? The horrid stench he'd first detected when he met Garvy by the wharves drifted out of the living room. There was cat litter added to it for sure, and blood he knew, but beneath that, something dead and decayed. Garvy had already told him he'd had dead cats in the bucket, and he'd just talked to Desiree. But how long had Taffy been there? *Not that long*, he told himself, *it couldn't have been.*

Drew tried to peek over Garvy's shoulder into what passed for the slanty one-bedroom apartment's living room.

"Oh, you want to come in?" asked Garvy. He opened the door a little wider, revealing a floor strewn with cat food cans and beer bottles. Even the instruments and weight set lay in disarray. The TV still stood in the corner, but he'd covered its screen with strips of electrical tape, all except for one little square in the center.

"Come on in, guys," said Garvy as he led them inward. "I've been wantin' to talk to you anyway. Want some tea?"

"Why, you all out of beer?" asked Rodge, pointing at the empties.

"Oh those aren't mine," said Garvy. "Those are from the bums. They come over. They bring me kitties. I give them beers."

Rodge stood over Garvy emphasizing his height. He put a large hand on the singer's shoulder and squeezed. "I think you're not feeling well," he said. "Better tell us where Taff and Dez are or you're gonna feel a hell of a lot worse."

Not since he'd pummeled that snot-sleeved jean-jacket dude had Drew seen Rodge seriously angry. Now the intensity in his eyes made his rage palpable. Yet Garvy gave him back a blank stare, as if not intimidated.

Drew firmed his grip on the steel dowel under his jacket. "You gotta tell us," he said.

"Hey, come on now man, I feel fine," said Garvy. "You know, I've never felt better. I mean, I admit it, man. I wasn't well there for a while, you know, when I was with the band. But I feel so much better now, praise His name. You know, John 3:16 man, 'for God so loved the world, he gave his only Son.' That's some radical love, man—like if you believe, you won't perish, but have eternal life. That's why I'm better, that alone, you know, because before I was incomplete, and now I'm full. I'm totally full, man." Garvy smiled, rolled his eyes upward as if he could see something beyond the ceiling.

"Look, cut the shit," said Buzzy. "Where are the girls?" He took a step forward, his hand gripping the hatchet low against his leather trench coat.

"You know," said Garvy, pointing at the wall's splotchy white plaster. "This is an old house. It has rooms people don't even use. They only use 'em sometimes. Like the abortion lady, she used to use 'em."

Rodge frowned. His eyes flickered to the blank wall as he tightened his grip on Garvy's shoulder. "This is your last chance. Where are Taffy and Desiree?"

A blast of sound exploded through the room as the TV switched on. A girl's high-pitched porno voice screamed *Oh my God, fuck it! Oh my God, fuck it! Oh my God, fuck it!* The movie was running, though most of the screen was blocked out by the electrical tape. Only the little square shone, full of pink shapes, which took a moment to identify as human genitals.

50

Garvy pointed with the remote. "Yeah, I only have that part showing, only that one now, you know? That's how you get to know where they are, and how I keep my sin low. You can keep it low, but you can't get rid of it. Only He can do that, He hath given us his only son… umpphh!!!"

Blood blew out of Garvy's lip as Buzzy smacked his face with the butt of the hatchet.

"Tell us where they are, fuckin' tell us!"

It took both Drew and Rodge to pull Buzzy off. Rodge kept hold of his arms while Drew stepped around and faced Garvy. "Tell us where they are or we're hog-tying your ass to the stove," he said.

Garvy coughed, looked from Drew to Rodge. "She's in the stove, exactly. How did you know? She's in the stove, she had to go there."

"Who?" barked Rodge. "Who's in the stove?"

"She lived hard, too hard. I used to think it was right but it couldn't be."

Rodge threw a punch, but something shot out of Garvy's jacket and blocked it. Drew caught a flash of something sharp and white. "Fucker," hissed Rodge, pulling his fist back. A streak of blood ran from finger to wrist. The wound was sudden and deep and the blood pumped fast with his heartbeat.

In that fraction of a second Garvy split away, sprinted through the kitchen door and out the back toward the rear stairwell. Buzzy moved to chase him, but Drew stopped him. "Wait," he said. "We don't know what's back there. We go together."

# 16

At first Buzzy looked surprised at Drew's commanding tone, but after taking a moment to peer toward the kitchen's shadowy doorway, he nodded and lowered his hatchet to a ready position. Drew saw then that the drummer's arm had changed again. He'd always been muscular, but now his forearm looked swollen along with his scabby, half-melted fingers, and all of it was pinker than the nastiest sunburn Drew had ever seen. His eyes looked puffy, too, like he hadn't slept in a while and his whole figure appeared hunched.

Rodge's arm also had issues. He had a deep puncture in his palm, along with a gruesome laceration running along his wrist.

"What did he cut you with?" Drew asked as he tore off a piece of his t-shirt and bound the wound.

"It actually felt like a bite," said Rodge. He shivered and was sweating a little.

"That'll have to do for now," said Drew. "You guys ready to do this?"

Rodge squeezed his hand into a bloody fist. "Definitely," he said.

"Okay, let's go," said Drew. He picked up the remote and shut off the yelping porn movie. For a moment silence settled around them like dust. Then they heard it, a muffled sound, a female voice had blended with the movie. Except that its wails were those of suffering instead of ecstasy, indistinct syllables that came in bursts, ragged, distant, exhausted.

"It sounds like it's on the other side of the wall," said Buzzy, tapping the greasy plaster. He gave it a kick with his boot, chipping out a teaspoon of white powder.

"He also said something about the stove," said Rodge.

"Right, the stove," said Drew, turning toward the kitchen. For a moment he considered calling the cops. They couldn't deceive themselves about how bad it was going to be. But there was no time to stand around and wait for a cruiser. And if they gave Garvy an ass-kicking before the cops got there, it could go badly for them.

"Come on, first the kitchen," said Drew. "Then we find a way to the other side of the wall."

They made their way slowly forward, Drew and Buzzy in front, Rodge behind because he had the reach. Drew handed Rodge the steel dowel and stopped to break a leg off the coffee table that held the TV. A pair of rusty nails protruded from the end making it a spiked club. Lighter than the dowel, it would probably break after a few blows. How many would it take to bring Garvy down? Drew grit his teeth at the thought.

As they crossed the threshold onto the patchy linoleum, they began to cough. The stench had thickened. Layers of red-brown filth oozed over the edge of the sink. It streaked the counter and spread onto the floor around chunks of bone and gristly flesh. A gray pot sat on the stove, lidless and covered in burn marks. A stiff cat's paw stuck out of the top. Drew thought of the tuft of fur he'd seen poking out of the five-gallon bucket and felt his stomach start to turn.

"What the hell," said Buzzy. "He's hunting cats?"

"Not hunting," said Drew. "Collecting. I saw him the other day. He says he collects the dead ones."

"To eat?" asked Rodge.

"Maybe," said Drew.

Rodge reached down to the burnt brown oven door. He opened it slowly, eyes squinting. Drew took a deep breath and Buzzy turned away.

Inside, a small ceramic casserole dish sat on the rack. Drew pulled it out and removed its stain-covered lid. The remnants of a half-melted picture frame lay within. The plastic was blistered and stank, but the photo of Mrs. Heisen was recognizable. It had been singed around the edges, her face circled, and a necklace with a cross drawn around her neck, but there was no mistaking the ill-fitting pantsuit. Across the bottom in magic marker was written: *Murderer!*

"I guess this is what he meant by 'she's in the oven'," said Drew.

Rodge shook his head, caught between relief and panic. "We gotta go, gotta keep going," he said, pushing the oven dish away. He strode toward the back door then slipped on something slick beneath the wall cabinets. As he crashed down, a door sprang open and belched out a heap of bloody fur.

"Get it off me," he cried.

Drew and Buzzy began knocking away legs and claws, rib cages, tails and intestines. They were pieces spilled from one of Garvy's storage buckets. *Just pieces*, thought Drew, though there was something repulsive about them he couldn't quite pin down, something beyond the decay.

They were shoveling rotten organs off Rodge and helping him to his feet when they heard a distorted "Meeeeooowwlll!" behind them.

"Holy fuck," said Buzzy, pointing with his hatchet.

The cat took a timid step forward. "Meeeeooowwlll," it repeated, a warped slant to its vocal cords. It was standing in the back doorway, at the top of the staircase. Its neck looked thin and broken beneath torn patches of fur. Only a few teeth remained in its gaping mouth. Its eye sockets were a pair of pink sores.

Rodge was still shaking and knocking bloody cat bits off him. "I think there's fucking fleas in this shit, get it off me!" He batted the stuff to the floor with the steel dowel. "What the hell's wrong with that thing?" he asked.

They watched as the cat moved in a parody of an affectionate feline, trying to rub its stiff spine against the doorway. It let off another burble of broken meows and dragged one demolished paw behind it.

"Is it alive?" asked Rodge.

"Not for long," said Buzzy. He reared back with the hatchet.

"No wait," said Drew. He grasped Buzzy's forearm and pointed as the cat limped into the shadows and down the creaky stairs. "Keep a few feet behind it," he said.

# 17

A yellowed harbor light glared through a half-curtained window in the back stairway. It lit a narrow passage between crumbling paint-peeled walls. Every few steps the cat peered back at them, its form a mere outline, its eyes utter absence.

When they reached the bottom of the stairs the stench that lingered from the kitchen contorted into a bludgeoning, gaseous rot. Drew's foot kicked the cadaver before he saw it was there. He fell back, stumbling over a five-gallon bucket on the floor.

"Fuck, it's the back door," said Buzzy. "Freakin' thing thinks we wanna get out."

"Maybe *it* wants to get out," said Drew as he righted himself.

He looked down at the body's torn checkered shirt scrunched beneath a wool sweater. A knit cap with a *Penske* logo lay nearby on the floor, and cracked leather boots only half covered black, swollen feet.

The sweater had been pulled up over the man's chest, revealing a once flabby girth with a shank of back fat gnawed down to the pelvis. A small gray balloon of an organ peeked out of a hole by his spine.

"Whoa, one of those cat-bums," said Buzzy.

The cat sounded a crooked meow. It settled on its front paws and began nibbling blindly at the pelvic bone.

Drew turned to the door, pushed away the window's ragged curtain and revealed the harbor's eroded bricks and broken wharves.

"Meeeoowwwlll," whined the cat. It gestured with its eyeless head, and Drew turned again. Behind them, just to the right of the stairs they had come down, he saw a second, narrower door. A new brassy lock gleamed above its knob.

They stepped back as Rodge bashed it in with the steel dowel and then climbed a second rickety stairway that ran parallel to the first. At the top they found another door opening into a side bedroom.

A single low-watt lamp dangled from the high ceiling, casting its dim glow over a filthy hardwood floor. An explosion of bloodstains spread outward from the far side of the room where Taffy's corpse sat propped against the wall. A gash split her face from the center of her forehead to her cute upturned lip. Bits of brain hung, caught in her spiky hair, and chunks of vomit streaked down her t-shirt to her mall-tanned midriff. She'd been stripped bare from the waist down, and her broken legs splayed at painfully odd angles, as if they'd buckled beneath an immense weight.

Rodge ran across the room and fell to his knees. "Oh my God, Taff," he muttered, pulling her off the wall and cradling her in his arms. His eyes opened and closed as he wept, as if unable to bear looking at her or not looking at her.

Drew forced himself to keep his focus, saw that the room had two other doors besides the one they had come through. One stood in the far corner and was closed. The other was just to their left and hung slightly ajar. Thinking it might be a closet, he tapped Buzzy on the shoulder and pointed with the chair leg. "You check that one. I'll check the other."

Buzzy nodded and they moved forward. Drew tried not to think of Taffy lying dead just a few feet away in her sobbing lover's arms. But they couldn't leave until they found Desiree. She had to be close, she had to be through one of the doors.

"Looks pretty that way, don't you think?"

The voice came from behind the closed door. Before Drew could answer, it opened, and Garvy emerged from the dusty shadows. He was holding a thick black machete with a streak of silver along the blade. But it wasn't the weapon that made Drew work to steel his stance—it was the string of severed cat heads he wore around his neck. Garvy's jacket was hanging open and their stubby skulls scratched against his bare chest. Bits of bloody vertebrae dangled as they hissed and rolled, as if still alive. They were eyeless like the cat they had followed down the stairway. Yet somehow they glared at Drew and Rodge, grinding their pale fangs. It must have been one of these that had bitten Rodge's hand.

Rodge stood and pivoted. "You motherfucker," he cried as he let Taffy's body drop and leapt at Garvy.

But Garvy knocked the larger man down as if he were half his weight. He kicked away the steel dowel, straddled his body, and raised the machete. As he held it poised, the necklace of cat heads shot out like a serpent and bit into Rodge's neck. With the strength of half a dozen jaws, they raised him up a foot off the floor.

As Drew ran to help, he saw Buzzy fall beneath another figure that was attacking him from behind.

"You bastard," Rodge gasped as he tried with his waning strength to grab Garvy's neck. He winced with pain as the cat heads chewed his flesh. But neither he nor Drew was fast enough to stop the machete. Garvy thrust it through Rodge's sternum, causing his chest to belch blood. All at once the cats let go and his body fell, quivering in a death rattle.

Drew dropped the chair leg, snatched the steel dowel, and bashed Garvy in the forehead. A dime-sized dent sent streaks of blood down his face. "Right, you're the hard one," he mumbled through bloody lips, "the hard one, like me."

He dodged a second blow from the dowel and came at Drew with the machete. The weapon gave him more reach and put Drew on the defensive. As he swung the blade again and again, the cat heads let out lungless wails, like a windstorm laced with the songs of tormented souls. They floated hypnotically before him as Garvy worked him steadily back toward the boarded up windows.

From the corner of his eye Drew saw Buzzy being attacked by what looked like the corpse of a homeless guy. But the body wasn't like the corpses he'd seen in movies—it flowed as it moved, its whole frame bubbling with movement as if from within. Its clothes were shredded, cat claws stretching out of its chest and arms. Its legs balanced on handfuls of foul, half-crushed paws and out of its neck poked a half-dozen hollow-eyed feline skulls.

*It's a corpse full of dead cats*, he realized. *The dead inside the dead, and Garvy was controlling them all, and they would all die again, for him…*

The heads on Garvy's necklace hissed at him, moving in unison, striking like a serpent with too many mouths.

Drew felt his muscles beginning to strain, heard the crack of crushed bone as he batted away a cat head with the dowel, but within seconds, another replaced it. He parried a swing from the machete and backed up another step. There was no way he was going to be able to outfight Garvy before he was up against the window.

On his left he glimpsed Buzzy as he wrestled with the cat-corpse thing. He'd fallen beneath it and Drew could see dozens of claws raking his flesh. He'd buried the hatchet in the bum's calf, which only caused one of the dead cats to chew off its host at the knee and leave Buzzy's weapon lying on the floor just out of reach. By his screams it didn't sound like he would be reaching for it much longer.

*Damn it*, thought Drew. *If I can free Buzzy we might have a chance*. He spun and felt the machete bite through his leather jacket in the back. Ignoring the pain, he ran over to where Buzzy was flailing on the floor. He kicked the corpse in the ribcage with his steel-toed boot and caused a vomitous caterwaul to erupt from the things within. The blow crushed a few, and sent more scattering across the floor.

Drew had successfully knocked off his attacker, but Buzzy was a mess underneath. Cat claws had shredded his clothes and flesh alike. Red gashes streaked his body from face to foot and he seemed on the verge of passing out from the pain. Drew turned just in time to parry another blow from the machete, but Garvy kept hacking at him as he let out a string of babble: "Thou art immersed in evil! Thou art a bastard, spawn of Behemoth! Leviathan!"

Garvy was forcing him against the room's front wall. The pain from the wound in his back wore him down. Buzzy was dying, Taffy and Rodge were dead. Could he make it back to the stairs? No, the scattered remnants of the bum's body were re-massing there, hissing hungrily as they pieced together their bloody bits of bone. Besides, the voice he'd heard screaming had been Desiree's, despite the wails of pain, he'd recognized it. As long as there was still a chance that she was alive he had to stay, even if it meant he would end up dead.

He landed a blow with the dowel to Garvy's stomach. It knocked the wind out of him and almost made him drop the machete. Drew considered a suicidal rush—it would mean a dozen foul cat fangs chewing him as he tackled the deranged singer. But if neither of them survived maybe Desiree had a chance.

With the dowel clenched in his right fist, he twisted and threw his left elbow into Garvy's chin. He shifted his weight and hit him again with the dowel, steel crunching bone. It knocked Garvy back a few steps, but still wasn't enough to topple him. The cats had hold of Drew now, and he could see a cold blue gleam in Garvy's eyes as he reared back with the machete to deliver the final blow.

Instead it was Garvy's skull that shattered as the hatchet clove through it. It came down again and knocked away an ear with a chunk of brains attached. The rest of him collapsed in a bloody mess atop the wailing necklace of cat heads. Behind him, holding the hatchet, stood Desiree.

She was stripped down to her bra and a torn pair of Garvy's jeans. Her body had fresh bruises, not unlike the ones Drew used to see on her in high school. She let out a sob, dropped the hatchet and threw her arms around him. Together they crumpled to the floor, quivering and breathless.

# 18

For a time they remained there, holding each other among the dead. Drew felt his consciousness slip away, for how long, he couldn't tell. When they finally stood, the few golden cracks of sunlight winking through the window-boards were melting into darkness.

No longer animated once Garvy had been killed, the corpses of the cats and the homeless man grew more pungent. Flies emerged from the shadows. They began crawling all over the rancid flesh, preparing their broods of maggots.

Rodge already looked stiff. His body seemed even longer dead than alive, his right arm extended across Taffy's purplish legs.

"He stripped off her jeans for the cross," Desiree said. "You make one sacrifice there when they come for you, but not the final sacrifice. Garvy said I better cooperate, too. He said they're more merciful that way."

"I don't understand," said Drew. "Who are?"

"The angels. He said he was talking to the angels."

"That's crazy," said Drew.

"Come," said Desiree. "I'll show you." She moved to the doorway from which Garvy had emerged, beckoning for Drew to follow. They had to leave that place, and yet something was compelling him to follow her.

When they crossed the threshold into the inner room, Desiree felt along the wall until she found a box of matches resting on a low shelf. Striking a match, she lit an oil lamp beside the box and raised it up.

Its glow revealed yet another dust-heaped chamber. The wooden floor bore many amorphous stains, the walls the same slew of cracks and nailed planks. But here there were no bones on the floor, and one of the windows had been left uncovered. It was open to the now full dark sky, from which blew a cold breeze accompanied by the lonely blur of a fog-choked moon.

Around its edges hung sets of hastily nailed shelves covered with clutter. Most of it consisted of camping lamps, votives, and jar-candles painted with saints and Virgin Mothers. All of it the semi-broken product of junk stores, trash bins, and religious gift shops.

In the center stood a cross made from a pair of twelve by twelve beams that were drilled through with massive bolts. A makeshift plywood footrest protruded from the bottom, and in the place where Christ's hands would have been nailed hung handcuffs.

"He kept muttering about it," said Desiree. "He said if she pleased them enough they would make him like them, he was becoming like them. He said he took her on Sunday morning like they asked and left her there both nights, but it wasn't enough. They wanted more of us. And more of that."

She pointed at a basket at the base of the cross. A pile of cash, some bills smooth and clipped, some crumpled in piles. Stolen, brought together hastily like the lamps and candles. Garvy was trying to gain something at the expense of his former friends. It had something to do with Sondra, and the worst of it was that Drew found himself grabbing the basket of money and stuffing it in his jacket. "Come on," he said, glancing at the cold blur of moonlight shining through the window. "We have to get out of here."

~*~

But when they crossed back through the other room, they heard a groan. It was Buzzy. "My God, he's still alive," exclaimed Desiree. They took hold of his shoulders and feet, managed to lower him down to the back door that opened onto the alley connected to the harbor's access road. Drew ran back up, snatched the keys off Rodge's body, and brought the van around. They found a box of trash bags in the kitchen and made a hasty nest for Buzzy's body. He'd stopped groaning, but was still breathing.

"He's cut up pretty bad," Desiree said as they drove slowly over to the East End. When they reached the apartment they stood him between them and brought him up the stairs. Drew hefted most of the weight, realizing he probably could have carried Buzzy on his own.

When they were inside with the door locked, there was brief talk about calling 911, but both knew they weren't going to.

Both knew a threshold had been crossed.

"Have some of this soup I made," said Sondra.

She nodded toward the stove as she stood kitchen doorway, fins wrapped around her like a snug silken robe. Drew looked at the lacerations that scarred her arms and legs. He thought of what had just happened to Buzzy, and wondered.

"Come on," she said, "just have some, it will make you feel better. And don't worry about Buzzy, I'll deal with him. Are the others coming?"

Drew dropped to the couch, unable to look back at her. He felt Desiree slide against him and nuzzle her tear-dampened face against his shoulder.

"I see," said Sondra. "Well, it's too risky to go looking for their bodies now."

Drew felt a numbness taking him over, a numbness that felt impenetrable.

And yet what Sondra said as she came into the living room snapped him out of his daze: "Anyway, did you find any money? Every little bit helps." He felt her hand tugging at his jacket, the same plying tug she used when she was undressing him. She found the crushed wad cash and pulled it out.

"How resourceful of you. You did well. Just think, if you'd waited any longer, he may have become a half-angel."

"A what?" asked Drew.

Sondra ignored the question as she lifted Buzzy's body off the floor. Once in her arms, he began groaning. She carried him into his bedroom and closed the door, leaving Drew and Desiree together on the couch.

# 19

Later they had some of the soup, and when they finished eating they slept. They woke early the next afternoon, wrapped tightly in each other's arms. He slipped into the kitchen to make coffee and noticed Buzzy's door was still closed. When he came back, Desiree looked dazed, with dark circles under her eyes. "Don't leave me," she said.

"I was just making coffee," said Drew.

"No, I mean tonight. After what happened, just stay with me again tonight."

Drew looked at the worn expression on her face. The red roots of her natural hair showed beneath the black locks. Her cheeks seemed shrunken and her lips parched. She held him against her, both of them stale with sweat and the faint odor of blood. "Please, just a little longer. You're the only one who understands what happened. You always were." she said.

It reminded him eerily of one of their teenage weekends, one in particular where they'd stolen away from the party into a bedroom, supposedly to make out. But that night she sat staring into the darkness. She made him lock the door and sit beside her. The entire night she had him hold her while she wept and said, "It just hurts so bad," and he said, "It's okay, there's nothing wrong with you, nothing wrong."

This time it lasted only a moment before she regained her composure, lifted her face and gave him a light kiss. "I'm sorry, I mean, it'll be all right. Pretty soon it'll be all right for both of us."

Drew searched her eyes. What did she mean? He thought of Sondra's words, her books and her wounds and her words. And he thought of her fingers digging money out of his jacket. Maybe Desiree was trying to tell him something.

"We have to go back to my place," she said. "We have to make sure things look normal. I mean, I always pay the landlord in cash. I take out the garbage and stuff. I… I feed his cat."

For a moment they laughed then went silent.

"Anyway, just stay with me tonight. Will you?"

Drew nodded.

~*~

They walked across town through the thick early autumn fog. When they arrived at Desiree's apartment it felt clean and pleasantly dorm-like. They found themselves giggling, stripping each other down and making love on the plush carpet. It felt innocent, simple. And yet they also both felt they were feeding on something that had grown inside Drew, getting their fix of a strength that was buoying them, changing them. Sondra had mentioned that when the three of them were together, she had not imparted strength to Desiree. Now Drew felt a stir in his center and an electricity in his touch. He realized he had transformed to the point where he could impart strength on his own. It felt good, and yet too late, as if he might not have time to change her enough to save her from the shadow that seemed to impend upon their every step. Still he tried, as if it might be a way of salvaging something from their past. Whether he wanted to admit it to himself or not, he wished it a way to keep a door open for their future.

When they were finished on the carpet, Desiree disappeared into the walk-in closet that served as her bedroom and began playing her bass. He lay back and listened to her thrum through meandering rhythms and muted melodies. She played an array of staggering metal riffs and even a few blues solos. Drew was impressed with the range of skills he hadn't realized she had from just playing the set list with the band.

When she returned they curled up together on her futon, held each other as they drifted into unconsciousness.

Drew woke the next morning recharged and ready to figure out a way forward. Maybe it wasn't all about the band or Sondra. Maybe it was more about Desiree. Maybe he needed to *be* with Desiree.

But first things first, he had to take care of the van.

He threw on his jeans, kissed her forehead and headed back across town. As he hiked back up the hill he realized the van wasn't where he parked it. Had he left the keys in it? He was sure he hadn't. He raced back to his apartment where he found Buzzy wrapped in his bathrobe watching the local news. He looked swollen, pinkish in the cheeks. The scars were faintly visible, but mostly healed.

"Where's Sondra?" Drew asked.

"I think she's doin' somethin' with the van," said Buzzy.

Drew turned to the window. The expanse of the bay and open ocean beyond seemed to glare back at him.

"Dude relax," said Buzzy. "She said you did a good job the other night. She said *we* did a good job."

# 20

That afternoon Drew waited in the apartment, sat on the bed with his guitar and watched the window for her return. The sun sank beneath the ocean's sharp horizon and a cloudy moon rose over the windswept bay. Hours passed without any sign of Sondra, and the longer he waited for her, the more he squirmed and sweated, feeling like an alien in his own body. Part of him wanted her to be there, and yet another part wondered what that wanting really meant.

The wind rattled the window and his flesh ached all over. The wounds from the brawl with Garvy had mostly healed, but there was something else gnawing at him. Something about her, as if she were devouring him the way the midnight tide devoured the granite shore.

He fell into a fitful sleep, dreaming he was walking across the room, reaching for the soaking book. Its cover throbbed like the surface of a wet, sickly lung. He reached while skull-head eels writhed and chewed at his feet, he reached for the book but couldn't grasp it.

When he awoke late the next morning he swallowed four ibuprofens and loaded a knapsack with a few changes of clothes. He searched the dresser drawers and then the entire room for the cash they had stashed away but didn't find any. Apparently she had taken it all. He headed for the stairs where he unlocked his bike but found it had a flat tire. Screw it, he thought, and began walking over to Desiree's.

~*~

By the time he reached her apartment and rang her buzzer it was late afternoon. He rang it again, and when no one answered he pushed open the broken security door and walked up the stairs. He tried the apartment door and the sound of his rattling startled her.

"Who is it?" she gasped.

"It's me, Drew," he said. "I need to talk to you."

"But I didn't call you," she said.

"Do you need to call for me to come over? Dez, it's me, Drew…"

There was silence. He heard soft steps on the creaky hardwood. A pause. Was she looking through the peephole?

The door opened. Desiree stood in her leather jacket, jeans, and boots. Her newly dyed black hair was clipped back and behind her he saw a duffle bag and travel guitar case.

"Are you going somewhere?"

Desiree looked at her gear as if she just noticed it. "Um yeah, I'm just takin' off for a while."

"Can I just come in for a minute? I want to talk."

Desiree nodded, but didn't meet his eyes. He realized as he stepped inside that most of the furniture was already gone. He sat down on a bare futon frame folded like a couch. But instead of looking at him she stared at the door and stairwell, as if expecting someone else.

"So you didn't recognize my voice?" he asked.

"No, I did," she said, finally meeting his eyes. "I wasn't sure it was really you. Anyway, what did you want to talk about?"

Drew patted the futon frame. "Sit down," he said.

Desiree shook her head.

He sighed, stood up and took a step forward. "Look, wherever you're going, I want to come with you. I should have said this a long time ago. But ever since we were young, I thought you and I would, that we'd…"

Desiree held up her hand. "Don't," she said. "Seriously, Drew, I know you're going through a lot, and I want you to be all right. But what you're saying, that's just not how it is. Not with us anyway."

"Dez, what are you talking about? That other girl, she's crazy, she…"

Desiree chuckled. "Now you can't even say her name."

"Who even knows her name?" he said, then stopped himself and embraced her. He waited, but her arms stayed at her sides. He let go and brushed the hair away from her face. Her eyes looked like pools of starless night, yet awake with the potential for new life. It was as if she respected their closeness, but after what had happened, only seeing it from afar could keep it intact. That and her nervousness, her looking around, her twitchiness, shot Drew through with an icy rejection that said this was different and more real than past partings.

When he leaned in to try and kiss her, she turned away. "Don't," she said.

He darted in again and she pushed him back. "I said don't, Drew."

They stared at each other, her dark mascara running down her cheeks. She wiped the smear across her eyes, then strode past him to the bedroom. "I have to finish packing," she said. "I'm getting out of here. Please, just let me go."

"But where are you going?"

Desiree shrugged. "New York first. Out west if that doesn't work."

She vanished into the tiny room where he heard her rummaging around. For a moment he felt like picking up the coffee table and hurling it at the wall. But he didn't touch it. He knew she was right, and it didn't help that there was still a part of him that thirsted to return to his apartment, thirsted for Sondra's touch. If he went there now, his last connection to Desiree would be cut, and yet something made him hesitant to leave.

"You're still here?" she said when she emerged from the bedroom. She added a hastily stuffed skulls-and-hearts patterned tote bag to the other luggage. "Let me get you a cab," she said, dropping the bag and digging in her pocket for her phone.

"No, I'll go," he said.

"Are you sure?" she asked. "It's getting dark." She nodded toward the window where the last rays of sunlight were disappearing over the Western Prom. He detected a hint of fear in her voice, even felt a pang of jealousy as he wondered what could be more on her mind than their parting. Her cell phone rang, and he stepped into the hallway as she put it to her ear. He descended the stairs without looking back.

# 21

"Desiree, it's your Daddy."

"Doesn't sound like you," she said.

"Sure it does, just haven't talked in a while. But's it's me, Desiree, it's dear old Dad."

Desiree hung up, dropped the phone on the futon frame. It buzzed again, but she didn't answer. She went in the bathroom, splashed cold water on her face. Her Dad only called her once a month, and he wasn't due. And these days when he talked to her, it was in his sober voice. The one he'd had for the last four years since he'd joined that *Heart's Promise* group. She remembered all those asshole social workers who said abusers never change, but with what she'd seen in the world, she knew there were always exceptions. She figured those guys were used to hearing wishful kids saying their parents were going to be those exceptions. But Desiree had gone beyond that, past caring, and yet as repulsive and corny as the *Hearts* Christian group was, it had gotten her old man sober and stumbled him into a semblance of responsibility.

The phone stopped buzzing and she heard a knock on the door. "Desiree, Daddy's back," said the voice. Its whiny rasp sounded uncannily familiar this time.

She caught her gaunt reflection in the mirror and remembered that childlike, pouty tone. She felt a pressure in her chest jabbing against her heart. She was at once afraid it might really be her father, and yet glad it wasn't Drew coming back. Severing her connection with him was cutting deeper than she anticipated. It was because that connection was not one that they forged, but rather discovered, one of shared alienation from their families. When they saw it in each other, they realized they were veterans of the same battle and wouldn't have to explain. The only difference was that she had learned of their enemy's true origin long ago. The cruel faces at church, the outlines of angels haunting her bedroom window for as long as she could remember. She had seen the cruel reflection of a deeper reality from the moment of her mind's earliest awakening.

The whine sounded again: "Des-i-ree, open up!" It was the regressive tone the old man always followed up with his fist. He'd pout like he was the kid while he dealt it out. She closed her eyes, the ghost of pain blasting through her skull.

Knock-knock. "Open up this door. Did you think you'd get off so easy young lady?"

"Fuck off," she called out, refusing to be sixteen again.

"Did you think Geronimo would get away with his little rescue? Did you think I'd let you run off like a band of gypsies?"

Desiree punched the mirror, sending a crack through her reflection. She hadn't heard her Dad's epithets for her teenage friends in years, and yet she was mostly mad because she hadn't been fucking rescued. Drew had come for her, and they'd fought their way out together. If they hadn't fought together, they'd be as dead as Garvy. They'd looked out for each other, like they had to when they were kids. She knew that time was past now, but it's what made pushing him off harder than she wanted. Because she knew more about what was happening than he did.

As if echoing her thoughts, she heard the whiny giggle by the door, then a voice: "Dez-zee, Daddy's home. Time to go to Sunday school."

The voice was tinny, and she felt tears welling because she couldn't tell if it was real or in her mind. She looked in the mirror again and thought about her father. Because it wasn't just the booze and the morning classes. It was something else she had seen, one Sunday afternoon, on a day he hadn't otherwise bothered her.

She was shuffling down the carpet in their house's upstairs hallway, had a book under her arm, was just going to her room. She heard creaking in the floorboards, and looked toward the bathroom.

That's where her father stood rocking on his feet. He rocked side to side, legs apart, standing in front of the mirror, the way she was now. He was talking to the mirror, and its glass was frosted, as if steamed. It was a blurry portal, at first hard to see, but she could tell, she could tell what it was. She didn't want to walk toward it, but found herself compelled.

She heard her father murmuring then: "Yes, I *want* you to in-dwell. I want you to dwell in my home. Ye shall dwell inside me, ye shall cut right into fat old me."

That's when she saw a torso in the mirror, a torso without a head. In the blur she made out its steel encased chest and shoulders. A sickening gleam radiated from its armor, a light that blended with the shapeless presence above its neck. From within the glass, a voice began to whisper: "We are coming. Do not be unready, bloodheart. Thou shalt be our servant, for there are truths in the book. There are truths about us and about the others. Among these truths is that thou shalt writhe like a dog, hungry to be kicked. Thou shalt say, thank you, thank you, thank you, while your bones are breaking, your body scrambling sideways like it's gleefully dancing. In this way, thou shalt be locked in an endless seizure crying, I'm glad I'm yours, I'm glad I'm yours, I'm glad I'm yours!"

"I want to do that," her father whined in the child voice. "I want to."

"For now, thou art still damned. Our respect is earned. Look upon my face, fear us, and fear what is coming."

Something slammed against her apartment door. "Fear us," the voice said, real and clear as the slamming continued and the wood cracked.

Desiree drew the pistol from her jeans. She'd taken it from Garvy's apartment and never fired it, only managed to spring the clip in and out and find the safety. She stepped out of the bathroom, knelt on one knee, and aimed it at the door, clasping the grip with both hands.

The planks splintered with a final blow, and a slender figure stepped inside. He had long red hair, and a grin like bird of prey tucked into his freckled face. The trench coat hung open, while his jeans and leather boots clung to his striding legs. She aimed at his chest, a chest that looked covered in gray scales. "Fear us," he said, hefting his sword over his head.

Desiree shot twice, her forearms kicking up with the recoil. The barrel flashed, and behind it her assailant cried out as he swung his sword.

Weightless, she felt, the world rolling end over end. A dizzying rush of blood poured from her neck, smearing her face. In those final seconds, she tried to fight off mournful thoughts of friends and family. Her dying eyes searched for the death wound she'd dealt out. Instead, as he reached for her hair, she saw only a pair of molten bullets stuck in the scaled armor that covered his chest.

# 22

Heading down Congress Street, he made a left on High and then right onto Cumberland Avenue. By the time he reached Franklin Arterial it was full dark. Unlike the night before, there was no moon to speak of, and the fog covered the stars with its wispy shroud.

To his left stood rows of slanted apartment buildings, a thicket of paint-peeled wood, woven with shadows. He wondered if they were watching him, as if the buildings themselves had eyes. He quickened his step, tearing through the fabric of the fog. A group of shawl-wrapped Somali women gave him a wide berth as he tried to cut around the senior citizens' center, as if he were some kind of threat. When he glanced back over his shoulder, he saw what they were really avoiding: three slender figures in trench coats, following him. Their tumbling curls and long lumpy coats made them look like they were on furlough from some kind of asylum. The hazy grays of their outfits blended with the fog, making them hard to track.

Drew cut a hard left into the Kennedy Park project, hoping they wouldn't notice. Instead the red-haired kid smiled and steered after him. Drew ducked around a block of the pre-fab housing, sprinting toward the highway. If he crossed at the right time, he could block their pursuit with a string of speeding cars. But when he slipped into the connecting alley he found red-hair had come around and perched himself in front of the guardrail.

"What's the hurry?" he asked. He stood with his trench coat unbuttoned, one hand holding it closed, the other stuffed inside. Like a modern day teenage Napoleon, he thought, except three feet taller with a grin like a bird of prey. Drew cursed himself for not bringing a weapon.

"We wanted to catch up with you," said the kid, "because you forgot something." He opened his jacket and pulled out a black tote bag printed with white skulls and pink hearts. *Desiree's bag.* The bottom was swollen with something round, about the size of a bowling ball. A patch of something dark stained the side. The kid moved his arm slowly, took aim and tossed it on the ground halfway between himself and Drew.

The tote landed with a muted thump. It rolled over and Drew saw a crumpled bit of a plastic garbage bag poking out of the opening.

"We didn't have a lot of time to pack," he said. "So we just sort of rolled up the important stuff."

A tingle shot down Drew's back. He wanted to scream and leap at them, but instead felt his mouth forming questions: "What is it? What's inside?"

"Just a friendly face," he said. "Go on, have a look. Have a look at the price of sin." As red-hair spoke he drew a sword from beneath his jacket. Its blade flashed like a star in the darkness, a streak of burning light drawn from a dream.

But for Drew it was a nightmare. He noted the blade's length, the weapon was within striking distance of where he had tossed the tote. He looked at the crumpled trash bag again and saw what might have been a shadow, or might have been a lock of dyed black hair, poking out. "Desiree," he said.

Red-hair chuckled. "Marvelous. With such powers of reason, it's amazing you didn't see things our way in the first place. Perhaps it's not too late. Come here."

But Drew noticed one of the crew had broken off from the others and disappeared behind the building. He was making his way around to cut off the other end of the alley.

Drew looked at the bag one more time. Maybe it *was* only a shadow, only a bluff. Desiree was on a bus, heading to Boston. She'd have a bowl of noodles there in Chinatown, then go on to New York. The stain wasn't a smear of blood from the bloody stump of her neck. The uneven ball in the tote bag wasn't the severed head of a friend he would never see alive again.

Red-hair took a step forward. Drew knew it was his last chance, and bolted down the alley. Glancing back, he saw a figure with hatred in its eyes picking up the bag he'd used for bait, the bag that had landed with a dead thump.

# 23

"Now you know they're coming for us," said Sondra. "So you know we're running out of time."

"But you lied to us," said Drew. "You pretended to help us, and instead you brought death."

"Death would have come one way or another. I brought you a chance at something else along the way, a chance to be a part of my world, and to help my people."

"But still you lied," he said.

They stood facing each other in his bedroom. She had her fins wrapped around her hips like lingerie, their tips extending down her thighs like garters. Her legs seemed to swim in front him, drawing him in despite his anger. Desiree was dead, and instead of listening to his own inner voice, the voice cloying him with the possibility he held some fault in what had happened, he felt himself slipping. He felt Sondra stifle his thoughts with her soft words and intoxicating presence. He struggled not to replace revulsion and grief with the yearning to touch her warmth and feed on physical bliss.

"I'm doing what I have to for my people," she went on. "They still have a chance, and that's no lie."

"But who are your people?"

"Atlanteans." She gave him that look of appraisal she'd given him the first day.

"But who are Atlanteans? What comes after page one in that book?"

"Look what I brought for us," she teased, producing a leather whip with a handle shaped like an anatomical part he didn't want to touch. "Oh come on, don't be a prude. I found you in a storm, show me some lightning."

He took the whip by one of its leather strands and tossed it against the wall.

"That's it," she giggled. "Sometimes it's tender, sometimes it's not. It'll all make you stronger, and I need you strong."

"What's in the book Sondra?" He turned her around, pulled her head back by her hair, making her laugh.

"What do you mean?" she asked. "There was a catastrophe."

"Yeah, there was a catastrophe. There were a lot of catastrophes."

"Just do this for me, Drew. Come on, one more time. What do you want, poetry? Something romantic? Ooh baby, hit me like a meteor hammering the Earth…"

He punched her in the jaw, cracking a tooth. She punched him back, breaking a rib.

They fell against each other, raining kisses while their hips writhed. Her scars opened into gashes that slicked their flesh with hot blood. He felt like they were drowning and on fire at the same time, igniting in each other something far wilder than love. Finally, after what felt like an endless, breathless, scalding shiver, they collapsed.

"That is strength," she hissed in his ear. "With that, even among my kind, you might hold your own."

"What do you mean might hold my own, what does that mean?" he asked.

"Occasionally we reward the worthy, those who are strong enough. If they're willing to pay the price, they may even earn a rank. But now we have to leave, we have to hurry."

"I'd say we've been paying the price all along," said Drew. "And I'm not going anywhere until you tell me who the Atlanteans really are."

"If you really want to know, then see for yourself," said Sondra. She rose from the floor and went to the window. "You're strong enough to turn the page now, so go ahead, do it."

"I will," he said, picking up the book.

"Drew," she said as he opened the cover.

"Yes?"

"Be tactful when you learn who I am. Humans aren't the only ones who aren't perfect. In the end, none are, not even Jarwhal's own. Yet some are more *tactful* about it than others."

Drew caught the reflection of her eyes flaring red in the window's glass, then turned back to the book. Skipping over the rising mural of a city in flames, he pushed through pages of strange script, characters similar to those he'd seen in the undersea cave. Toward the middle he found a passage that had been translated into English in the margins:

*Chain Molech's legions as common pigs for slaughter, and cast them in the darkest regions of the sea. Make for them living graves in the remotest depths, in the festering abscesses in the rock. There cast them down where water drenches the boiling bile of the Earth. Writhe will their prison as a wyrm squirming through submarine lava, endlessly destroyed will be their corruption, in the lightless regions of the sea.*

"Now try the mural again," she said.

Drew flipped back to the first page and beheld a comet-like object hurtling through space. It had what looked like a palace on it, and upon a throne in the center of its vast pavilions sat an immense, faceless figure admired by choir after choir of winged beings. Drew watched as two of the beings stepped before their leader and seemed to engage in a debate. He couldn't make out their words, but could tell that the debate was evolving into an argument. It became more and more heated, until the crowds of the winged figures burst into a battle. Their melee spread out of the palace, into the air, and then out among the stars. Groups of them seemed to meld together then break apart to fight separately, and then meld together again. They appeared as bizarre globes full of the armored figures rocketing around a humongous planet he thought might be Jupiter. As the globes crashed, the beings within exploded outward, savaging each other with vicious blades and bleeding into open space. When one side began to gain an advantage, the other plunged toward the sun. Before they reached it, the victors fell upon them, hurling them toward the small blue planet he recognized as Earth. Their feathers burned and their faces melted. Their armor splintered with lances, swords, and bizarre axes that looked like cupids with blades in place of arms.

When the mass of the vanquished impacted the ocean, a gigantic gray worm rose from its depths. It swallowed them as they floundered among the waves, its gaping mouth round and ringed with slate-like teeth. It looked like a deranged eel with a jaw large enough to bite a mountain off an island. After devouring nearly all the decimated host, it dove downward, its bloated belly stretching and twisting with the shapes of its suffering contents. Its most swollen segment stretched into the north Atlantic, a cold empty expanse below the southern tip of Greenland.

Two armored beings with radiant feathered wings followed the worm as it dove downward. They bound the thrashing beast to the ocean floor with chains that remained burning even beneath the raging waves. Into the worm's very body they carved a prison, an architecture of diseased coral and stone. As they worked they pulled the mutilated bodies of the damned through the suffering beast's wounds and bound their flailing limbs with manacles, sealing them into wretched cells. The beast began spinning from the pain, churning up earthquakes, volcanoes and putrid bile that flooded over the city of writhing corpses in an endless cycle of catastrophe.

One of the winged figures cried out, its mouth moving in mismatched rhythm with the words, as if it were being simultaneously translated: "Be thou contained in the belly of Yormungund! Thou contingent of Molech, Yormungund Atlantis be thy despicable prison!"

~*~

Tears streaked Sondra's eyes as he closed the book.

"So do you understand now what I am?" she asked, spreading her leathery wings and displaying her naked, flame-scarred body.

Drew was silent. It took all his strength not to look away from her.

"I am a descendent of those who survived the first war. It was only the strongest of us who were able to carry on, who were able to carve a city into the great serpent, our slithering undersea prison. Immense as it was, in truth, we occupied but one small segment of the topmost circle of Hell. Because of this we were for a time able to elude the angels sent to hunt us down. But all the while we were still suffering. Some of us went insane from the constant pain, the burning wounds inflicted on our bodies. Others were strong enough to continue a shadow war against the angels on the Earth's surface. Still others contented themselves to improve our stronghold, for they had slipped their chains and bred with the humans. They sought to swell the ranks of our army, succeeded in the process of generating a litter of half-breeds to share in our misery.

"The angels eventually renewed their assault, increasing the severity of the cycle of catastrophes you saw when you first opened our book. We were reduced to sealing ourselves into catacombs, expending what strength we had left to bolstering our last defenses. That is why only you can open my brother's sarcophagus, for its glyphs ward that no being spawn of angels shall ever open it. And yet for all of our various defenses we could never hide what our city beneath the sea really was, who we really were. And so, now you know what I truly am."

"Yes," said Drew. "You're Atlantean."

_*_

An hour later they lay on the floor beneath the window, bodies entangled and breathless. Minor burns pocked his flesh from sliding over her smoldering wounds. The pain was nothing compared to the pleasure of her touch, and despite the scalding heat, his muscles and bones yearned to gorge again on the strength their joinings imparted. But this time Sondra pulled away, leaving his broken rib only half-healed as her eyes flicked to the window and the ocean beyond.

"Please, not yet," he whispered.

"But we have to hurry, they know I'm here now and they've mustered their strength. They're coming for us, not half-angels like Garvy and the one who attacked you in the lot. I'm talking about the ones who followed you, Brinsdale's minions, his *saints*."

"Well you're right about one thing," he said. "I still don't understand, which is why there's something else I need to know."

"What is that?"

"That you promise you'll stay with me. If I decide to help you, I need your promise you won't disappear."

She looked at him again with the gaze of appraisal. "That depends on whether you fulfill the covenant."

Just then they heard banging on the apartment door. Sondra stood, leaned out the window and looked, then dashed back to the closet.

# 24

"They're here," she said, pulling out a wrinkled trash bag. Her eyes were lit with a vicious glow as she drew out two swords. Their hilts dripped with blood-colored stones, their blades terminated in serrated tips.

"Angels use Oorinic steel, but we use both Oorinium and Plutysium. They are equally deadly, though Plutysium is rarer."

"Where the hell did you get those?" he asked.

"What, you think that cash we made was just for beer? Weapons cost money. These weapons cost *a lot* of money."

The banging sounded again. Drew took the sword, felt its weight.

"Now go welcome our guests while I check the other exits."

"But…"

"Go," she said, pushing him out of the bedroom.

~*~

As he approached the front hallway, he could hear Buzzy's voice: "She ain't here, so why don't you dudes go back to blow dryin' your hair."

Drew had to steady himself when he stepped into the hall and saw what had become of the drummer. A film of sweat covered his body, soaking his t-shirt and jeans. Cracks webbed his elbows, leaking pinkish blood and chunks of stringy white cartilage. His forearms had swelled into a pair of large red claws lined with uneven and rotten looking teeth.

"Hey, Buzz, what's the matter?"

Buzzy casually raised a claw, pointed through the open doorway. "These guys say they're lookin' for Sondra," he said.

Drew gripped the hilt of his sword, kept it low along his leg as he peered past his roommate toward the stairs. Sure enough it was Brinsdale's crew. This time the shorter, dark-haired kid stood in front. He was straight-mouthed, with his hands in the pockets of his trench coat. Behind him stood the tall one with the red curly hair, glaring at Drew with his gem-blue eyes.

"Just let us have a look inside," the dark-haired kid said.

"No-can-do, dude," said Buzzy. "In fact, you oughta just step on back." The drummer proceeded to throw the weight of his misshapen arm against the kid's chest, knocking him against those behind him.

At this the red-haired kid slipped his hand inside his coat, looked past Buzzy at Drew. "You gonna try me this time?" he asked. "Come on now, don't run off like a little prick, like a little *bastard.*"

He took a step forward, causing Drew to raise his sword.

"The sad thing," he continued, "is that by now you must know who she really is, and *what* she really is, and yet still you follow her. Well, I guess when it comes to Hell, it takes garbage to know garbage."

Drew stepped out onto the landing and stood shoulder to shoulder with his roommate. Buzzy raised his claws, flaps of curdled puss leaking through their cracked shells. "Say it again," he said, "and see what happens."

"Zechariah, wait," said Brinsdale as he emerged from behind his henchmen. "There's still time to reason with one another. We don't have to have any more bloodshed if you just let us take the demon. You who are lost may yet be found, you who are condemned may join us and yet be redeemed."

For a moment nobody spoke. Drew's eyes flicked from Brinsdale to the red-haired kid he'd called Zechariah. He wondered if they were as confident as they acted. Beside him he noticed Buzzy looking at the floor, like he was searching the beginnings of regret, like what the preacher said about redemption had planted a seed in his mind.

Buzzy opened his mouth to speak—a fraction of a second after the dark-haired kid swung his dagger. It slashed open his swollen elbow, causing him to howl in pain. In response Buzzy threw out his claw, clamped onto the kid's head and squeezed.

A sickening pop sounded. The kid's body hung quivering, bones cracking as brains bulged in the fissures. His dagger dropped from his hand and clattered down the stairs. The odor of feces rose from his twitching legs.

Zechariah thrust his hand into his coat and drew out the five-foot sword, its blade lined with spiked lugs. He swung it against Buzzy's claw, shattering the shell and causing him to drop his victim.

Before Drew could respond, Brinsdale was at him with his own sword, and it took all of his speed to parry his attacks. The rotund preacher was amazingly fast, and chewed his lower lip as he swung his blade, drool rolling off his chin like a glutton at a feast. In two blows he drove Drew back across the landing, his blade whipping and howling as it slashed, almost too fast for Drew to track. It was all he could do to back pedal into the apartment's doorway and try to hold them off there.

As Drew struggled to push the preacher back, he felt hot blood splash against his cheek. He turned and saw Buzzy grasping the sword Zechariah had thrust through his chest. His good claw clasped the blade, while his other quivered as it tried to clamp onto the hilt. Zechariah bore down, keeping hold of him like a fish on a gaffer. After ratcheting the sword through his gut, he flung Buzzy's body against the floor. Buzzy's torso curled into itself as he let out his last blood-choked breath. Zechariah stepped over him, adding his blade to his leader's attack. He glared at Drew with his hawk-like visage as the two of them lunged forward. "For truly," he said, "it is better ye die by my sword than suckle the eternal venom of yon whore."

Zechariah slashed from above while Brinsdale thrust low to catch Drew in the ribs. They pushed into the apartment this way while Drew parried with sweeping arcs. He absorbed the blows with painful shocks running wrist to shoulder. He tried a rapid parry and lunge, and felt a brief exhilaration at his newfound strength when he finally stopped their advance.

Zechariah snarled as he slipped on the pink slime oozing across the floor from Buzzy's corpse. Drew pressed the attack, drove him back out to the landing. Feinting left, he slashed right. He took off a clump of the kid's red curls as the blade bit into his neck. Zechariah opened his mouth as if to scream, but sprayed blood instead. Drew pulled back then lunged forward once more, thrusting the sword through his enemy's stomach. A tangle of intestines quivered across the hilt as he tore to the side, cutting Zechariah nearly in half. When he withdrew the blade, the body fell atop the slop that had been Buzzy.

But the time spent outmaneuvering Zechariah came with a price—Drew felt an explosion of pain behind his knee. He collapsed on his back, breaking off a piece of the banister and getting the wind knocked out of him.

Brinsdale's fist followed after his sword, grasping a lock of Drew's hair and pulling him to his feet. His eyes stared with a cold fury and his right hand pressed the tip of his sword against Drew's jugular. "Tell me where the succubus is. Tell me and I'll make your death quick," he spat.

"No need to look far, Reverend," said the voice behind him.

Brinsdale had no time to answer. He was screaming in pain from his severed foot.

Sondra leapt over the man's heaving belly, picked up Drew and pulled him across her shoulders. But when she turned to plunge her blade through the preacher's heart, gunshots sounded from inside the apartment. Something large-caliber opened up three large holes in the hallway's walls, blowing white clouds of plaster into the air.

At least one slug hit Sondra, tearing open her wing, yet she managed to leap down the steps and into the street. There she swung Drew around and held him beneath her belly, lifting them into the dusky sky despite her wound. Gunshots rang behind them as they flew out over the bay and plunged into the water.

# 25

Drew's flesh tightened, bruised itself against his bones as they dove deeper and deeper. Like an organism at war with itself, the strength imbued by Sondra now competed with the continuous blood loss and shock of hurtling downward. He kept the sword gripped close to his body, even as he felt like his skull would shatter and his brain burst like a dead jellyfish.

His mind felt warped and starved when they finally slowed among the silent valleys of the ocean's floor. His eyelids wavered with the immensity of the darkness, scratched open here and there with slashes of wispy light. They were coming toward the undersea mountains from another angle this time, a crevasse cut like a wound into the Earth's crust. He began to glimpse strange things, bloated whales with crab encrusted jaws, moth-like rays with tails like trails of skulls, and blind squid caught in their own tentacles, gnawing hungrily on their own flesh. He felt vomit pushing to pour out his throat, lost consciousness and regained it only when they burst into the grotto, choking and clawing at the charred brickwork.

Before he'd even caught his breath, Sondra was dragging him down the tunnel by his hair. His limbs hung limp, save his right hand, which kept a grip on the sword's hilt and dragged it clattering along the bricks. She brought him coughing and gasping to the circular room ringed with sarcophagi. There she threw him at the feet of the tall figure in the jeweled robes.

"Take hold of the latch," she cried. "Take hold, bloodheart, and release my kindred!"

Though blasting through the saltwater had had a cauterizing effect on his leg, the wound still pulsed with pain. Drew put down the sword and had to crawl to reach the great grimacing statue. Hoisting himself up on the thing's boot, he took hold of what she'd called the latch, a valve-like wheel set into the figure's right palm.

Slowly he swung open the heavy stone door.

A brief groaning sounded, then silence. At first he saw only shadows thrown by the glowing crystals on the walls. Then out of those a greater shadow emerged, an utter absence of light, shaped by flames that oozed over its skin.

The gigantic demon stepped forth, at least twenty feet tall, though Drew couldn't be sure in the strange proportions of the cave. His face seemed to mock human perfection: chiseled cheeks, steely black goatee, and coals of eyes that glowed with an almost professorial twinkle.

Yet the rest of him was a naked monstrosity. Flaming boils trailed across his chest like ranges of tiny volcanoes. They moved as if alive, running through his charred skin like lice. Bloody lava spewed from their cones and occasionally they burst, leaving craters in his flesh.

"Cherylith, my suffering sweet," he said, taking Sondra's hand.

The succubus closed her eyes, turning away as she received his caress. Her lips and eyelids glowed crimson, as if that were how a demon blushed. The giant reached around her skull, turned her head toward his and kissed her deeply. She whimpered as he pulled her slender body against his.

Drew stepped forward. "Hey, I thought you said he was your brother," he said.

Sondra kissed the monstrosity again, then squirmed away. For a moment she looked confused, turning back and forth between Drew and demon. She shrugged. "Well, technically we're all related."

"You bastard!" he cried, lunging for the beast.

The demon stepped to the side, allowing Drew's body to crash into a stalagmite. The brittle stone shattered, leaving crystalline slivers in his skin.

Behind him the demon chuckled. "I am in fact a pureblood," he said. "Cherylith, however, carries a touch of the humanum." He leaned over and brushed back Sondra's hair. Out slithered his forked tongue, which he ran along the length of her neck.

Sondra closed her eyes, sucked in a deep breath and held it. When she opened them again, tears had formed, and she turned to face Drew.

"But I thought you needed me," he gasped. "I mean, I knew what you were, but I thought... I thought you said..."

The gigantic demon laughed beside them. "You foolish bloodhearts, always thinking everything revolves around you. The succubae were ours long before they pretended they were yours to satisfy their perverted caprices."

Drew opened his mouth but Sondra interrupted him. "Just don't say I lied to you," she said. She gazed at him, eyes aflame as her kinsman clamped a steel collar around her neck. He hooked it on a chain which he fastened to his heavy belt, then jerked it once to test the drag. Sondra fell, legs splayed. Her kinsman chuckled and reeled her back up by tightening the strap.

"But you can't do this," said Drew. "This wasn't our deal, you said nothing of this."

"Drew," she said, voice raspy from the pressure of the collar. "You don't have much strength left. You can barely get to the surface, let alone back to the city."

Drew glared at her kinsman. "Maybe I'll use my strength for something else," he said.

The demon tucked a grin into his combed goatee, flecked with just a touch of puss from the boils on his neck. "You would martyr yourself for a whore," he said. "How charming. Even so, you wouldn't get far without this." He reached down and picked up the longsword Drew had left leaning against the wall beside the statue. Its Plutonic steel glimmered in the cave's dim light, one of the few things Sondra had said could harm her kind. Clasped in the demon's grip, it was now a world away, though there was only a yard between them.

"Then I'll go," Drew said. "I'll take your lie and I'll go."

But before he returned the pool, he caught Sondra's reflection among the cave's crystals, dozens of tearful eyes gazing out of their facets. "Don't say that," she said. "Never say I lied to you."

# 26

The Coast Guard patrol found him tossed by the waves amid a torrential rain. They said he was lucky he was even spotted. How long had he been without his kayak? Without being reported missing, he was incredibly lucky.

He didn't bother telling them he had the strength to swim several more days, maybe even make it to shore, if he wanted to.

But then something occurred to him as he glanced at the small framed print of Saint Michael hanging in Captain O'Leary's cabin. Swallowing the pain killers offered by the medic, he said he was feeling better already, please pass his gratitude on to the whole crew. When they reached the pier and they asked if he had any family in the area, he said no, but he'd appreciate if they could call his pastor, Reverend John Brinsdale.

~*~

For two days Brinsdale kept him in a concrete room in the basement of the old police armory. There were no windows, no visitors, and very little food.

On the morning of what the kid who brought him the bread said was the third day, Brinsdale came for him. He was wearing a tan jacket and slacks, and moved deftly despite the new prosthetic foot. Around his waist hung the sword he'd used to slice open Drew's leg. The sight of it gave him a shiver, but he also noted it was a full foot longer than the sword the demon had taken from him, and its blade several inches wider.

"We could do things to you," said Brinsdale.

Drew began to answer but paused—the preacher's right hand hovered over the sword's hilt, the clasp on the scabbard already unhooked. A single stroke could open Drew's chest and splatter the concrete walls with his blood. He decided to remain silent.

Brinsdale frowned across his large, square jaw. "All right then, son. I'll bite, but out of caution, not curiosity. Why did you come to us?"

"To make an agreement," said Drew.

"Then you've come to your death, son. We can no longer recruit you. You are weak, contaminated, and untrustworthy. I will behead you." As he said this, the preacher pulled his sword out a few inches, eyes flickering with something bordering on pity, but only bordering.

"I didn't come to join you," said Drew.

"Then perhaps you know where we can find the succubus, and you came to have her done as she did you?" The preacher cracked a grin. "There is no honor among the damned."

This time it was Drew who tensed as if he would leap from the floor. "She chose me," he said. "And I wouldn't sell her to the likes of you."

Brinsdale huffed, released his sword hilt, and punched Drew in the jaw. He caught the back of Drew's head with his left hand and yanked him back up as he spat his words: "You murdered Zechariah! You murdered him and you will suffer the consequence!"

Drew breathed into the pain, let his mouth bleed: "You hunt them, don't you," he said. "Your superiors reward you for hunting them down. Except this time you lost. You thought you could overwhelm us. You thought you were pros."

Brinsdale chewed his lip. "You may be right in that the wench wasn't worth Zechariah," he said. "But that won't save you, son. If you tell me where she is now, I may renew my offer of a quick death."

"I told you that's out of the question. But as I said, I came here to make an agreement. If you help me with what I need to do, there's something in it for you."

"If you're looking to take revenge on her," said the preacher, "you're in a poor position for it."

"True," said Drew. "First you need to give me your sword."

# 27

That night he paddled the kayak by moonlight. His guitar, some bottled water, and what he'd borrowed from the preacher were strapped into the bow. Someone more cautious might have wondered how to find the island amid the fog-swathed shadows. But Drew pushed briskly through the waves as if the darkness itself were his beacon.

When he reached the rock outcropping, he dragged the kayak up the bank and took a swallow of water. He used his flashlight only a moment to lay a tattered blanket between the pines and arrange his things. When he was finished, he sat cross-legged on the flannel with the guitar on his lap.

He didn't need to see to play the minor, bass-heavy dirge. And though there were no words, his mind and heart whispered an incantation that was an invitation for Sondra to meet him again upon the island.

Soon he glimpsed her shadow cut against the moonlight, wings pressing against the rising wind. Her eyes glowed against the blackened clouds, her body glistened with its patina of red scars and smoldering cuts. When she landed and kissed him, her lips still burned, and her breasts still pressed against his ribs as impetuously as on their first night.

"I will always return to you," she said. "As long as any part of us exists."

"By exists, you mean in Hell?" he asked.

"I mean anywhere." Sondra licked her lower lip. He noticed her teeth were cracked and mouth bleeding. "I gnawed through my chains while he was meditating," she said. "By now he's rising out of the ruins, on his way to finish us off. I might have only come here so we can die together."

As they kissed he held her tightly, as if he'd offer her a chain of his own. In turn she sucked at his flesh with her jagged maw, smearing him with blood and small burns.

"Don't you understand me?" she whispered. "We're running out of time."

"You're right. But we do have this."

He reached beneath the blanket and pulled out Brinsdale's sword. Unbuckling the scabbard, he bared a few inches of its blade.

Sondra shuddered and gave him the look of appraisal once more. "It appears I wasn't wrong to help you," she said. "It appears humans aren't always stupid after all."

"No," he said, brushing back a scalding lock of her hair. "We're occasionally cunning. But like you said, we're running out of time."

Drew pointed into the misty distance at a massive shadow moving toward them beneath the water. "Here, take it," he said. "Take the sword."

Sondra took hold of the scabbard and drew forth five feet of Oorinic steel. She held it between them, extending its hardened length toward the sea.

"But Drew," she said, "how do you know that what my brother said about succubae wasn't true? How do you know you're not just a whim, and I won't kill you then trade the sword for my freedom?"

"Because if Brinsdale doesn't receive your brother's head, our covenant will be broken. The angels he answers to, who right now could give a damn about a lost succubus, will chase you down and kill you."

Sondra kissed him, caught his tongue in her broken teeth as if she would cut through, then released. The wind was getting stronger, and the fog swirled with an impending gale. "So we'll face him together," she said. "Because you can make strong anyone you choose—but the one who turns your gift into a favor they can return, that's someone worth taking to Hell and back."

~*~

The demon's torso rose from the waves like the projection of a rotted corpse against the night. His body had grown to an immense size, and his muscles flexed as he heaved his sword over his head. His once thin lips and trim goatee stretched into a snarling jaw full of foaming fangs, and the sight of him held Drew transfixed. For a moment, as the sword descended, he assumed himself a willing attendant at his own execution.

But before the blow connected, Sondra sprang into the air and blocked it. Though much smaller than her brother, the length of Brinsdale's blade allowed her to parry her enemy's blows. She twisted and parried as she flew, and the swords rang against the whistling wind.

Again and again she slashed at her brother's misshapen flesh. Yet despite her attacks and his already his oozing wounds, the demon pumped his sinewy wings. He rose fully from the ocean, picked up speed, adding momentum to his assaults.

Like a bullet fired at a charging beast, Sondra kept flying headlong against him, body trailing a streak of flames. Drew dove into a crevasse between the granite boulders just before they barreled back down to the shoreline like meteors slamming into the earth.

~*~

Any exhilaration that he survived the shattering of the island was obliterated by the terror of coming-to in the freezing water. Drew's body was swirling among the waves as the clang of steel echoed above him. A flash of lightning split the sky, and he glimpsed the warring demons' fiery forms exploding against each other.

He coughed out a throat full of brine as he mustered enough strength to swim, keeping just behind their wave-crests as they crashed over themselves. As he thrashed his way closer to the combat, Drew saw Sondra lose hold of her sword. He followed it with his eyes as it plunged downward, its glimmer sinking into the ocean's gray-black abyss.

Gulping a mouthful of air, he dove after it. He cut his palm as he grabbed the blade with his left hand, then clasped the hilt with his right and swam upward.

The closer he got, the harder it was to look straight at the gigantic pureblood. The demon was becoming a sickness of ill proportion, an image caught between the human-like figure he'd seen in the grotto and a smear of electric fire. The look on his face was one of untold viciousness, all fangs and eyes as he slashed at the succubus. She pressed her attack in despite, recoiling from his blows like a serpent. She hurtled herself at his neck, tearing with her burning claws. The span of her wings made her look like some great vampiric bat ripping at the throat of a massive bull upon which it was crazed to feed. Though larger and stronger, the pureblood could not fend off her ferocity, and brother and sister came down again, still fighting as they impacted the water. Drew noticed that the surge caused Sondra's glow of fade, become weaker under the strain of keeping up the momentum of her rapid assault.

Drew pressed on, though his lungs were on the edge of collapse. He stayed beneath the surface as the demons fought along the peaks and valleys of the waves. Finally, they twisted downward, as if the giant were trying to smash his sister against the ocean floor. A mass of sharks formed behind them like an undersea storm cloud, hovering in anticipation of the coming feast.

Drew swam as close to the beast as he could, felt pure hatred and malice radiating from his body. *Well*, Drew thought, *I have some malice of my own.* He lunged forward and plunged the sword into the demon's broad back, stabbing him just left of his spine, as if he were harpooning a whale. Clinging to the hilt, he twisted, driving the blade as deep as it would go.

The giant opened his mouth in a silent scream. His body soared upward, bursting out of the water. Drew felt a rush of air as the demon's wings opened behind him, and yet he never had a chance to take flight—Drew grabbed the beast's hair with his bloody left hand, pulled out the blade, and hacked into the back of his neck.

The pureblood made an awful choking sound as his body fell forward into the oncoming waves. Drew could feel Sondra's strength added to his own as she took hold of her brother's mangled goatee. Using the leverage she provided, he continued hacking through the demon's neck. Spinning through the storm they clung to their quarry, remained rabid with their purpose as he sawed through gristle and bone, only letting go when the pureblood's head disconnected from his body.

As Drew made his final cut, he heard Sondra pronounce incomprehensible syllables, *her brother's name*, he thought, *his true name, and a curse upon it.*

When she was finished, Drew knew the demon was slain. Withdrawing the sword, he was overcome with exhaustion and his body began to sink. Above him he saw Sondra swimming, her ember eyes maintaining a faint glow. It was up to her now, and he wondered what she would do. She had insisted she hadn't lied, but it was possible she had become weak and wounded. Drew could only hold his breath and hope, as her glowing figure dove toward him, that she had enough strength to bring them both back to the surface.

# 28

A few hours later they cruised slowly into the harbor in a lifeboat stolen off an oil tanker. The name on the outboard motor was written in Cyrillic, and the two of them in the rusty aluminum craft dappled with rotted red paint looked like a pair of castaways. The succubus sat curled up in the bow, her wings shriveled and scarred like they'd been torn from a diseased bat. Maybe she really had been nearly dead when she dove for him. It was a different class of wound, he'd learned, that demons inflicted on one another.

The craft zigzagged between moored sailboats and yachts. As they came in closer to the city, Drew angled left and made for the rotted wharves along the south end. They could tie up there and he could use the phone in the rehearsal space if the door was open. He had no shirt or shoes and his jeans were torn but other musicians and hangers-on around the building would likely assume he was just hungover.

Drew turned and checked the steel chain hooked to a peg on the back of the boat. The succubus had tied it well and it held fast. A few dozen yards behind he could see the archdemon's head. She had strung the chain through its mouth and neck so it dragged through the waves like a bloated fish. A few of the sharks that tried gnawing it lay tangled in its hair, teeth still in its scalp. His flesh is poison, she had said, but they still couldn't resist.

As they neared the first of the abandoned wharves Drew killed the motor and they drifted beneath the splintered pilings. Cats slithered among the slivered wood, took up positions in the shadows and stared with dozens of gleaming eyes. Drew made his way out and across the gravel road toward the studios. The door turned out to be locked, but he saw one of the panhandlers from Munjoy Hill digging in a trashcan over on Fore Street.

"It's money if you tell the preacher I'm down here. The one up on the Hill. Go and tell him I'm here."

The vagrant gave him a skeptical look from head to toe. Only then did Drew realize as he stood shivering and shirtless in his torn jeans, that he too, was covered in bruises and lacerations.

While they waited for Brinsdale, Sondra submerged the archdemon's head a few hundred feet out. Even the drunken fishermen used to the harbor's filth would have recoiled at the sight of it. When she returned she sat with him in the back of the boat holding the chain, staring back at the cats.

~*~

By sunset Brinsdale still hadn't shown up. Drew sat shivering in the autumn night, salt water teasing his thirst as it lapped against the boat. His wounds were peeling, they itched and oozed blood. He planted the sword's tip in the bottom of the boat, leaned on its ornately carved crossguard, and coughed until he wracked his lungs.

"Cherylith," he said, pronouncing her real name for the first time.

Her dark silhouette remained still and staring.

"I guess that's what I call you now, huh? What are we going to do, Cherylith, once we settle with the preacher? I mean where are we going to go?"

At first the succubus remained silent. The fog thickened, making his wounds sting. When they were surrounded by the mist, she spoke. "Maybe the Dominican Republic," she said. "Someplace like Santo Domingo, or maybe Mexico City, where we can live on cash and melt in. Someplace like that I can help you heal."

Drew coughed and nodded. Instinctively his hand shot down, scooped a handful of saltwater and splashed it on his forehead. It only made him feel more like he was burning up. It dripped down his cheeks like fiery tears, and rolled across his chest, burning.

"I need something to drink," he said. "I'm really thirsty. I won't be able to talk to him or nothin' if I don't get something to drink."

The succubus stood up, the look of appraisal needling him this time. She giggled, murmuring, *"You think you're thirsty now..."*

"Wait what?" he asked. "What did you say?"

"I said I would start healing you now, but can't until I've recovered myself."

She put her hand under his chin, lifted it, and kissed his lips. Memories of mesmerizing nights spent in his room flashed in his mind. "I'm going to risk going ashore," she said. "Keep hold of the chain and the blade. If they come and I'm not here, you'll have to defend yourself."

Drew nodded, moved to the bench in front of the motor. He laid the sword across his lap and took hold of the chain fastened to the dead demon's head.

"Good," she said. "I won't be long."

But as soon as she left, he was leaning again. He heard the sword thunk on the bottom of the boat before he passed out. When he came-to, she had already returned and was emptying a cheap duffle bag across the seat.

"Spring water," she said. "and a beer and some canned fish." She laid out the food on a plastic bag. He managed a half smile.

"Just like old times," he said.

"Old times indeed," she said.

The succubus straddled him and sat down on his lap.

"I'm sorry I passed out," he said.

"It's all right," she said, stroking his hair. "You've nearly fulfilled the covenant."

"I thought I signed up to lift the lid of a sarcophagus."

"You agreed to help someone who was trapped. More or less." The demon gave a warped yet wry grin. "Drew, listen to me, we're almost finished, almost free. Once we honor our contract with Brinsdale, we can be together. Here, I got you this." She passed him a little brown bottle of hydrocodone. "It'll help a little, though, to use one of humanity's subtler expressions, it might knock you on your ass."

Drew took the bottle and swallowed a couple of the pills. Cherylith climbed off his lap and took up position in the bow. There she peered through the thick fog in the direction of the wharves. Drew wondered, as he watched her, just what kind of worth she really saw in him. She had needed him to open her brother's sarcophagus, which was something he'd commanded her to do. But had she predicted Drew would fall for her enough to help slay him? And now she said he'd agreed to help someone who was trapped, which meant help rid her of the preacher. He wondered where it would end, whether this was about freeing her from being anybody's thrall, or about whether it was about making him a thrall himself. He tried to shake off the thought as he reached for the beer. He hoped the light booze and the pills would kill the pain enough to make him at least a little limber. He tried to rest as the hours passed, until the first rays of dawn pierced his eyes like slivers.

He took hold of the sword by the grip and stood up just as the heavyset figure of Brinsdale emerged out of the morning fog along Fore Street.

"Good morning to you," he said. "A testament to His Majesty, every dawning day."

The succubus didn't answer. "Pull in the chain," she said, and leapt to the back of the craft where she helped Drew haul the swollen head of the archdemon to the surface. Waterlogged, it looked like a giant maggot, with erratic, poisoned crabs stumbling in and out of the depressions of its eyes and shark-bloated hair. Its lips twisted in an eternal mockery of what might have been anger or laughter, steeped in a bottomless mire of pain.

"For He hath given His only Son that we may enter paradise," said Brinsdale.

"Save it, Reverend," said Cherylith. "We have what you wanted, and we brought back your sword."

The preacher looked at the weapon in Drew's right hand. "Ah yes, my angelic blade," he said. "An early longsword forged in Wales around 1280. It was a gift for Edward Longshanks, from a humble Welsh craftsman disillusioned with rebellion. But the English king didn't like what he thought were Celtic carvings in the hilt. He cast it aside where it nevertheless found rebel blood in the hands of a foot soldier who ambushed Llywelyn while he was on his way to rally his troops. So you see, vengeance finds its way home after all, particularly when it is righteous."

As he spoke Brinsdale pulled aside his trench coat and unbuckled the sheath of another blade. It occurred to Drew that something was wrong—it was both Brinsdale's gesture and the way the succubus was standing, her wings spread and muscles taut. Her eyes boiled with bitter light and her clawed fingers looked rigid and poised to strike.

Drew followed her gaze and saw that she was scanning the windows along the second and third floors of the crumbling brick buildings. The streetlights cut the fog just enough that he could see figures among the broken panes of glass. They were crouching down behind the barrels of their rifles. A few had scopes and all were thrust just a little too far forward, the young men hoping Brinsdale had brought them along for a taste of the real thing.

But for each unskilled and overzealous acolyte, Drew knew there was another like Zechariah, poised and ruthless, marking exactly where he would put a bullet.

Around the wharves the mangy cats teemed, their eyes sparkling with blue fire. Brinsdale had brought out his minions en masse to finish hunting a demon. And yet even this conflict, in all its strangeness, still had rules. It was the unearthly strength with which Cherylith had imbued Drew which allowed them to slay the archdemon. He wondered what the real prize was, the prize for which Brinsdale was willing to risk his entire flock.

"Drew," said the succubus, never taking her eyes off the preacher. "Cut the chain with the sword and give him what he's owed."

With a single slash, Drew cut through the chain and held it out for the preacher. Brinsdale nodded and a pair of burly young men emerged. They took hold of the chain and dragged the head in among the trash-strewn rocks along the shoreline.

"Now give him the sword," said the succubus. "Just do it so we can get out of here."

Turning the blade around, Drew held the sword by the crossguard so

Brinsdale could take hold of its grip—Drew held it out, but the preacher didn't grasp.

"No, keep it," he said. "Consider it a gift."

"Very funny, Reverend," said Cherylith. "Drew, drop it on the wharf. Don't give him a legitimate reason to summon an angel."

"But I am giving him the blade of my own free will," said Brinsdale. "For He hath bestowed free will upon us, Drew. And you know, I've changed my mind about you. I've decided it's still not too late."

Drew looked from the preacher to the succubus. Though Brinsdale was smiling, they both looked like wolves ready to pounce.

"We don't have much time," hissed Cherylith.

Brinsdale gave a nervous chuckle. "Why do you think she encourages you to give up the blade, Drew? What exactly do you think she'll do with you once you're out of sight of land? Weak, unarmed, and alone? Not what she did in your bedroom, Drew. Such infernal affections won't seem so kind the next time she has you alone."

Drew turned and looked into Cherylith's eyes, gone from orange embers to white-hot coals.

"Don't believe him," she said. "Drew, we've come this far, we're almost there. Give him the blade and I can get us out of here."

A shot sounded, like the muted crack of a whip. Cherylith's body spun right. The sound came again and spun it back to the left. The succubus fell to her knees, a bullet hole in her shoulder and another in her ribs. A splatter of her flesh coated the aluminum seat behind her.

"Well it won't kill her," said Brinsdale, "but it'll slow her down a little. I mean, if you really want to risk staying in the boat. Just hang on to that sword though, Drew, and we'll put a few more slugs in her. We'll give you a fighting chance. In fact, if you bring us back *her* head, you could replace Zechariah. Why not bring us back her head, Drew, since you've had your fun with her? Come on, show us you're worth our gift."

At this Drew recalled what Cherylith had said to him on the island: … *you can make strong anyone you choose—but the one who turns your gift into a favor they can return, that's someone worth taking to Hell and back.*

And then something else, what was it? *Occasionally we reward the worthy, those who are strong enough. If they're willing to pay the price, they may even earn a rank…*

But could she be believed? She said so many times she wasn't lying, but though shrewd, Brinsdale had never really deceived him either. In that moment Drew felt a strange and sudden emptiness from the city that surrounded him. He felt cruelty from the little city by the sea, a gray empty trap that gnawed and gnashed at his heart. He had never felt so dead, and for a moment he closed his eyes. He wanted nothing other than for a great hazy hand to reach out of the decayed streets and bricks and crush the mind that had been held prisoner despite its youth—but instead, in that moment, it was a different vision he received.

Like a dream, like what it must be like to have your life pass before your eyes at the moment of death, the images came—he saw himself and he saw Desiree, they were together in a small field by a cove. It was a warm overcast day, and they were surrounded by friends and family. Desiree's trucker father was giving her away to Drew, who was ready with a ring to place on her finger. Reverend Brinsdale was officiating and Buzzy was the best man. They said their vows, both said, "I do," and kissed when Brinsdale said they may.

But just as Drew was taking his lips from hers, he felt them turn cold. He stepped back and saw that the best man wasn't Buzzy but Zechariah. He was laughing and holding a sword. He saw that it was red with blood from passing through the bride's neck. She stood a moment, unable to smile above the black cut across her throat. Her head fell on the ground, looking up at him, forever unable to smile, while beside him Zechariah was laughing, her father was laughing, and Brinsdale was howling while the wedding party flickered with flames.

Drew opened his eyes. The reverend was still staring at him, his look as eager as those of his rifle-toting minions in the windows. In a flash Drew reached out with his left hand, pulled the preacher off the dock. His two hundred pounds of muscle and fat crashed down, nearly swamping the aluminum boat. A bullet sank into Drew's calf and he heard Cherylith screech in pain. But he had the preacher up on his knees and the blade of the sword against his throat before they could finish him off.

"What the hell are you doing?" cried Brinsdale. "You stupid little punk! You stupid little trailer trash punk!" As he choked out his words, he struggled against the arm lock, nearly breaking free. "You'll be damned for this," he cried. "You don't know what you're playing with! You're a fool to throw away your soul, throw it away on a demon whore! Don't you understand? You'll be damned for this, forever!"

Drew bent his head down so that his lips were close to Brinsdale's ear.

"I'm counting on it," he said.

Behind him he glimpsed Cherylith's bullet-riddled body as it rose into the air, a slash of crimson in the fog.

"You fool," choked Brinsdale. "You don't understand."

"I do understand," said Drew. As he spoke he heard the ruckus of the preacher's shooters as they ran closer. "But here is what you do not—that I go to be with my own."

A bullet shaved his scalp, knocking him back, but not forcing him to release his grip. A second bullet clipped Brinsdale's shoulder as the preacher hissed a prayer through grit teeth. As Drew steadied his blade, he wondered how it would go for him after the shooters took him down. He wondered if he'd serve Cherylith herself, if they'd give him to someone like her brother, or if they'd all just watch him burn, one more soul in a sea of the damned. Drew turned and gazed at the succubus as she flew further out into the fog, wings beating strongly despite her wounds. For a moment she gazed back, eyes flashing like stars in the distance. Keeping his eyes on hers, he dragged the blade across Brinsdale's throat. "See you in Atlantis," he said.

# Below The Bridge

"Come," she said, beckoning them below the bridge. Burke and his friend Terry followed the pale woman around the corner of a giant pylon. Her figure carved a moon-like crescent as she moved toward the river, and the fabric of her dress clung to the sway of her hips.

"Dude, I can't believe she's with you," said Terry. "What is she crazy?"

"She's a ghost," said Burke, striding ahead of his friend as she led them around a second pylon, the last before the water's edge. There the sloping rubble siphoned little light from the skyscrapers across the river. Even New York City was dimmer at 3:00 a.m., even on Halloween night.

"Come to me," she said to Burke, grin glowing with a silvery sparkle. His eyes wandered down to the low curve of her breasts, the rippled muscles beneath her ribs, the gentle V beneath her hips. "Tonight is the night you can release me," she said.

"Release her?" said Terry stepping up beside them. "I thought you wanted to get with her."

"Shutup!" snapped Burke. "Don't talk about Margaux like that."

"Hey man, chill out, I didn't know junkies were your thing."

Burke scowled but didn't answer his friend. Why should he? Terry had everything—tall, good looking, computer job in the city, his own apartment, two freakin' girlfriends, sometimes three. He wondered sometimes why his friend even hungout with him—probably because Burke tended to buy the drinks at the bar, tended to pay when they went out in general.

"Look man, why don't we just go back to the party," said Terry. "I bet Donna can introduce you to a friend. This whole place just smells... bad..."

They wrinkled their noses at the dank air, the mix of salt flats, sour fish, and something more putrid.

Margaux stepped closer, peeled off her dress and stood naked. Her hair looked brighter than before, as if teeming with its own light. Her breasts swelled on her chest and her feet clung to the sloping gravel, legs slightly apart.

"Damn," said Terry. "For a junkie, you look pretty good."

"Will you stop talking like that?" said Burke. His friend didn't understand. Just because Margaux was a ghost didn't mean she was bad. But he couldn't blame Terry for trying to be rational about it, so he just said, "Margaux and I are together. We meet here."

"Then what the hell did you bring me for?"

"Because she asked me to. She said I needed to bring a friend on the night I released her. And you're like, my friend."

Terry's face changed, the sarcastic grin melted to sympathy. "Hey bud, s'all right, man, you don't gotta talk that way. It's cool with me if your girl wants you to bring along, um, company."

Burke felt his friend's hand on his shoulder as tears welled in his eyes. Terry's grip was firm and reassuring and it was gestures like this that made him think sometimes the network specialist hungout with the office temp because he really *was* a nice guy. Burke wondered if maybe he shouldn't have done this after all. Maybe the sarcasm and the mean stuff Terry said around girls sometimes was just his own way of being imperfect. Maybe it was this imperfection that created a true bridge of friendship between them.

"So what exactly did you have in mind, baby?" Terry asked as Margaux came in close enough to touch.

Margaux smiled, the rictus of her grin going up a little too far on one side, revealing the long-toothed, somewhat misshapen contour of her jaw.

"What I had in mind was getting the hell out of there," she said. She pointed behind her at the pylon, a place where high water erosion had worn the masonry off the granite. There, in a cavity emptied of blocks, lay a dead woman, vicious stab marks gashing her dress.

"But, d-damn…" stuttered Terry. "You really are…"

"A ghost," said Margaux.

Burke was so focused on his friend's revelation he hardly felt the gentle tickle of Margaux's fingers along his wrist. Only when he tried to raise his right hand and put it on Terry's shoulder did he realize she had handcuffed the two men together.

"Wait," he said. "I don't get it, what are you doing?"

The apparition giggled, her skullish jaw swiveled beneath her glittering eyes. "No, you don't get it in so many ways, Burke, but that's what I like about you."

Beside him Terry's muscles tensed like he was about to break free by pulling off Burke's arm. Instead his friend answered his startled gaze with a grin. "Wow man, your girl's even kinkier than I thought," he said.

Before he could answer, Margaux caressed Burke's cheek and turned his face back to hers. "Don't mind him," she said. "Come with me."

Her shimmering image guided them through the crumbled stones to where her body lay like a thrown away doll. "They don't make dresses like that anymore," she said, pointing at the crimped velvet. "And that bastard didn't care much for it when it was new in 1929. No matter, I don't like to talk about him anyway. All that matters now is what *they* say, the ones in the robes who fly inside the walls. They say I have another thirty years to find someone to weave the spell on Veil's Night, you know, tonight, when things are thin." She twisted her hips before Burke's mesmerized eyes, made her belly into a luridly impossible corkscrew, and yet somehow no more lurid than the crooked corpse that lay behind it.

"I might feel a little better if someone at least busted out some shiny leather," said Terry.

"I told you to stop that," Burke snapped.

"Pay him no mind," said Margaux. "It's me who matters now. And I like you so much better than the others. You're different. Not many will follow a girl below the bridge you know. Only guys like that old Joe Zilch, who couldn't even kill me right and got me stuck here. But you're not like him, Burke. That's why I needed to cuff you. Just because you don't get it, even though you're down on your luck, you still don't want to hurt anyone. That's your problem, Burke, you don't even want to hurt the *bad* guys."

Burke shook his head, looking at her figure as it swam and swayed before him. With every word she hovered closer, bumping her knee playfully against his. Her presence felt airy and heavy and dead, opposing beauties hitting him like a drug.

Terry's voice interrupted his trance. "You're right about Burke," he said. "He is a nice guy. Too nice for you, I think."

"Sacrifice shutup," barked Margaux. "Burke," she continued, voice softening, "I need you to listen to me. I handcuffed you together because I don't want you to get scared at the last moment. Remember, you agreed you'd give me anything."

"But I don't understand, what do I have to do?"

That's when the corpse righted itself among the filthy stones and began to scrape across the gravel. Despite its jagged wounds its limbs appeared pliant and swift. It charged into the flickering apparition and merged with it. Even as the men grimaced in terror, the half-beautiful, half-distorted abomination that was Margaux took hold of Burke, clasping him by the back of his neck.

"Kiss me Burke," she said. "If you want to keep your promise, you have to kiss me."

Burke felt all pins and needles, every inch of him compelled to run. Beside him Terry's body went heavy, falling into an awkward half-collapse. Burke tried to turn away from Margaux, but before he could, her lips touched his. They felt at once hot and cold, and the slime they secreted like honey and filth.

A gnawing shock shot through his gums as they sprouted a set of dagger-like fangs. The top row grew so quickly they cut into the flesh of his chin. They would have reached halfway down his neck, had not a second set on his lower jaw pushed them outward.

"That's more like it," said Margaux. "Now eat your damn friend!"

Burke turned and looked at Terry as he struggled in the grime. He was trying to loosen his wrist from the cuff, and had turned his hand blue-white with the effort. "No, wait," said Terry. "No please, just wait, just lemme go, please..."

"Hurry up," cried Margaux. "Just do it and don't let him whine."

Burke felt the heaviness of his jaw, the new shape of his teeth. He opened his mouth as his friend begged: "Please man, seriously, I know I took your money man, but that's it, please, I don't want my parents to have to bury me, man, please, for my mother, man, for my mother!"

Burke blinked. He'd never met Terry's mother or anyone else in his family. But that wasn't Terry's fault, just like it wasn't his fault that Burke was the one who hungout below bridges, wondering where he'd land if he jumped. Damn it, what was he doing? He turned to the apparition that still held him in its grip.

"I can't," he said. "I can't eat Terry."

"Don't you understand?" hissed Margaux. "He doesn't care about you. He never cared about you. He's a jerk. Why do you think I asked you to bring him and not your *own* mother? Or that secretary you thought about inviting from the office? Because he *deserves* it. Don't you trust me, Burke? Don't you want to know the real *me*, underneath?" Margaux swept a hand over the tender flesh beneath her belly. "We made a promise to each other Burke, and now it's like you don't even want to *know* me!" Tears seeped from the corners of her eyes while her lips managed a camera-worthy pout. Burke felt a pang of sympathy in his heart. His mind turned lascivious again, despite Terry's squirming.

"Hey, Burke, wait," cried Terry. "What are you doing man? Fucking wake up, please! You gonna do what she says? For all we know somebody dosed

95

the party punch, bad trip, that's all!"

Burke snarled, saliva dripping from his fangs. "I. Meet. Her. Every. Night. She's always been so... *good* to me, Terry. She is *good*, and I want her."

But Terry clasped his leg with his free arm, shaking his head. "No, no, please don't say that. I admit it, I hung around you just for the free drinks, in the beginning. But then I saw you were a really nice guy, man. I didn't want nothin' bad to happen to you, I wanted to help you out tonight, bring you to the party, because you're really my friend man, please, don't... umphhhhh..."

Margaux's half-rotted foot kicked Terry in the cheek. "Eat your friend, Burke," she said. "You have to do it now."

The apparition's voice sounded more serious in its quietness, but it also allowed Burke to hear Terry sobbing. He leaned in close with the teeth, and heard his friend chanting in a hiccupped whisper: "Mama's here, mama's here..."

Burke felt his new jaw twist in disgust. "Jesus," he said. "I can't. I want us to be together, Margaux, but..."

"Burke," she said. "This is your last chance, and if you don't, I will."

"You better not," Burke growled, shaking free of her grip and snapping at her neck. An inhuman wail exploded in his ear—he'd hurt her and she collapsed at his feet.

"Please," she said. "Please!"

It was as if all her wounds were bleeding at once, the gash from his bite, and the old slices opened by the killer's knife. She leaned up on one elbow. "Please Burke, if you're not going to do it then please..."

He fell to his own knees, brushing back her silvery-dead hair. He felt her press her breasts against his chest as she wept. "Please what?" he said.

"Please... give me back my teeth!" She planted a brutal kiss on his bared fangs, and with her snake of a tongue ripped the fangs from his mouth.

~*~

*Wow, that was close,* thought Terry. *It looked for a minute like temp-boy mighta gone for it.* He watched as Burke's empty mouth sucked at the night air. His throat looked an empty hollow, his old teeth lost in the bleeding soup that were his gums. His body quivered where it knelt and he reached out with one hand to the friend whose life he had just saved.

*Ah, what to do with temp-boy,* he thought. *If only he could break out of the handcuffs and take off. If only corpse-kitten didn't look so disgustingly delicious…*

"Well," said Margaux, stepping between them. "It appears choice number two will have to do."

She flashed the upturned grin, baring the teeth. This time the look was more knowing. It was a look Terry had seen on coke-head chicks in bars who were going to put out for a few bumps, a look that spoke of dark exchange.

"So what do you think, Terry? Are you game?"

"I just want to get out of these handcuffs."

"Is that really all you want, Dapper-D?"

"Well," he said, looking straight into starry eyes superimposed on empty sockets, "I wouldn't mind taking you down on a nice piece of sand between the rocks."

"Accept my terms and free me," she said, "and you can take me any way you want."

*Yeah right*, he thought. *Only he had to find insurance on her promise. He wasn't as foolish as his friend.* He turned to Burke who'd withdrawn the supplication with his free hand and was now using it to staunch his wounded mouth. *The teeth*, he thought. *She'd been afraid of them when Burke had turned on her. It had taken a kiss to get them back. All he had to do was hold onto the teeth and he could keep her under control.*

"Sure," he said. "I accept."

Margaux giggled. She brushed his teeth with her tongue as she kissed him, causing them to lengthen into fangs.

~*~

*Ha, they're mine*, he thought. *Now corpse-kitten really was screwed, so to speak. Such was the fate of the desperate.* But before he took his pleasure, there was something that had to be done. He reached out with his thumb and forefinger, raised Burke's chin, applying a little pressure as he guided him to his feet.

"Wha-whath are y-you d-doing?" Burke muttered through his blood-swamped lips.

Terry shook his head. "Burke my friend, when at the mercy of a momma's boy, there's only one thing you can do."

"Whath's that?" Burke asked.

"Cry for your momma."

"But *I'm* the one who had merthcy on *you*," he muttered.

"Exactly."

Terry clasped his friend by his hair, as if he would kiss him, then plunged the saber-like teeth through his neck. He clamped down, pressing through his esophagus and out the other side. Having shut him up, he withdrew, moved down to his chest, split open his sternum and tore out his heart. The blood emptied in a rush. He hoped temp-boy caught a glimpse of his heart speared on his fangs, saw rubbery organ meat sliding down his throat. A final reminder nothing comes easy for fools before he collapsed in the muddy gravel.

"And so," said Terry, catching his fang-stuffed reflection in a puddle as he turned to Margaux, "are you ready to pay the price of your release?"

Margaux smiled back as she unlocked the handcuffs. Her body looked a dance of the solid and ethereal, of blood and silver. "Kiss me and take your reward," she said.

"Yeah right. I think I'll just take door number two," he said, grabbing her by the hair. He twisted her around and thrust his pelvis into the soft shadow above her thighs. "Irony's a bitch," he said, forcing their conjoined bodies against the ground. As they rutted, the scent of salt, musk and burst capillaries mixed with the sour copper of her old wounds. He delighted at the eager thumps that punctuated her shocked whimpers. He reveled in the way her mouth grinned and grimaced at his deliciously indecent path of attack.

After their bodies quaked, released, collided and released again, he rolled off into the gravel. "A cigarette," he said, climbing dizzily onto a granite block. "Not that I want to squander my time."

"Do whatever you like," she said, taking her own seat among the stony shadows. She pulled in her lanky limbs and gave him her skullish stare, doe-eyes deformed by slashes of the city's lights. "Only kiss me once more, just once more."

"Sorry honey," he said. "Wouldn't want you to have the old chompers back now. Besides, by morning you'll be as free as our friend." Terry nodded at Burke's corpse. Even through the river's fog, he could see Burke's gouged open chest, ribcage reaching upward like a crimson hand. Final gesture of futility, of one ever abandoned by hope.

*And what about corpse-kitten?* He glanced back at her dead, doe-eyed stare. *Was he any worse off than her? How insane and hopeless had she become to not care what means her freedom came by?* Well, she'd taught him one truth about eternity. That freedom was fused to power in death as well as in life. It was there for the taking, for those with wits enough to seize it.

The crackle of the police radio interrupted his thoughts. It was answered by a voice much nearer and clearer. "Copy," it said.

Terry turned to see three Dodge Chargers pulled up between the pylons, lights washing the granite with their red and blue glare.

"What the hell did that?" asked one of the officers.

Terry turned again and saw that Margaux had moved, was standing between the pylons opposite the police car.

"All right," said Terry. "I'll kiss you."

Margaux grinned, her body gone a glistening blur. Her breasts and hips looked swollen out of themselves, more engorged even than when their bodies had been fused.

Her grin widened into a smile.

"I'll kiss you," he cried, taking a step closer.

Behind him he heard the police officers' steps crunching toward them. "Sir, raise your hands and turn around. Do it now."

Terry turned and looked over his shoulder. Not because the officer ordered him to, because he needed to see where they were, needed to see if he had any time.

Instead he saw his reflection in the puddle again, fangs bloodied with the gristle of his eviscerated friend.

"Get on your knees," barked the cop, louder this time. "We're not playin' games here. Get on your knees with your hands raised." He held his gun in a two-handed clasp while his partner deployed the backup behind their cars.

"Of course you don't have any time," said Margaux.

"But I thought you wanted to be free," he pleaded. "I did what you wanted, just kiss me! Kiss me!"

As he spoke, the first gray rays of an overcast sun touched the river. The apparition lurched toward the pylon, the niche where they'd first seen her body.

"Please," he pleaded. "This is Veil's Night or whatever the hell you called it, you're going to be free! What do you care?"

The apparition chuckled. "Oh that," she said. "How did they used to put it? There's a sucker born every day. In fact there's another one all lined up for our big date. Real eighties man, big-guy. Cold War vet off the Korean DMZ. I told him I wanted to meet him on Veteran's Day, the day I was killed by that pinko squatter, the only day I can be released."

Terry felt a lump rising in his throat.

"Stop talkin'," said the cop. "You have the right to remain silent. We're not playin' games."

Terry watched as the apparition's blurry figure stepped into the shadows and wrapped the destroyed dress over its shoulders. In its torn state the crimped velvet looked almost robe-like, and her eyes, the only part of her face he still recognized, glowed an infernal orange. "If you're lucky they'll institutionalize you," she said. "A few years' respite before you fulfill your end of our... agreement."

And for a second, just before they pressed him down and cuffed him, Terry glimpsed them through his tears—the robed forms in the wall cavity, the twisted horns and hair, the agonized eyes full of hatred. "Well played," he heard. "Two more souls for Jezzrael. She uses astral projection to great advantage. You could learn from her, Adriel. She plays to rival the archfiends themselves."

# The Red Path

Liam put the rusted hatchback into all-wheel drive and slinked up the s-curve to the top of the hill. There he picked up the private road that led west toward the lake. He lit up a joint and counted a mile and a half until he passed the mansion on his left. Through the trees he glimpsed its pointed gables and dark windows. Funny to think with his new receptionist gig he felt like a million bucks. He didn't need a mansion, just enough to get him his one bedroom apartment in the better end of the student ghetto, by the hospital.

*Maybe that's why Kelsey agreed to come out to the lake with him*, he thought, as he smoked and drove. He had somewhere of his own to take her back to after they swam. It wasn't much, but it was *his*. He didn't have to invite himself over to her place, or even worry about any roommates anymore. He'd spend the day watching her getting in and out of the water, hair damp and glistening, bathing suit swollen with her breasts. After, he'd suggest they go in town, hit a bar early, then maybe go over to his place for a movie.

He chuckled at his daydream, pushed the gear back into drive as he coasted the down slope. Really he'd be happy if she agreed to meet up with him again. Either way, the fact she'd finally called him back was something to be glad about.

Liam counted another two miles on the odometer until he reached her cottage. The small, winterized log cabin didn't look like much from the outside, yet it had a refinished interior and solar panels on the roof. To live out here had to cost her something.

*All right with him*, he thought. They probably worked her pretty hard in that sales department at the Whosy-whatsit Engineering Company. And he was definitely mature enough not to mind a woman who out-earned him.

~*~

She met him in the driveway with her key in her hand. "Why don't we take my car?" she said.

His words caught in his throat as he took in the sight of her. Kelsey had changed since the summer before. Although he'd seen her once since then, it

101

had been winter, late at night at a bar, and she'd been wearing a thick jacket on her way out. Now her blue fleece top hugged a torso slim with muscle. It didn't quite cover her stomach, which flashed a sliver of tan, rippled flesh.

The corporate gym was treating her right.

But she was already headed toward her car.

"Hey, wait," he said. "We can take mine, s'okay."

"Checked your tires lately?" she called back.

Liam looked down. He definitely had not. And they did look a little deflated. And hey, if he didn't mind the lady out-earning him, why would he mind if she drove?

"Hey no prob," he said. "Just let me grab the six-pack."

Liam grabbed the bag of beer, locked up the car, and headed over to her hybrid-SUV.

~*~

She let him pick the music as they made their way northwest toward the lake. He chose a set of tunes by a teenage girl guitarist who'd made some fame online with her articulate renderings of acoustic blues and complex folk pieces. He felt thrilled when Kelsey asked who it was and seemed to like it.

The small victory made him relax some, and he decided he was glad she was driving after all. Truth be told, he'd been a little nervous about navigating the maze of lakeside dirt roads to the public access site. With her, the GPS was doing the work for them. It was all good, and he wondered how she'd take it if he offered to crack a couple of beers.

Instead he grabbed the passenger's hand grip as the truck jostled across a small boulder in the dirt road. Although the day was warm for late spring, a wall of clouds had come in fast and obscured the sun. It cast penetrating shadows over the pointed pines. The drizzle it brought with it weighted down their needle-clustered branches.

By the time they reached the shore, the drizzle turned into a steady rain.

"Maybe we oughta just stay in the car and knock a few back," he said.

Kelsey turned to him and smiled, her faint freckles visible beneath her tan. Her eyes were clear blue, skin silk-smooth. Although he knew it was the same girl he'd had a fling with the summer before, and he'd thought her beautiful then, this was something else entirely. He wondered if it was some kind of spa treatment she could buy, or just some odd brand of confidence.

He'd wanted to surprise her with something too, wanted to work out and get in shape. And though he had built some muscle, he only texted her photos from certain angles, because his beer belly was, well, still a beer belly.

"I thought we came out here to go for a swim," she said.

"Maybe wait 'til the rain lets up?"

"Gonna be wet anyway," she said with a wink, and let herself out of the car.

The wink made him feel a little better and he climbed out into the rain, six-pack in hand. He told himself to take it as a good sign that she was still into getting in the water.

"So whatchya been doing with yourself lately?" she asked as she removed her fleece top.

Speechless again, he didn't remember her chest being quite like that. Must have been the weight she'd lost in the middle. And her bathing suit was indeed a bikini, though she left her cut-off jeans on, just put her wallet in her backpack and her sneakers on a rock.

"I… well, I just got a new job," he said.

He took off his boots and stuffed his crumpled cash and keys in his socks. When he was down to his own t-shirt and cutoffs, he sat down on a rock and popped a beer.

Kelsey chuckled. "You don't want to go for a swim first."

"One before, the rest after," he said.

"Suit yourself," she said, diving down.

He watched as she swam out into the middle of the lake. She kept her head down, turning to the side when she needed to breathe. She did a few diagonal laps, and just when he started to wonder if she gave a damn that they came there together, just when he started to think maybe he should have brought his damn car after all, she turned around and powered back to shore.

"Water's warm once you're in," she said as she stepped onto the pebble beach.

Liam nodded, stood up on the rock and did a sloppy cannonball into four feet of water.

When he swam back to shore, she was grinning and wringing out her hair. "You didn't want to take your shirt off?" she asked.

"It was already wet," he said.

She shrugged, and as if in answer, went back to the car and fetched her fleece top along with a pair of towels. She handed him one without bothering to ask if he'd brought his own. The rain let up, though the clouds had darkened. He took another sip of his beer, then mustered the courage to towel himself off.

While he stripped off his shirt, her wet bathing suit plopped onto the hood of the truck. She stood in front of him naked, the tan lines from the bikini accenting the narrow angle of her stomach where it led down to her sculpted thighs. She didn't turn when she looked up and caught him staring.

Kelsey raised her eyebrows. "You didn't bring an extra pair of jeans?" she said.

Liam shook his head. He turned and dropped his cut-offs, realizing in an instant his answer had been to show her his pale backside. *What's the matter,* he thought, *ashamed to show the front?* But that hadn't been the reason he'd turned. No, it was because he realized then she was something else. Her being there couldn't possibly be related to anything like romance. Whatever happened the summer before obviously wasn't what he thought it was.

~*~

On the way home she cleared her throat and said, "Liam, there's something I have to talk to you about."

He didn't answer. He blinked against the shadows cast by the wan sun's weak attempts to cut a sliver in the clouds. The pines cast their branches into the road like spiny strands of a great broken web. He'd drunk five beers and his stomach sloshed like giant ampoule of anesthetic.

"All the texts and emails," she said. "And the pictures. And the time last winter when you followed me around the bar, and the time I ran into you when I came out to get my mail, and you were parked by my house."

Shit, that's right, he realized, he *had* driven out there late one Saturday, passed out in his car and nearly gotten himself a DWI on the way home. If he'd bothered to lift the coffee he'd bought from its plastic holder, bothered to get himself out of there before she'd seen him, he probably would have...

"What about them?"

"They're inappropriate, Liam."

Silence as they passed through the pines. The dirt road rose with a patch of broken boulders, jostling the SUV.

"But we know each other," he said. His voice sounded way too whiny. He pissed himself off. "I mean, we knew each other. It's been over six months and I've hardly seen you."

Her lips pouted. "Well, you're right. We knew each other. And that's why I'm bothering to tell you in person. I wanted to tell you back in the water, but you were hardly even in the water."

"Coulda come out and told me over a beer."

Kelsey chuckled. "Strictly cocktails these days, you know, the calories." Her hips shifted on the heated seat. "Anyway, I really don't have time for this anymore. If we have to have this conversation again, it will be at a hearing, because I'll be getting a restraining order against you."

Liam turned toward the window, face flushed.

Kelsey sighed, took his hand and gave what felt like an attempted supportive squeeze. "Look, I guess I never thought of you as bad at heart. We had some good times, and I like how you're, you know, kinda laid back. I'm okay with a little of that in my life, if you can just call first and be an adult about it. That's why I'm giving you one chance, you know, not just calling you last summer's drunken mistake."

"You just did," he said.

"Right," she said, letting go of his hand. "Frankly, Liam, you have no idea what it's like with a job like mine. It's become a career, really. A company like Qwillon LLC is not some burger bar or faded state agency. We're in the midst of a buyout, we're restructuring. We're laying off and expanding at the same time, and I just don't have any time for sloppy slow balls like the kind you're pitching when…"

"Holy crap, lookout!" he cried.

The SUV jostled over a gouged out patch of road. Kelsey flicked on the high beams against a cloud of dust, and they caught a flash of something gigantic. It looked thick as a tree trunk, and was covered in spiny hairs. There were others behind it, a tangled group of them. They were wrestling, throwing each other to the ground. The SUV skidded once more, and this time they saw what looked like colossal steel hooks scraping together. Mandibles, thought Liam, in front of a pyramid of eyes. He felt the vehicle tilt as it slammed into the giant exoskeleton. Nausea hit him like a club and his head swam with dizziness.

Before they could get out, they felt a thump on the window. There was something else out there, a hunched figure that ran up to the car on their right. It was a man, breathing heavily, and letting out low sobs. "My son," he chortled, "My son, my son!" He pounded on the window and waved something that looked like a short, thin stick.

Liam reached for the door latch when the vehicle jostled again, as if from an earthquake. The car spun around, and he found himself looking through the slanted windshield at a second cluster of mandibles and eyes. A spider, he realized, a spider big as a Mac Truck. Beyond its vertiginous size, this one looked broken and demented from a crosshatching of vicious wounds. Its skeleton crackled with jagged fissures, and its hairy jowls seemed sunken and wrinkled. The other spider held its head in its mouth, and was sucking deeply from its quivering body.

*Cannibals*, thought Liam.

The SUV gave a slow roll to its left and fell on its side. The weight of the wounded beast pressed down beneath its attacker and crushed the vehicle's front end.

"Damnit move!" Kelsey cried.

She pushed against Liam and the door simultaneously, and was able to force it open a crack. Her strength was impressive, and when he added his, the tip of the spider's leg rolled away and they lifted the door open.

They crawled over each other to get out. No words passed between them as they made awkward tugs against vinyl, plastic, and metal.

They fell into the road amid the beasts' lurching shadows. An ammonia-like odor rose from the dying spider, and the air swarmed with deer flies that mashed themselves in Liam's blinking eyes. He snatched a muddy towel from where it lay, began batting them off just as another leg crashed to the ground behind them.

The beasts quaked like a pair of dark mountains, living slag from an avalanche. They blocked the entire road, flooded it with fallen spines and torn pieces of their bodies.

"We gotta push past," said Kelsey.

"No, go back the other way, just one leg over there, we can climb over it."

That's when the man who had run past their car emerged from the dust.

"Please help me, it's my son," he moaned.

Kelsey shook her head. She leaned down and picked up a fallen blade-like sliver from the spider's exoskeleton. She held it in front of her as the man approached.

By the time they could make out his face he'd come within arm's reach.

"Back off," said Kelsey.

"My son," said the man, tears trailing from his eyes. "Oh God, my son." From where he now stood they saw he was not holding a stick but a small arm. A pair of thin bones jutted from where it had been broken off at the elbow.

Before they could answer, the spiders rolled back toward them. Again they slammed down on the SUV, shattering its windows. Glass flew like shrapnel, and the weeping man buckled and fell. The beasts did not relent, their log-sized legs scuttled and scraped against each other. The aggressor's body surged and flexed with its momentum and squeezed a pair of baggy sacks above its fangs. Liam felt a spatter of the ammonia-like liquid on his face and began to cough.

"We gotta help... we gotta help this guy," he rasped.

Instead of answering, Kelsey gave him a hard shove into the ditch that ran along the road. He landed on a torn piece of abdomen, its spines puncturing his jeans and stabbing into his leg.

"What the hell," he cried.

Kelsey crawled through the muck and crouched beside him. "You need a weapon," she said. Her eyes shifted. She took in his wound, asked, "Can you walk?"

"I... I don't know," he said.

They heard crashing and snapping as the last of the car broke apart. The delirious man had risen to his knees, still crying, "My son, my son," as he crawled and bled into the gravel.

"No way to help him," Kelsey said. "But at least I got this." She held up a roll of duct tape.

"What the hell's that for?" Liam asked.

Ignoring him, she produced a buck knife from the pocket of her cutoffs and opened the blade.

"Can't we just run out through the woods?" Liam asked. He tried to stand, but felt a burn in his thigh from the spider's hair, like splinters on steroids. *Ha, he had tweezers back in his apartment, but he'd need a giant pair for these.* His head swam, he felt dizzy, and the ammonia smell made his nose and lungs sore. "Venom," he mumbled.

He stood, wavered, and leaned against a small pine. The spiders stilled for the moment, their silhouettes all segmented angles against the sky. Kelsey knelt over a broken oak branch. She pushed back her mud-caked hair and lashed her knife to the branch. Liam blinked against waves of blurriness. His friend's face looked all angular, her shirt torn and filthy over muscles, trained and taut.

*Like some kind of tribeswoman*, he thought.

"Hey, Liam, get with it," she said. She waved the makeshift spear in front of his face. "Take the weapon. We have to push through."

"No," he said, head heavy as he shook it. "The woods. We'll make it out through the woods."

Liam turned away and took stumbling steps toward the trees. His eyes picked out paths through the waterlogged mounds of moss and clover. A mist arose, mixed with darkness, clouded the skeins of branches, and muddled the smears of puddles. He knew the paths were fake paths, not something worn by human feet, but just tricks the growth patterns of the pines played on his eyes. And now with everything aslant and his steps off-rhythm, he could trust what he saw even less.

Stepping over a broken birch, he put his hands over his ears to block out the warped cries of "My son, my son!" he could still hear coming from the direction of the road. He also heard Kelsey grunting with effort, and felt the ground shake with the weight of the resumed and shifting battle. The mist thickened, and he coughed. When he reached out, his hand touched something sticky.

Blinking in the last rays of sunlight, he saw before him a white wall cutting across the trees. Like someone set a piece of blank paper perpendicular to the forest floor. Its surface was silken, as if made of a minute stitch of tightly woven hair. He barely touched it, and had to rip hard to pull away.

*A giant web*, he thought. *We are caught in a giant web.*

Liam turned and headed back toward the road. Despite the ammonia dizziness, and the sore drunkenness left over from the beer, he forced himself in Kelsey's direction.

He began a half hop, half stride, leaned on the trees as he moved over the uneven ground. He braced himself to jump over a dark puddle surrounding a granite boulder, when the ground shook beneath his feet. An explosion of dust and rubble burst above the road and sent another heap of flak through the trees.

"Kelsey!" he cried, sloshing through the water, making his feeble leg move faster.

When he broke through the tree line he saw the aggressing spider had flipped and thrown its prey. Its gnarled hulk lay splayed across the road from where their car had rolled over. Kelsey stood between the two of them, jacket pulled over her head, bare legs beneath her shorts riddled with wounds from the flying debris.

"Stay there," he called out. "I'm coming."

When he reached her she strained to stand. She breathed against the pain and handed him the makeshift spear fashioned from the branch and buck knife.

"I told you the only way out was through," she said.

Liam felt a streak of anger amid his surge of adrenalin. He may have been a broke, fat bastard, but he was strong enough to carry her out of there. He looked both directions on the road. On the down slope where they'd been driving sat the cannibal. Now that it had flipped its prey it appeared semi-sedate, like the idol to some thousand-eyed god. Its fangs hung twitching beneath the fat, venom-drenched sacks, making it look as if it already hungered again.

"What are you waiting for?" Kelsey hissed. She struggled to break out of his arms.

Liam turned in the opposite direction, where the carcass of the slain spider lay across the road. Its body curled in a crescent, with legs jutting upward like the spires of a tormented city. It looked dead and devoured, save for a red path that wove between its broken parts.

The blood came from the father, himself bearing a gruesome wound to his torso. He shambled forward, carrying his son's severed arm back toward the lake.

"We have to go back," said Liam as he hefted his friend's weight.

"We can't go back," Kelsey said through clenched teeth.

"Damnit, Kel," said Liam. "That thing's trying to kill us. I'm trying to take the quickest way out of here."

Kelsey twisted in his arms. The body he'd seen so smooth and supple now writhed and contorted itself. He smelled the rank sweat of panic. Squirming out of his grasp, she turned around and hit his jaw with a right hook. He fought the instinct to slam her back, even as she picked up her make-shift spear from where it lay in the road.

"I tried to give you this," she said.

"I didn't want it," he said.

"You should," she said.

"If I thought it would work, I would," he said.

He watched as she turned and made her way down the dirt road. She bled from wounds in her arm, legs, and stomach, and kept correcting her course when she drifted toward the ditch.

As the beast tracked her with its eyes, Kelsey raised the makeshift spear as if she'd hurl it into their quivering cluster. In response, it stretched its venom-swollen palps, a seasoned killer entertained by the seriousness of its prey's efforts.

"Come on, you have to help me find my son," came the man's voice from behind.

Liam turned and met his eyes. His glasses hung slanted, one lens cracked, the other missing. His canvas cap and shorts mocked the day a middle-aged father set out to the lake for a picnic with the son whose severed arm was now turning a blotchy purple.

He beckoned and shook his head as he muttered something unintelligible to himself. Liam took one step, then another and followed him down the path. *I will not turn around*, he thought, even as he heard the suction of the venomous palps.

As he moved he heard gasps and grunts he knew were Kelsey's. His head swam with new waves of dizziness and nausea. Involuntary thoughts teased him from within: *she'd have sounded something like that in his bed. Ha, ha, if the day had gone differently, he still might have been hearing that sound.*

⁓*⁓

Liam followed the man down the red path, through the dead spider's carcass. Mud stranded with rivulets of blood slicked his boots. A buzzard landed on a segment of leg to his left, pointed through a cloud of flies to a giant, broken piece of the beast's thorax.

There he saw the turned-over car. The woman lay twisted in the passenger seat, her pale arm stretched toward the children's seats in the back. One of them was fully crushed by the collapsed roof. In the other sat a boy in a baseball cap, missing an arm. His face was so puffy he looked stuffed into his shirt. His skin was as pale as his mother's. He stared back at Liam with sunken eyes, and then blinked.

He began to move his lips: "My arm," he rasped.

Liam turned away, overcome with nausea, while behind him stood the weeping man. "My son," he said and waved the purple arm.

Unloading his stomach into the bloodstained mud, it was all Liam could do to stay on his feet. His dizzy brain forced him to keep walking, look for a place to get past the car.

That's when he felt the spiny arm wrap around his ribs and lift him up.

One of the palps still attached to the dead spider's head held him before its wall of eyes. "So you're one of ours," it said in a voice that sounded like a swarm of buzzing flies.

"What? No, no, I'm sick, I'm just sick."

"The venom," said the spider.

"I need to get away, go home. I need a doctor."

"He was a doctor," it said.

Liam squirmed inside the palps. He felt the spines dig deeper as he rotated and looked. The man held the boy's arm like a club as he screamed into the crushed car. Liam heard moaning, and when the man took a step closer to the wreck, the mother crawled out, voice wheezing and whistling from the lacerations in her neck: "Don't you lay a hand on him," she cried. "Don't you hurt that boy!" She pointed at the bloated, one-armed body.

"Why doesn't he help them?" Liam asked.

"They don't need any help," said the spider. "They know the way of things here, it is implicit."

Liam's head swam. Within the spider's eyes he watched the reflections of the clouds of deer flies, so many the outline of his torso crawled with them. He reached beneath their mass, seeking a deep itch with fingers that could not scratch.

"I tried to help my friend," he said.

The mouth opened, teemed with maggots as it choked out its words: "Bee-al-zee-bul is your house now."

"What?"

"Master of the lofty House of Flies, for gluttony is sloth."

"I don't understand," said Liam.

"You are confused, you've been confused about who you are. Although it was a fate of sorts for you to perish with this one whom you thought you loved, you should never have consorted with her ilk. She is not like you."

"But I like her. She's... she's beautiful."

"That may be true, blood-hearted son of men. But you must understand where you belong. There has been an accident, William—a head-on collision. It was the doctor's fault, it turns out, though it makes little difference in your current state."

"I feel sick," said Liam. He looked around the road as the flies thickened. They bit him, and his skin burned and itched. The doctor's voice alternately moaned and whined about his son while his bleeding wife chastised him. Liam looked back at the rise in the road and saw Kelsey's silhouette cut against a ghastly white moon. She hacked at the beast that assaulted her with fangs and forelegs. It scuttled forward and backward, legs boiling with inhuman dexterity. She fell and it bit her. She rose again and slashed at its face.

"She is a fighter and she will not surrender," said the spider.

The movements of the figures in the distance rekindled Liam's nausea. The beast relaxed its jaws, let him fall, and he began a stumbling run down the red path toward the lake. He vomited again where the water lapped the shore. But where it had been clear and blue earlier in the day, its now fetid stench hit his nose and triggered dry-heaves. He felt the spider's palps stroking his back. The deer flies parted for its caress, and Liam saw its eyes reflected in the moonlit water.

"Your friend climbs the mountain of Purgatory, but few who do so find redemption. Most fall again, eternally struggling, never content. You on the other hand, are damned, and shall gnaw and shall burn."

The flesh on Liam's back swelled. Beside him a one-armed boy chased a blown-off baseball cap into the shallows, only to shriek as the water turned to blood around him, steamed as if it were liquid fire. Liam felt his own screams rising with the dry-heaves in his throat. The spider pushed his head down, submerged him in the scalding heat, and then pulled him up again to gasp at the rank air.

"Ye who resides in the province of the slothful shall ever reap the torments of the Master of Flies," said the beast behind him. Fangs pierced Liam's stomach as his head was dunked again.

Time lost its shape as his body melted and reformed, was torn and reformed, again and again. At first he hoped it would end, or he at least would forget himself. But something would not let him, and each assault felt as fresh as the first. Somewhere inside he hoped Kelsey was still fighting, for he did not regret how he felt for her. It was a side effect of his memory remaining intact. A side effect of suffering's necessity that he remember who he was. Which also left another strength in place, one that gods and devils could not comprehend among the slothful—that salvation had, from the start, been a pointless task for one made as he had been, and yet eternal suffering was effortless.

# Blood Balance

Numb from drink, he felt their fists as if wrapped in a blanket. They were hurting him, but he was barely conscious. He heard one saying, "Cut him, just cut him." The other saying, "No, not here," but he knew they wouldn't wait long.

He threw a last right hook, knocking one down, but the other rained punches on him until he couldn't move. He felt his wallet slip out of his pocket and his jacket slip off his shoulders. The blade was the only thing left. He forced his eyes open enough to see what he'd earned from a life of sloppy drinking habits. He gritted his teeth, expecting the edge on his throat, but it never came.

Instead he saw a woman's silhouette as it stepped out of the shadows behind his attackers. She pulled something from inside her leather jacket. Before he passed out, he heard the men squeal in pain.

~*~

When he awoke he was a little sore, but somehow not hungover and broken. He was in his apartment, naked on the bathroom floor. She had hosed him off with the showerhead, and when he stood and looked in the mirror, a flood of memories poured through him—Emma's lean body entwined with his own wounded, bleeding frame. He'd gone from the danger of a brutal mugging to a reckless sex session with a friend he'd never even kissed. Somehow he'd found the strength. It was as if in his drunkenness, he thought his wounds were worse than they were. He was choosing to die in her arms instead of heading for the ER. Savagely they'd ridden each other's bodies, and all the while he'd thought he was embracing Emma and death simultaneously. Instead, he awoke feeling like his wounds were not as serious as they should have been —they'd already begun to heal.

As if in answer, he found a note she had taped to the mirror: *You owe me. Meet me tonight at the gas station.*

~*~

113

Roy took another shower, threw on a pair of jeans, steel-toed boots, and a t-shirt. He headed out of the apartment, strode over Grant Street's broken glass and yellowed cigarette butts. At the end of the block, he cut through a row of slanted townhouses and made a left on High Street. He found Emma waiting in front of the gas station's convenience store.

"'Fraid you weren't gonna show," she said.

"Yeah, listen about last night, that was some crazy shit. I haven't been myself lately, too much booze, and I…"

"Shhhh," she said. "Never mind that. I'm in a bit of a bind myself. I need your help with something."

"Sure, I mean, anything," he said.

"Hope you mean that."

"Why, what exactly are we doing?"

"I need your help getting my check," she said.

"That's it?"

"Getting paid ain't always easy. It's my boss, or I should say, my old boss, he's kind of a jerk. So are the other guys who work for him. Just feel better if you'd come with." Emma smiled through strings of matted, badly crimped blond hair. She smelled of weed and her midriff leaked out of an old Sabbath t-shirt two sizes too small. He didn't even know how much older than him she was, late twenties, maybe thirty. And yet for all her retro-street swagger, she retained a certain leanness of muscle, like a vet or an athlete, which combined with her lush skin and wry smile, always turned heads.

"I appreciate this, Roy," she said. "You know, you're all right. I know your barback gig's not bad, but you shouldn't shortchange yourself. You have more admirers than you think."

*Odd*, he thought, *for her to talk to him like that.* He was doing her the kind of favor a lot of other guys would do for free, just to get her attention. Although she'd always come in the bar where he worked and been friendly with him, he assumed it was because he kept a respectful distance. He had to wonder, now that he was up and about, if those knuckleheads really would have knifed him the night before. Instead she'd taken him home and taken him to bed, and it had done something. Hadn't it? He'd taken such a pummeling, and here he was, already up and catching his stride.

They left the store and she guided him across the parking lot hand-in-hand. "You know, I should never have worked at *Luggins Lounge*," she said. "Johnny Luggins is a creep. He encouraged the waitresses to wear shorter skirts, like sleazy and indirect, talking about getting better tips and stuff."

"Sounds nasty."

"He is. And let's face it, there's nothing worse than working for creeps and jerks."

"Except being broke."

"Well, that's debatable. And anyway, there's cash in this for you. Something better than leftovers from the tips jug."

He thought of the dwindling pile of wrinkled ones in his sock drawer. "Yeah, I suppose I could use it," he said.

Once over the Franklin Arterial, they cut through the yards of rotting Victorians, the abandoned mansions of long-extinct sea captains. Dozens were condemned and covered with the signs of demolition companies, themselves out of business. On the other side of a chain link fence topped with razor wire, they snatched a cup of coffee and a smoke at a bodega, then rounded the last alley before the harbor.

"Didn't know they still had bars out this way," said Roy. "Guy must be hard up."

"Yeah well, don't underestimate Luggins. He has a house out by the golf course, and a couple of beamers. He keeps this place open like, I don't know, like it's some kinda pet."

They kept walking east until they reached the piers, crossed the railroad track to where the old industrial harbor lay. There a diner and a laundromat did business serving crews of sailors and the occasional trucker. Across an oily lot stood *Luggins Lounge*, a two-story roadhouse with boarded-over upstairs windows and a snake of red neon above the downstairs awning. When they got closer, he saw the neon made a cursive "L" in the center, though it doubled well for a glowing, mangled serpent.

A screech sounded somewhere in the fogged over lot.

"What was that?" asked Roy.

"Dunno, probably a cat."

It sounded again, and Roy squinted into the mist where he saw shapes moving.

"Is that a kid back there?" he asked.

He heard the screech again, and a low moan. A door slammed behind the restaurant. Had he seen a woman's face, and a small boy's? He moved to walk around and peek into the lone window on the structure's collapsing back addition, but Emma took his arm.

"No, we go in the front," she said. "Don't wanna trespass, don't wanna give the old man an excuse to use his cap-gun. Come on, this way, here we go."

A neon beer bottle with a label that read OPEN hung over the glass entrance. Roy braced himself as they pushed inside. At six-three, one eighty, he was a little on the slim side for bouncer work. Still, he'd done okay in the army, and a boxer friend had shown him some moves. What bothered him as they moved across the lounge's mottled, whiskey stained floor, was an underlying rankness—a rot like the time he'd cleaned out a warehouse full of rats' nests. Like a carcass cooked and gone spoiled.

"Hey, Bryce, Lug here?" asked Emma. She raised an eyebrow and leaned her tight t-shirt on the bar.

Bryce the bartender scowled. "What the hell you doin' here?"

"Getting my check."

Bryce stood taut, polyester dress shirt clinging to his skinny frame. "Lug said he let you go."

"Yeah, I know, like I said, I just want my check."

"Well you ain't got a check, so you and your ass-out bulldog can fuck off on outta here."

Roy felt his arms tense. He let shit like this roll off him most of the time, but he didn't like the way the bartender glared at him through his greasy bangs. The chump was holding the beer glass like he was ready to break it over his head. It was looking like making the first move might not be such a bad idea.

"There some kind of problem?"

Roy turned and saw a man step out of the shadows. He had thick arms, tousled white hair, and a mustache. His gigantic stomach stuck out of his unbuttoned dress shirt, and the white wife-beater underneath was covered in brown stains.

"I said, is there a problem?"

"Lug, wait, let's take it easy," said Emma. "Just let me do what I gotta do, just let me get my check."

"I told you not to come back here," he said. "Now you done did it." In a single motion he pulled off his belt and swung it at Emma. She ducked and stumbled back, knocking over one of the bar stools. Roy picked it up and used it to parry the next blow.

"Now you done it," cried Luggins. "Gone on and friggin' done it!"

When Roy turned, he saw Bryce had Emma in a choke hold. He felt pain explode in his calf as Luggins swept low with the belt. He managed to throw a punch as he lost balance, but it only sank into the man's fat, grease-stained stomach.

"That all ya got, hotshot?"

They were the last words he heard before Luggins's belt whipped across his forehead, followed by his boot.

~*~

Roy awoke secured to a sink, opposite Emma. They were behind the bar, their backs tight against the shelf of liquor bottles. Triple wrapped plastic handcuffs bound their wrists to galvanized drain pipes. He thought it was odd to have two rows of sinks behind the bar. Usually the ones behind the bar were placed there for ease of emptying and washing glasses, like he'd done a thousand times.

But the sink that ran along the underside of this bar looked like none he'd ever seen. It stretched across like a rectangular, cast iron tub. The white porcelain was chipped off and covered in brown and red stains. The thing was making suction sounds and emitted a stench similar to the one he'd detected when he first came in, only colder, like metal could die and decompose.

"Don't make 'em like they used to," said the man at the bar.

This one had white hair and a mustache, too, but he wasn't Luggins. He wore a knit cap offset by a platinum necklace. Another old guy seated to his right still had some wisps of blond in the haggard beard that dangled over his wrinkled collar. A third stood on the end wearing a sport jacket and relatively clean shirt, just one gloppy stain beside the loosened tie.

"The fuck you lookin' at?" said knit cap guy.

"Don't answer," said Emma. "It'll only make it worse."

Roy turned his dizzy head and caught a glimpse of her flushed, tear-stained face. When he rolled his gaze upward he saw the men at the bar had a line of soup bowls in front of them. They were eating spoonfuls of the chunked gravy-like brown liquid that stained their shirts.

"Yeah, the young bulldogs ain't like they used to be," said Luggins. He was standing to the left, wiping the shiny silver faucet with a dirty rag. "Your grandfathers would be ashamed," he said to Roy as he rubbed the nozzle. "Not 'cause you can't punch, but 'cause you're so damn take-the-class-again slow."

Knit cap guy cracked up. "Ha! Take the class again! Play it again, Sam, take out a loan while you're at it, ha, ha, ha!" He took a spoonful of his slop and slurped it into his mouth, smacking his lips with his tongue and wiping his mustache with the back of his hand.

The one on the end in the sport jacket belched, and Roy felt the metallic rot intensify in his nostrils. It was the cooked variety this time, the slop in their bowls, the burnt version of what was in the sink.

Beside him Emma made choking sounds. Her throat looked lumped with nausea. She seemed to be trying to say something, but before she could, Luggins said, "Ahhh fuck it." He flipped over his wrist, and there was no mistaking the human stomach's curved gray shape as he dropped it in the sink. A growling sounded, a garbage-disposal grind with a throaty, almost vocal quality. The sink's skinny legs quivered with the vibrations, the faucet throbbed. Out poured a stream of brown liquid into a bowl Luggins held beneath it. He threw the lever for the hot, adding a stream of red.

"Here ya go, Hank," he said, sliding the bowl across the bar.

The man in the jacket smoothed his tie, lifted his spoon and blew. "A little vinegar if you would," he said.

"Why don't ya ask bulldog for some vinegar," said Bryce, stepping in front of Roy and leaning down. "I mean, he already got the piss kicked out of him."

His boot connected with Roy's face, and he was out again.

~*~

When he awoke he was looking at a haggard woman's face. It was connected to her shoulders and nothing else. A clavicle stuck out like a chicken bone, and her blond hair was smeared with blood.

"I wish bulldog boy could save me," said the head in a gravelly high-pitched voice. It wagged back and forth like a puppet, and Roy could see Luggins' fat fingers clamped on its scalp. "Oh wait, it's too late, most of me is sink-soup now."

The sink vibrated behind him as he spoke, its legs bucking and dancing on the concrete. The men at the bar were gorging themselves, shoveling in brown lumps from their bowls. Their eyes bulged in their sockets as if feasting on the sight of their own hunger. Jacket-man grabbed a Lysol bottle filled with orange liquid. He mixed it with the red and brown lumps in his bowl then picked up the whole thing and poured it into his mouth, juice running in streaks out the corners of his lips.

"Nothin' better than eatin' through a sink!" he growled.

The others hooted, nodded, slurped.

"To the sink! To the sink with all of 'em!" cried knit-cap.

Roy pushed and strained against the plastic handcuffs. He managed to break one strand and roll over into a shelf of liquor bottles, smashing half of them and landing himself in a pool of glass. His foot kicked the woman's head out of Luggins' hand. The old man coughed up a piece of brown sludge and brushed it off.

"The hell with her," he said. "Let's do the kid."

Bryce nodded, rolled up his sleeves and brought up the bound, unconscious body of the crop-haired boy he'd seen in the alley. Roy tried to tell himself it was a mercy that the kid was at least unconscious. He tried to tell himself the head wasn't his mother's.

When the bartender lay the kid before the sink, the entire apparatus began to rumble. Red liquid bubbled in its drain, steaming brown chunks spiraling around in it.

"And the Great Dragon was thrown down, that Ancient Serpent, who is called the Devil and Satan, the deceiver of the whole world—he was thrown down to the Earth, and his angels were thrown down with him," chortled Luggins as Sport-Jacket came around the bar and helped Bryce lifted the child over the length of the sink.

"We gotta do it now," said Emma.

Roy turned to where she was cuffed beside him. She was clutching a belt knife in her right hand.

"You had a knife all this time?" he hissed.

"Yeah," she said.

"Give it to me!"

"No," she said. Emma slithered toward him and began sawing at his handcuffs.

The men at the bar chanted, howled, and belched over the sink. In response the sink filled itself to the rim with boiling liquid. A sulfuric reek arose, mingling with the stench of death, and before his eyes the length of steel began to melt and warp. It became coffin-like, with a figure appearing etched in its side. Like a relief sculpture carved into a sarcophagus, there appeared the figure of a hideous naked man. He was lying back, on his elbows, face deformed and chin pointed. It looked sharp like a crescent moon, and above it an alabaster horn protruded from his head. The man was at once still and tilting, at once silent and laughing.

Beneath the figure's muscular steel body, shrouded figures teamed like vermin. Their wretched hands held him above their heads, rotted wrists snapping from the weight, only to be replaced by others. The steel figure's hands wagged and made flapping motions, his legs vibrated atop his sea of bearers like a child in a bath of souls. "Dona suus," he said in a sick, sing-song voice. "Dona suus omnium!"

Roy felt Emma's hot breath on his neck as she whispered to him: "Listen to me," she said. "You're gonna smash the bottles on the second shelf, right there, with the grain alcohol. I'm gonna cut Luggins, then when I light it up, you're gonna grab the kid and run outta here."

"Are you crazy? I thought we were coming here to pick up your check!"

"You will pick up my check. But first you will run out the back the door beside the walk-in freezer. Anyone in there need help, you give it to them."

Roy tried to ask another question, but Emma's blow connected with his chin. Her arm was like a baseball bat. His head exploded with pain and his torso smashed into the shelf of liquor bottles. A second wave of glass and alcohol spread across the floor. He glimpsed a flutter of Emma's fingers as she dropped the lit matches and streaks of fire zigzagged in all directions.

The howls from the men at the bar changed from ecstasy to agony. Roy picked up the child, hooking one arm around his flaccid body. He half vaulted, half rolled over the bar's burning planks. He kept rolling to douse the flames touching his and the kid's clothing. The ceiling was already billowing with smoke and the lights had gone out. A weak streak of streetlight allowed glimpses of burning, bleeding men staggering in all directions.

Luggins drew a pistol, but was already choking and falling to one knee. Emma cut sideways, slashing open his giant stomach. As he fell bleeding, she leapt up into the shadows, catlike, narrowly avoiding the steel arm that reached out of the smoke for her neck.

Roy, too, was choking. His eyes were burning and blinking as he forced himself to stand and run for the exit. Casting a glance over his shoulder he saw something in the smoke. He made out the outline of a horned head and fanged visage. The figure moved with thudding steps, tearing men apart with its steel arms, mauling them with the alabaster horn above its pale white face.

When its blank eyes met Roy's, he stumbled over a table and collapsed before the walk-in freezer's door.

But before it could reach for him, Emma leapt down from the rafters. She dodged the thing's blows and scratched her blade across its body. Flames engulfed them both as they locked in melee, and the figure's great white head laughed even as it was immolated.

Roy got to his feet, lifted the boy, and took hold of the freezer door. He found it locked, then remembered the door beside it that Emma had mentioned. He shouldered the thin plywood open, moved down a narrow hallway, and there found a small, paint-peeled storeroom. A woman and two children huddled in the corner. They were hog-tied, wrists to ankles, and tied again to an old radiator with twine that cut into their elbows.

"I'm gonna get you outta here," he said. He was looking for something to cut the twine when he found another door, locked at the top with a sliding bolt. He popped the lock and found himself looking out on the bar's rear parking lot. It didn't take long to find a beer bottle, break it, and come back to cut the twine with the shards.

But even as he sawed at it and the boy he'd been carrying came-to, none of them spoke, nor rose to make their escape.

"What the hell's the matter? We gotta get outta here! The place is on friggin' fire!"

The gray-haired woman looked up at him and squinted. "Are they all dead?" she asked.

"They will be. So will we, if we don't get out of here!"

The woman nodded as Roy roused the boy and girl at her feet. The girl looked a little older, maybe eleven, the boy maybe eight or nine, like the one he was carrying. They could walk, and he guided them outside as they heard sirens in the distance. It was only now hitting him that if Emma was still inside, she probably wasn't ever coming out. He'd seen the flames engulf her but somehow thought she'd had a plan, that if he'd carried out the kid like she'd asked, she had her own way out.

Roy turned back to the storeroom only to see the old woman was still inside. "Come on!" he shouted.

But she shook her wrinkled head. She turned as he ran toward her, then scurried into the black smoke that was billowing in the hallway.

"Damn it," he coughed.

When he turned back to the parking lot, he saw the two boys wandering in a stupor, and the girl walking quickly away from him. The sounds of the sirens were getting louder, and a white van with a blue police light sped into the lot and pulled up in front of them.

"Fire Department's on the way," said the driver. The man in the passenger seat leapt out and opened the van's rear door. He wore a blue jacket and work boots, and was grabbing a first aid kit and blankets from a shelf.

"Is this an ambulance?" Roy asked.

"No, but I'm an EMT," said the man. "Your arm looks pretty bad. Get in back, I'll wrap it for now, they can look at it at the hospital."

The driver had gotten out and was tending to one of the boys. The other lay beside him, unconscious again.

"There was a girl," Roy said. "She might need help, she's over there," he said, pointing.

But the girl was running full tilt across the railroad tracks toward the shoreline. *Where was she going?* he wondered. The driver followed her with his eyes, then returned to the van and got on the radio. He said something about three recovered, smoke inhalation, third degree burns.

That's when Roy realized his arm was awash in pain, his shirt scorched and partially melted into his triceps. He let the EMT help him into the back where the unconscious boy was strapped to a stretcher, and the other boy was sitting on the floor clutching his knees.

"For the pain," said the EMT, giving him a shot in his uninjured arm. Roy nodded, felt the numbness take hold, then let himself fall back.

~*~

When he came-to he lay on a cot in a small room with three others that were unoccupied. One window, facing a brick wall, let in a minimum of sunlight. After lying still a few minutes he sat up, dazed. He pushed aside a food tray with a stale sandwich, and opened the door.

It led to a well-lit cement hallway, which he followed to a lobby in front of a small windowed office.

"Where am I?" he asked the woman at the desk.

"The infirmary," she said.

Roy looked around, trying to orient himself. Bulletin boards hung on screws in the cement. They held calendars too small to decipher, a list of what looked like phone numbers, and a string of keys. A poster beside the reception booth depicted an angel, classic blond hair, flowing white robes, wings. And yet there was something about the poster—no words, the halo above the figure's head white instead of gold, its edge sharp. Beneath the angel's robes he saw the glint of armor.

"Well, Mr. Keller, I see you've come around."

Roy turned and faced a man with a shaved head, dressed in a robe. His attire seemed familiar and yet distorted, a kind of cassock combined with a priest's collar.

"I'm sorry... I must have blacked out," said Roy. "I don't... I don't remember coming to this hospital."

The man smiled. He was clean shaven, yet had the five-o'clock shadow of one with very pale skin and very dark hair. He placed his hand on Roy's shoulder, cold fingers brushing his neck. He turned him gently and escorted him down the hall. It was the type of gesture he should have shaken off with a warning, like "Don't touch!" But he still felt dazed, almost as if a drug had gauzed the inside of his mind.

"This isn't a hospital," said the man. "Although, if you think about it, the very term 'hospital' was brought about by orders like ours, so in that sense, our organization has been your most authentic host indeed."

The man glanced at more images of angels and what looked like saints decorating the hallway where they walked. They made a left and entered an office. The plate on the door read *Reverend James L. Hathaway.*

The Reverend gestured for Roy to sit on a folding chair, and took his own seat behind his desk.

"You must be groggy," he said. "Would you like a cup of coffee?"

"Um, I'm not, I don't..." stuttered Roy.

"Two coffees," said the Reverend.

Roy looked over his shoulder and almost toppled the chair—he hadn't heard the boy approach. His eyes wore charcoal gray circles, the body beneath his white robe was bone-thin. It was the boy he'd carried, the boy who'd been with the woman in the lot.

"Yes, Reverend," said the boy, and vanished.

Before Roy could speak, the Reverend cleared his throat. "Ahem, well, first things first. Considering your recovery is on track, and your wounds have stabilized, I'd like to congratulate you on a job well done. I am presenting you with this check, pre-endorsed by Emma Christiansen, in the amount of one hundred thousand USD."

The Reverend slid a blue rectangle across the desk. Roy saw Emma's name on the pay-to-the-order-of line. The Reverend turned the check over, pointing to her signature and the endorsement where she signed it over to Roy. But it wasn't the dollar amount or fact that she had signed it over to him that made his stomach queasy—it was the single word in the memo line, in blocky letters as if from some old typewriter: Exorcism.

"You may have large shoes to fill, but do not be afraid, my child," said the Reverend.

The boy returned with the coffee. He bent over the table, resting the tray carefully, as if afraid to spill a drop. Roy noticed something funny about his walk and when he looked down saw a kind of ankle bracelet made of plastic that spanned both feet. Like a restraint stretched just wide enough to allow him to walk, with an electronic box on the left side, three green lights lit along the top.

"Sugar?" asked the Reverend as the boy shuffled out of the room.

"But I don't understand," said Roy. "I mean, Emma was doing some kind of… some kind of rescue?"

The Reverend chuckled. "I suppose that's one way to look at it, though I think recovery would be more accurate."

"But those people, that thing," said Roy, trying to push the image of the burning steel man from his mind. "They were being kept, they were being killed."

"Indeed. And now they have been returned to us."

Roy looked at the word on the check. "By us you mean a church? By exorcism, salvation from a demon?"

"A demon yes, salvation, well, you see, Roy, there are things about our world which the layman and the novice do not see. These things can be difficult to understand for some. Emma understood them. She understood them well."

"But that kid, he'd been kidnapped right?"

"Not exactly, Mr. Keller. You see, the demon's minions, Luggins and the rest, they purchased him from us."

"You *sold* them?"

"Yes, there are always some among us who are not a good fit with the organization. For it is written, 'Servants, be obedient to them that are your masters according to the flesh, with fear and trembling.' You really can't have one without the other." He paused to stir the cream into his coffee and take a swallow. "They work as runners, cleaners, porters, like the boy you just saw. But there are times when their best services are as commodities. A former soldier like yourself must know that even in the worst of wars there is business to transact with the enemy."

"Then why the hell did you rescue them?"

"As I said, not so much a rescue as a *recovery*. This particular fiend opted not to make good on his payment. Perhaps he sought to open a new front in our conflict. Well, either way, our assets have been recovered. And our exorcist made the ultimate sacrifice in doing so."

Roy looked at his arm. A twisted river of scars from third degree burns ran from his shoulder to his knuckles. He knew the wound was serious but for now it was making him think of something else—the old woman who could have come out again, the old woman who willingly walked back into the flames.

*Nothing worse than working for creeps and jerks.* Emma's words swam in his mind as he watched the Reverend pull an object from beside his chair and lay it across the desk. She had said that line in the present tense, and hadn't been talking about Luggins.

"Our exorcists carry this sort of short sword because it is easily concealed," he said, drawing the blade from its sheath. "It's broad for its size. Of course, there are situations that call for heavier weaponry, but this will do to start. We'll itemize the cost of your equipment of course, and you can pay us once you cash your predecessor's check."

"You're fucking recruiting me," said Roy.

"Recruiting indeed. Here, take it, it's yours."

Hathaway slid the sword across the table, pommel turned toward Roy.

"And if I refuse?"

"How could you refuse? You're either with us or with them. Or I suppose, you could put on an anklet and be with *them*." He nodded toward the boy who Roy hadn't realized had been standing silently behind him. His eyes looked even wearier, a bead of drool dripped from his chin, and bruises had formed on his neck where something had bludgeoned him.

Roy snatched up the sword and pointed it at the Reverend.

"Oh, I see, well, you'd never make it out of here alive. We have others like you who guard us, and still others even stronger before whom you'd faint if you but gazed upon their visage, let alone faced in combat. I'm sorry Mr. Keller, but you've really only one option."

"Yeah, only one," said Roy. He thought of the night Emma had found him outside the bar and brought him home. He knew then he owed her his life, but hadn't known what that really meant.

Roy stood and spun around. He gripped the sword close to his stomach, put the strength of his torso into the blow that cut cleanly through the boy's bruised neck. A smile spread across the boy's face as his head tumbled from his shoulders.

Roy turned back to the Reverend. "Will you call your guards?" he asked.

The Reverend studied him where he stood heaving, spattered with dark blood.

"Not if you accept my offer," he said.

"I will," said Roy. He handed the Reverend the sword, took the check, folded it, and bent down on one knee. The old man came around the table, touched his shoulders with the flat of the sword's blade. He was speaking, half English, half something that sounded like Latin. Roy wasn't listening—instead he thought only of Emma. In freeing the boy and his mother the only way they could be freed, in torching the demons' nest, they'd profited over pain by a meager margin. Now it was his turn, for all the times he'd come home blind drunk and finally gotten what was coming, now it was his turn to pay the blood balance. He rose, a servant of angels, reluctant but ready, for the first commission in the work of his Lord.

# Little Gray-Green Men

Fin Transle slashed his finger on the stack of photocopies. The bead of blood tumbled over the bank's logo and down the side, touching every page. *Damn it*, he thought, *I'm fired*. Across the hall, Executive Vice President Hodge looked up from his desk, gritting his teeth. He pressed the mute button on his conference call. "Mr. Transle, you appear accident prone," he said.

Wrapping his finger in a nearby napkin, Fin kept his focus on the bloodied financial reports. There was no saving them. Instead he pressed the print command and sent them back through the color printer. He was already re-collating them when Hodge finished his call.

"Ten minutes, they'll be all ready," said Fin. He ran downstairs with the stack, dropped them in the copy room, and dashed down to the sidewalk for a shot of espresso from the deli.

All in a sweat when he returned to his cubicle, he dropped the reprints into the binder. He was just catching his breath when the espresso slipped and spilled soil-colored liquid all over the new book. "No!" he cried, tearing off the first page.

"What's the problem now?" asked Hodge, emerging from his office.

Fin juggled the stained pages, sliced a paper cut into the tip of his nose and sent another spurt of blood over the tabs.

"Oh Jesus," he said.

Hodge walked up to him, frowning into his silver goatee. He met Fin's eyes with his own.

"I'm sorry," Fin said, reaching for the mouse.

"There's no time to be sorry," said Hodge. Beneath where the VP's hands hung at his sides, Fin noticed a weird twitch in his pants. A string of lumps jiggled above his thighs, like he had pockets full of rats.

Fin nodded, forcing himself to stay calm. He needed this job. Rent was due, Anna's tuition was due, and the fridge was empty. Though the agency had already been through a dozen temps with this firm, he knew he'd be number thirteen if he didn't get it right.

He was just turning away from old-jiggly-pants, back to his computer, when Mallory, the woman who'd hired him, rounded the corner.

127

"I'll handle this," she said.

Hodge gave a curt nod, and returned to his office.

When he closed the door, Mallory gave him a bright smile. She had the easy-going attitude of most of the young analysts; her form-fitting suit claiming hipness, sex appeal, and business acumen in a single sleek swoop. The sliver of cleavage that blossomed out of her open collar offered a casual and constant insult to second-wave feminism, and she winked at Fin like flirting was just another way of wringing more water out of the temp towel.

"Don't worry," she said. "You just have to relax and focus." Her tongue flicked across her lower lip and as she bent over the desk, her platinum hair brushed against his wrist. "The old man just gets a little cranky when he's hungry. Why don't you leave the new copies with me and call it a night?"

*No*, thought Fin. *This is a test. This is what got the other temps fired. Knock off early and they won't call you back.* He decided to ignore Mallory when she offered a second wink, and went back to reprinting the reports.

This time he supervised the copying himself, and asked the operator to make two printouts of the master, just in case.

"Now they want two copies?" said Valko, shaking his head.

"It's my fault, I spilled coffee on the first stack," said Fin.

The copy operator shrugged as he slid the papers into the machine. "Hey man, it's okay. I'm going back to Bulgaria anyway, where there aren't so many freaking aliens."

"Excuse me?" asked Fin.

Valko stepped over to the counter and pointed at the ringed planet that made up his screen saver. "The bankers," he said. "They're aliens. Spawn of Nibiru, you know, Planet X?"

"Sorry man, I'm not into conspiracy theories."

Valko shrugged again, his accent thicker when he spoke: "They are farming us, my friend. Do you spend no time on the Internet? It is no conspiracy, but rather it is an unfortunate fact of life."

~\*~

Fin returned to his cubicle with two boxes, set them beside Hodge's inbox and emailed him that they were done.

Hodge threw his door open, strode out of his office and tore open the covers. "I wanted them spiral bound, but this will do," he said. "I suppose you want another coffee?" As he spoke Fin felt hypnotized by the deep blue eyes framed with wavy gray hair. Mr. Hodge had an arch air about him, like a Shakespearean actor, except the black suit and tie were all corporate. "Mr. Transle, I want to show you something," said the banker, pinching his neck with such nonchalance it almost didn't feel like a pinch at all.

He guided Fin into his office, across the gold-trimmed carpet and leaf-patterned furniture, past the glass case of medieval swords and daggers and on to the window. "If you're going to buy some coffee, Mr. Transle, don't go out *there*," he said, pointing down into the alleys that snaked from the street into the shadows behind the bank.

Fin was perplexed but decided to play along, since Hodge seemed to have forgotten his mistakes. He stared where the banker was pointing, saw a woman with a fur coat and garter belt walloping a man in a leather jacket with a huge, club-like purse. In that moment it seemed ludicrous that for him, manipulating papers stood between having an apartment and being ass-out on the street.

"Do you think you'd do as well out there?" asked Hodge.

Fin craned his neck, tried to follow the couple's trajectory as they scurried between the dumpsters. He wasn't sure. He didn't answer.

"I thought not," said Hodge. "Tell you what, Mr. Transle, why don't you spend your money in-house, use the espresso machine in the pantry. In fact, here." Hodge reached into his bulging pockets, his hand jumping around like he was chasing a rat. When he pulled it out he was holding a stack of crumpled bills. Fin caught the steely blue eyes again, hardly believing this guy had really gone from belittling to magnanimous.

"Oh dear," said Hodge. "It seems I have only large bills."

Fin looked down at the old man's hand, saw twenties, fifties, hundreds, and flashes of what, if he didn't know better, were even larger denominations. *Weird though, how they seemed to straighten and stretch between his fingers.* It was like Ben Franklin was peeking out at him, his eyes a pair of zeroes, bloodshot with gray veins. Fin blinked. The bills looked crumpled again.

"Something wrong, Mr. Transle?" asked Hodge. "Why don't you just use your own money for now and later I'll get change. In fact, later I shall spring for dinner."

Hodge smiled, put his hand on Fin's shoulder and escorted him back into the hallway. When they reached the lobby, he pointed out the door to the pantry then turned off toward the elevators.

~*~

Fin was cursing when he reached the vending machines. Little plastic packets of sugar and powder that were supposed to pass for coffee. He should never have listened to Hodge. Freaking aliens, Valko had called them. Yeah right, with food like a space station.

He popped out his phone while the machine gurgled out his coffee. Anna's picture showed on the screen. She was wearing reading glasses and a turtleneck, sitting in a café with her geology books cradled on her lap. He recalled how his brother had shaken his head. "Now I know why an attractive female gives you the time of day, let alone dates you. You're putting her through school. Sucker."

But he knew it wasn't true. Anna kept her word, they moved in together. They were in love, but it was also like they were best friends. He didn't need to show off her good looks, never asked her to put her hair down or do anything to pump his ego. And it wasn't like they were prudes—they had gone to a Halloween party as Adam and Eve, wearing real fig leaves between their legs and nothing else. It's just, he didn't need to show it off. He knew what he had, kissed his fingers, then touched them to the face on the tiny screen.

"Awwww, she's a lucky girl."

He turned around and saw Mallory standing behind him. She'd undone another button on her shirt; her breasts seemed swollen and skin flushed. "She's a lucky girl, Fin, and you're a lucky guy. It's getting late, though. I'd like you to come to my office now, find out just how lucky you are."

Mallory stepped close and gave him a dizzy stare. Her pupils floated slightly upward and he was struck by their violet-blue color. Like Hodge's, but darker. *Could they be related?* That made it even more disgusting.

He could feel the warmth of her soft body as she pressed against him. He pushed her gently away. "I just want to do my job," he said.

Mallory nodded, kissed his wrist. "Your decision," she said, eyes lingering before she disappeared around the corner.

~*~

Fin was entering his overtime on the agency form when Hodge reappeared by his desk. "Alas, they wouldn't give me change," he said.

"Excuse me?" asked Fin.

"They wouldn't give me change for these bills. Now they're upset."

"Who's upset?" asked Fin.

The answer came in a splash of gray-green bills flooding his desk. Hodge was drawing money from his pockets by the handful like they had no bottom. Fin jumped back against the printer as the flood of presidents rolled toward him.

"Are those… are they… moving?" he stuttered.

Hodge made no answer, only licked his cracked lips as the bills stretched themselves out. Fin recognized little Jackson heads with blown back hair, bald Ben Franklins, and a high-collared, inky-eyed man that looked like an underfed Winston Churchill next to the number 10,000. The gray face lit up and stared back at him, its mouth open, baring fangs.

"Not familiar with Salmon P. Chase, Mr. Transle?" cried Hodge. "He did a great deal for the slaves, you see!" This time there was no subtlety to Hodge's pinch. He seized Fin by the neck and dragged him into his office. Upside down and on his shoulders, Fin clawed at the carpet. Behind him he saw throngs of marching bills, tiny gangs of Ben Franklins opening and closing their mouths, tearing their own paper with their hungry chewing.

Fin's world turned over again as the old man lifted him and handcuffed him to a steel loop attached to the wall. He saw Mallory perched on Hodge's desk between the phone and computer, stripped down to what looked like a shiny black bikini and torn fishnet stockings. Beside her lay a pair of daggers and a plate of crackers and cheese. "I tried telling you," she said, pointing behind him.

Straining his neck to gaze down the hallway, he saw through the open door into Mallory's office. Behind her desk an empty shelf ran along a large window that opened onto a fire escape. "I was going to give you a chance, Fin. Now I'm too hungry to care."

Hodge closed the door, cutting off his view, and Fin could no longer hold off the shrieking and weeping. The swarm of presidents scuttled across the floor, hesitated long enough to leak green saliva, then began to bite. A Ulysses S. Grant went first, gnawing through his shoe into his foot. Then an Andrew Jackson shimmied to his knee, straddled him with his bony little slacks-clad legs as he bit hard enough to grind bone.

With the same expectant air he had when handing him files for copying, Hodge stepped across the room, took a dagger, and slashed him across the ribs. "That ought to expedite things," he said.

A dozen presidents' beady eyes went wide as they leapt off their paper, Grants and Jacksons, Franklins and Lincolns, all fluttering upward like famished insects slurping at Fin's blood.

Hodge reached out, plucked an engorged Lincoln off Fin's neck. He placed his wriggling, blood-giddy body on a cracker with some brie. "Not Nibiru, son of Ooloo-Elan," he said, taking a bite. "Voivúderu, Voivúderu Durúsium in the service of Jarwhal most Hallowed." The old man's eyes flared as he took a few more fattened presidents back to his desk.

Mallory came after, swaggering over in a grotesque mimicry of a striptease. "You're so loyal to those you love," she cooed. "It must make your blood thick like milk, like crimson cream." She poked his wound until a Ben Franklin popped off. She pressed him into Fin's hand and forced him to stuff the president's now pink-gray body into the hem of her stocking.

"We don't eat them all," she said, snatching up the little man and biting off his head. "Most of them will go in the ships. The spawn departs, but the bills remain. I mean, most of us are half-breeds anyway. But the little gray-green men, they're another species altogether. They remain connected to their celestial spawn, and wherever invested, their vine shall bear fruit, as directed on High."

With a small key, Mallory unlocked the handcuffs and brought Fin over to the desk. All pins and needles and too weak to fight, he felt sustained only by her whispered promise that cooperation would hasten his death. She plopped a stack of envelopes on his lap even as his body buckled in the old wooden chair. Facing the window he could see a trail of crystalline saucers the size of Christmas ornaments, lights red and blue, green and gold, streaming upward into the starry night. Inside their bubble tops, crowded like blood-swollen dolls, sat the presidents, eyes agog at the onrushing sky.

As he gazed at the departing ships, she made him assemble his final set of envelopes. He stuffed them one at a time with the husks of the bills, blank centers already refilling themselves with their respective portraits. *How many would he get through*, he wondered, realizing that not minding the overtime had a whole new meaning. An insane laughter shook his wounded ribs as the fuzzy blackness closed in… then he paused—one of the addresses—his own, his and Anna's…

"Oh you noticed," said Mallory, leaning close while behind her Hodge dripped brie and blood from his teeth. "I think it's only fair to compensate her for your loss and deliver this one myself. After all, she's smart, your girl. I only wish she'd direct her studies toward something more business-oriented, and do something about that look. Well, maybe I can win her over. If not, it doesn't matter. I'm sure you got her heart all fattened up with loyalty, all fattened up with its blinding, crimson cream."

# A Gentlemen's Agreement

"But why would he pay me a thousand bucks to sleep with his wife?" asked Trev as he stepped off the subway.

"Because Glaston's rich, and dudes like him are always looking for something new. Like, forget threesomes, this guy's probably had like, tensomes."

"If that's true, then he's already seen this show for free. Why's he gotta pay me?"

"Well, there is one thing about his wife…"

Trev stopped walking. He stood on the elevated train platform, car exhaust rising from below like fumes out of a sulfurous pit. "What, she's got a disease?"

"No, she's dead," said Renny. He spun on his heel and started down the rusty steps that led from the platform to the street.

Trev sprinted after him and caught him just as he stepped onto Broadway's mottled concrete.

"That some kind of joke?" asked Trev.

"You know I don't joke about business," said Renny.

His friend gave his trademark ironic smirk, assuring him that his ambiguity was the only trait on which anyone could depend.

They continued east through the darkness and the humidity, following the above-ground track that seemed to hug the earth like a gargantuan insect made of steel. It injected the streetlights with a flood of shadows as they passed rows of bodegas and blasted brick buildings. The bag-clutching vagrants looked a shade filthier in the poor lighting, and despite the occasional wisp of neon, Trev had an odd sensation he was losing his sight.

"We turn south over here," said Renny.

Trev followed him around a sharp V of a corner, past a park with a statue of a wigged Eighteenth Century dude who, in the murky light, looked like a hunched hitchhiker. They came upon a block of tall mansions topped with half falling-in roofs, trapezoidal turrets, and heavy, slate shingles. Among them stood one structure in good repair. A new wrought-iron gate lined its trimmed front yard, and glass lamps glowed among its storied ledges and twisted dormers.

134

"Looks like at least somebody keeps stuff up around here," said Trev.

"Heh," said Renny. "More like *restores* it. Old man wants to be a hipster or something. Anyway, don't worry, he's cool. Just remember, it's a grand."

Trev looked at his friend grinning under his matted curls. Despite the heat, Renny wore a vintage olive drab military jacket with a red, black, and gold German flag patch on it.

"So, how much are *you* getting?" Trev asked.

"What? I get a grand, too."

"For doing nothing?"

"Hey man, it's a finder's fee," he said, shaking his head. "Like, information ain't *free*. Besides, you get to do this hot chick."

"I thought being dead made you cold," said Trev.

Renny pushed his glasses up his nose and looked at Trev askance. "Come on. Pretty soon we'll both be a grand richer."

They stepped up the stone stoop and rapped on the door with a knocker that looked like an inverted steel scepter.

A tall, gray-haired man answered. He had a long face and a cropped mustache. He wore a jacket and collared shirt, but no tie. The clothes were form fitting, yet his gaunt chin and raised eyebrow still gave him a touch of old-world aristocracy.

"Welcome, gentlemen. A pleasure to see you again, Renny." He turned to Trev. "I'm James Glaston."

"Nice to meet you, I'm…"

"No, no. Don't take it personally, but your name's not necessary. My one sticking point, as you might say, in an affair I'm otherwise entirely comfortable with."

Glaston led them out of the vestibule into a small parlor with arched windows and a set of ornately upholstered furniture. He handed Trev a narrow glass and filled it with a syrupy liquid poured from a crystal carafe. He poured another for Renny and then the last for himself. "To a woman's pleasure," he said, raising a toast.

The two young men raised their glasses and sipped. Renny began coughing and Trev set his down without actually swallowing any. He could tell by the smell it was vintage, yet disgusting sherry. Either way, he thought it better not to ingest anything on this "most unusual of errands", as his host might have called it.

Glaston smirked as Renny took another painful sip. "I suppose I should have gotten you a pair of cold beers," he said.

Renny scowled and pounded the thick wine like it was a shot of bourbon.

"Indeed. Well, onward gentlemen," said Glaston, and led them out of the parlor into a kitchen. They swept around a stained oak island and came to a bolted steel door. "This will take you to the basement. My wife is there. As you can see, I left the money on the cutting board." He pointed a bony finger at a neat stack of fifty dollar bills.

Renny stepped toward the cash, but Trev didn't move.

"Um, Mr. Glaston?" he asked.

Glaston raised his eyebrows. "Yes?"

Trev wanted to ask if the old man was planning on watching, or had a camera hidden down there, or if there was anything else he needed to know. But he realized then it didn't matter, he wanted the money and was doing it anyway.

"I'm… I'm sorry. Nevermind."

"Then I'll take my leave," said Glaston. "Renny, you have my number. Text me if you need anything. And as for the young gentleman entering our service, do be gentle with Grace, she's but a slight thing."

"Um, sure," said Trev.

Glaston smiled. "Please also remember we have a deal, will you? That you promise we have a deal?"

Trev nodded.

"Good then," said Glaston, finishing his last sip of sherry.

When Glaston was out of the room, Renny turned to his friend. "Check it out." He fanned the bills with his thumb. "A thousand bucks."

"Should be two," said Trev.

Renny shrugged. "He's probably waiting for the deed to be done before he gives us the other half."

Trev looked at his friend, the nerdy kid he'd grown up with in Forest Hills. He wondered if he could walk down those basement stairs and close the door with no one but Renny standing guard. When they were in high school, he'd always thought Renny might have ended up a scientist or a stockbroker. Instead he'd decided to become half artist, half street hustler and all of neither. Not that Trev's acting career had been going anywhere lately. He'd once had a decent role in an incarnation of *Jesus Christ Superstar* on Broadway, and then a few minor roles in Shakespeare in the Park. That's how he knew the recent dry spell was a fluke, and how he knew it was going to happen for him someday—it really was—if he could just survive in between. For now, the important thing was that he'd seen windows along the basement wall on the way in. If worse came to worst, he could escape through one of those.

"Tell you what, Renny. Why don't you just front me the money? You can get the rest from Glaston later."

Renny paused, concern knitting his sweat-smeared eyebrows. "Hey man, I don't think…"

"Or I won't do it."

"Well then I guess I gotta," Renny said, and frowned.

"Great." Trev peeled the fistful of clammy cash from Renny's hand, then turned and made his way down the stairs.

~*~

The door closed behind him with a quiet click and for a moment he was blind in the darkness. After a few steps, he saw a blue glow ahead of him. The light was enough to reveal a rough cement floor. He sucked in a breath that tasted of dust and earth with a hint of something sour underneath.

As he moved forward, he saw that the blue glow came from a snake of track lighting wrapped around the base of a rough-hewn wooden coffin. The coffin rested at a slant, as if it had been shoved there, and the lid was held on with a hasp, as if it were normally padlocked on the outside.

He realized then that he had expected leather and red velvet, soft whips and fake instruments of torture.

But what stood in front of him looked so… dead.

Trev glanced from side to side, trying to spot the windows he'd seen on the way in. But the light from the plastic snake cast itself only a few feet around the coffin's base.

He tried to force himself to take a step closer, to reach for the hasp. The lock had been on the outside—to keep something in. But wouldn't now be the only time they needed the coffin? This had to be some kind of fetish game, where she lay inside pretending to be a corpse, which was why he had expected the whips and chains. So what was with the hasp? Maybe they kept something valuable in there, stored something in there all the time.

The coffin began to shake. The lid clattered against the base. Something inside was moving. Trev wanted to turn and run back up the stairs, but tried to keep still. *For the money,* he told himself. And yet another part of him wanted to see it—like some diseased mental appendage to his passion for acting, something kept him transfixed on the wooden box.

He took a step forward as the lid began to lift. Something flashed in the blue light, a shape imprinted on his eyes that wrenched his stomach…

…but no, there was only another string of lights laid into the interior. These were soft white, and within their contours he saw a woman's figure. Yes, it was Mrs. Glaston rising up out of the coffin. Her body's curves looked fluid in the gray satin slip that clung to her breasts. Her nipples pressed against the material, unabashedly hard. The track lighting gave her pale skin an almost silver sheen, and when she reached out and pulled him against her, he smelled a touch of lavender in her thick blond hair.

When he finally broke off the kiss to catch his breath, he beheld her stone-gray eyes and smeared maroon lipstick. Mrs. Glaston giggled, and they bit at each other playfully. Her lashy eyes, her darting tongue—every move she made seemed so alive, so fresh—that it offset the icy coldness of her skin.

"I'm Grace," she said, "and I like a lot of attention." With a raunchy giggle, she raised her slip and revealed the ripple of flesh between her thighs.

Trev lowered his head and began kissing his way down her pelvis, mutual caresses making it feel so easy. Within seconds, she'd pulled him up, turned around, and pressed him against her. She twisted her spine and their bodies twined together. A sweep of her lavender-scented hair and the musk of their mounting rhythm intoxicated him.

"Tell me I'm beautiful," she said. "Tell me I'm a beautiful woman."

She sounded almost absurd to him—almost—except for a dizzying knowledge that maybe Grace Glaston was not well treated, and maybe it was her way of consoling herself about what the old man was making her do. The near Victorian modesty of her words contrasted with the increasing speed of their bodies, the yelps and whimpers more and more tawdry. And somewhere in the darkness he heard other whispers, stark profanities echoing and scuttling in the shadows. They were vile, crude words of the flesh, churning like an undertow beneath the rhythm of their rutting.

And yet the increased speed and roughness lit her up like lightning. She started ramming herself back at him, whispering between her throaty moans, "I'll do anything… *anything*… for you. Because you're here… because you'll say I'm beautiful… *forever*."

~*~

When he woke, they were lying in the coffin with the lid open. Her head lay against his chest, her fingers playing softly with his lips.

"You were the best of all of them," she said.

He grinned. "Well, I hope your husband wasn't the only one who got his money's worth."

"Oh, I don't care about money," she said. "We are alike now, and we're together. That's all that matters."

Trev rose up on one elbow and looked into her stony eyes.

"What do you mean, forever?"

"I mean you're staying here, like you promised."

"Hey, I never said anything like that, babe. I gotta go."

"But your family only gets the ten thousand dollars if you *stay*. And it's too late now anyway. Once that door shuts, there's no going back. If you try, you'll only make it worse."

*Ten thousand*, he thought. *Damn it, Renny. That asshole, as if he were going to give Renny a pass when he got out of this mess.* "Okay, listen," Trev explained. "I'm telling you, there must be some kind of misunderstanding. I've got to get out of here."

Grace began to sit up, then rolled over and nearly pinned him to the bottom of the coffin. "Don't kid around with me like that. I thought I knew you."

"Knew me? You just met me."

Trev tried to push back at her, but she was surprisingly strong. He had to feign relaxing his muscles, then suddenly slip backwards on his thighs just to sit up. "Look, we can take a break and maybe have another go, but then I gotta split."

"But you promised you'd stay forever."

Something in the look of her eyes, her tangled hair hanging between them, gave him a shiver that made him slide back again. He twisted and tumbled out of the coffin, jumped up and ran for the stairs.

But when he reached the top, he found the door was locked. He batted it with his fists, slammed into it with his shoulder, but it didn't budge. *Damn it, Renny*, he thought, *what the fuck were you thinking?*

He dashed back down the stairs, slamming past something that grabbed at him with an icy hand.

"Wait! You can't leave this place. You can't leave me!"

The hand was strong, the grip like steel.

"Let go of me," barked Trev, shaking his head and trying to catch his breath. He was afraid to turn around and look at her—he knew something had changed. And yet he couldn't break away. Instead, he said, "Okay, all right. I'll stay. Please, just let go."

When he felt the grip loosen, he pulled free and sprinted. He heard a shriek behind him as he zigzagged through the darkness. The rap of rapid, hammering footsteps sounded, and he was afraid to turn around. *I have to find a window*, he thought, as he ran on and nearly slammed into the cement wall.

"You must not leave," cried the voice behind him.

"You must be nuts," he cried back.

But the shiver in his bones betrayed his disbelief. Her hand had been so *cold*. It infected him with a chill that grew within him as he made his way along the wall. Further ahead, he saw a dull light. Had to be the window he'd seen on his way in. He dashed for it, tripping over something as he picked up speed. The something moved, and the sour smell he'd detected earlier exploded into a cloud of rot and putrefaction. Something began lurching behind him, its slower footsteps joining Mrs. Glaston's rapid scuttling. He saw the sliver of glass just as another icy hand grabbed onto his ankle. Before he could scream, he felt something bite—a gummy mouth sprinkled with rotten jigsaw teeth tearing into his calf.

He turned and threw a left hook into bony flesh backed by brittle bones. When he turned again, he jumped atop a crooked shadow, vaulted upward from its torn, moaning torso, and grabbed the lower ledge of the window. It only had one pane, but was locked with a rusty deadbolt. He felt the jigsaw teeth clamp onto his foot this time, and heard Mrs. Glaston's footsteps thumping closer.

With a final push from the heel of his palm, he threw out the deadbolt and lifted the glass. Brooklyn's humid mix of garbage and exhaust seemed fresh compared to the basement's stagnant rot. He hoisted himself out, and despite the pain in his legs, and the fact that he was only wearing a tank top and boxers, sprinted all the way to the subway station.

~*~

The security door to Renny's building, usually broken and ajar, was shut tight with a new lock. Trev spent a nervous twenty minutes standing and swearing until someone coming out allowed him to slip inside. He climbed the stairs to the third floor and rang the buzzer to his friend's efficiency suite. He could hear the warped rhythm of trance music rising out of rattling speakers, and if he listened carefully, a girl's laughter and the popping of a bottle cap.

"Come on, open up!" he hollered, pounding on the door.

"Ah, shit," he heard from inside. "Okay, okay, I'm coming."

Renny opened the door, wobbling drunkenly in his black mesh t-shirt. Behind him stood a willowy brown-haired girl in a black halter top with the eroded logo of some metal band stretched across her breasts.

"Wow, man. What the hell happened to you?"

Trev stood there in the slightly too-small denim cutoffs he found on a stoop on the way over. He must have looked ridiculous with the ends of his boxer shorts sticking out from under them—ridiculous and scary, considering the laceration on his calf and bleeding wound on his foot.

"You tried to screw me! You said it was about screwing Glaston's wife, but it was all about screwing *me!*"

He took a step inside, and Renny didn't try to stop him. It only took a few seconds to look around the efficiency's black painted interior and spot the slightly swollen pocket of the olive-drab messenger bag where he'd stuffed the wad of bills.

When Trev pulled them out, they were still half stacked, like Renny had been counting them when he'd arrived. For once, Renny kept his mouth shut while Trev sat down on the leather couch and counted out six-thousand dollars in fifties.

Renny waited until he had stuffed them into the pocket of the filthy cutoffs, and then said, "Okay man, that's cool. And an extra thousand for you for your leg. It's cool, man. I don't want any trouble."

"I don't know if it *is* cool, man," said Trev. "You don't understand what it was like!"

"Hey, whoa, spare me, man." Renny popped open a bottle of beer and handed it to Trev. "It's a mellow scene here right now. Look, this is Jenicka, she works down at the bar. Her friend's here, too, she's just in the bathroom… Hey Nicky," he called. "Come on in here for a second."

A small, sloe-eyed girl in an oversized t-shirt emerged from the bathroom. She had a mane of thick black curls spilling down her shoulders and grinned wryly as she sniffled and kept touching her nose with her knuckle. "Oh, cool Renny, so you did call a friend. A cute one. Nice to meet you, boy."

Trev noticed Nicky trying not to stare at his bloody leg as she extended her hand. He shook it and sipped his beer. The girl was over eighteen, but not by much. The whole time, Renny smiled at him like this little party was on purpose, like it was part of his original plan. He turned up the music and said they'd have a couple more drinks, then go play pool. Yeah, his partner Trev was way cool, they pulled a lot of scores like this. Trev opened his second beer and wondered if his wounds weren't all that bad, just an attack from some nutcases in a rich dude's basement. He'd earned his money, more than he'd ever made in a single day by far. He could even afford to go to the hospital later, but now it was time to relax.

Three thuds sounded against the door. A few seconds of dead silence, then the thuds came again.

"Who the hell is that?" hissed Renny.

Trev jolted to his feet.

"Who is it?" called Renny, pulling his hand out of Jenicka's jeans and rising from the couch.

But the knocks didn't sound again. The door had no peephole, so if they wanted to know who was there, they had to open it.

"You get it," Renny said to Trev. He moved into the kitchenette and threw on his drab jacket. Sweat was pouring down his face and his hands were shaking. Jenicka stayed on the couch, picking at her long nails, and Nicky moved to the bathroom door, clutching her elbows.

"I hope it's not the cops," she whispered.

Trev turned around and began walking towards the door. Even though it would suck, he hoped it *was* the cops. Yes, it was only the cops. Maybe even a detective without a crackling radio who just wanted to ask a few questions.

He opened the door and poked his head into the hall. The ensconced lights and manila carpet stretched in both directions. He was just about to wipe the sweat from his forehead when he looked again.

There was no mistaking the shape coming toward him: angled at shoulder-height, tapered at its base, the coffin was standing on its end as it slid down the carpet. It seemed to jump at him, the lid clattering, the nails creaking and moaning. It was on top of him before he could shut the door, its lid blasting open and forcing him back.

*"Liars!"* the thing hissed as Trev stumbled into the apartment.

Screams erupted around him, and Renny began hollering for him to move out of the way as he aimed a heavy pistol at the doorway.

But the thing coming at them was undeterred. It left the coffin hovering lid-open in the doorway as it leapt out and charged at Renny. Trev glimpsed a white wraith of a skull atop a tattered gray robe. He could tell it was Grace Glaston from the tufts of matted hair. But it was hard to look straight at her, for her eyes had sunken into her head and left black cavities shaped like a pair of permanent, backwards tears. Through gashes in her robe, he beheld the terrible change in the body his lust had so recently devoured. What had once been sumptuous flesh had imploded into purulent rot clinging to black bones. Her teeth were a jumble of broken nubs, and her nose had fallen off.

"Filthy liars!" she hissed again, grabbing Renny by his skinny wrist and prying away the pistol. She snapped out the clip and dumped the bullets across the floor.

"Get off him!" barked Jenicka, grabbing the corpse by the forearm

Mrs. Glaston turned to the young girl, her skull wobbling on its bloated neck. Each time she opened her mouth the stench of decay erupted into the room. A dribble of soil and saliva ran out of her throat, obscuring her words as she let go of Renny. She pried Jenicka's hand off her forearm, picked the girl up by the neck, and threw her against the wall, cracking the plaster.

When Jenicka's body hit the floor, she began vomiting blood.

Nicky already had the fire escape window halfway open, and Trev lifted her over the sink and pushed her through. When he looked back over his shoulder, Mrs. Glaston held Renny by the neck. With a wave of her rotted arm, the coffin floated closer, then turned sideways and hovered a few feet off the floor. She began pushing Renny under the lid, his screams mixing with the heavy bass from the sound system. Her back apparently broken, Jenicka could only lie and moan while the corpse kept stuffing Renny inside. A row of rusty nails hung out of the lid and bit into his body like teeth. Trev felt his stomach turn over as his friend was chewed in half. When his legs fell to the floor, she picked them up and fed them back into the quaking wooden case.

Trev tried squirming out the window after Nicky, but the apparition grabbed him by his belt and yanked him across the counter. Her arms felt steel-strong as they propelled him against the kitchen floor. Lungs empty of air, he stretched his mouth into a silent scream as Mrs. Glaston pulled Nicky off the fire escape by her hair and shoved her head into the coffin's mouth.

The coffin lid raked her body inward, one bite at a time, her bones quivering, her arteries pulping on the rusty nails.

When Mrs. Glaston turned Trev's way, her face looked all skull, her teeth all rot like the coffin's nails. His breath returned to him and his scream exploded through the apartment. But when he managed to stand, he found she had moved lightning-fast and was standing in front of the sink, between him and the window.

She was smiling now, silvery-blonde hair cascading down her shoulders. She looked as soft and beautiful as when he had first seen her in the basement.

"Why are you running away from me, Trevor?"

"Because you're a monster! You're crazy! You can't bring me back there! You think I'm going with you now? After this?" He swept his arm across the apartment's carnage, Jenicka's broken body gone still amid the bloody strings of flesh fallen from the coffin's teeth.

"But you promised you would stay," said Mrs. Glaston.

"But I didn't," said Trev. "That's not the deal I made."

"Your friend, he promised…"

"He lied!"

"…and you confirmed it, with my husband. And with me."

"So I lied too, big deal. It's fucking New York! Just take your money!"

"Trevor," she said, her voice deeper. "Be careful how you choose now, if you don't want to end up like the others. You can choose to come with me, and it can be how it was before, like this—" She smiled into her flushed cheeks, ran a finger over the supple curve of her thigh. "Or it can be like this!" she barked, flesh falling from her face until it was a bare skull licking its teeth with a gray tongue. Her nails grew long on her dirty hands and she took hold of Trevor by the neck and pressed him toward the coffin. Its lid opened and shut, clattering hungrily.

"Live with you or die? Is that it, is that all?"

The skull smiled. "No, die with me or die with them. Lie sweetly with me or be devoured."

Trevor sank to his knees, tears blending with sweat and blood on the kitchen floor. There was no choice. There was no option to the coffin's void. Here, death was filth, splayed all around him. But in the basement the coffin had been smooth and soft, and Grace's body had been sweet. Insane as it was— insane as *she* was—going with her was a better forever than having his flesh shredded on the apartment floor.

"Okay," he said. "I'll stay with you."

The skull face smiled, going smooth and fleshy again.

The apparition led him outside and they began walking east beneath the moonless night. The coffin floated ahead of them, then vanished into a mist that rolled in off the East River. Billows of fog drifted in as they turned south along Bushwick's sloping side streets. It was late enough that most of the people out were small groups of drunks, and there were fewer of these as they made their way through the industrial blocks leading back to the slum of rotting mansions.

Grace held him by the hand, her flesh soft and cold. She kept her face turned away, looking ahead. He had the oddest feeling, like a four-year-old following his mother, wondering if she was mad or happy.

A giddy giggle hiccupped in his chest. *She promised me this was right,* he thought, knowing at the same time that his mind was not.

~*~

When they reached the mansion, she guided him through the iron gate. He swayed toward the stairs but she shook her head. She turned to him, the flesh of her face shrunken and frowning. "Why do you think you can go there?" she hissed. "That's my husband's!" She yanked his arm, dragging him toward the basement window he'd broken.

She pushed him, glass cutting his arm as she shoved him through. He screeched as his ankle hit the dusty cement and snapped. For a moment, he lost consciousness. When he came-to, the track lighting looked dimmer than before. He could make out the wooden coffin with its jagged nails returned to the center of the floor. All around him he could hear scraping sounds, broken bodies crawling out of the shadows and taking hold of his limbs. Some bit him, others lifted and dragged until he was heaved into the coffin.

Step-by-step he heard Grace lumbering toward him. He reached upward, brushing her tangled hair. With a cold hand she threw down his arm, slamming the coffin lid when he tried to rise. In the darkness, he felt blood oozing from his arms where the nails cut him. He wouldn't last long losing this much blood, and yet his eyes flooded with tears.

When the lid lifted again, her face was a rot of maggots and filthy teeth. She kissed him with a shove of her gray tongue, laughed black blood across his cheeks. She bit his chest, digging into his ribs and causing him to bleed even faster.

And yet he wouldn't lose consciousness. "Please," he said as she slid her dead body over his, grinding with her hips, raking with her claws. "You said it would be like before, that if I stayed with you, it would be like before."

"I lied, Trevor." She twisted his neck and bit into his forehead, leaving a tooth in his eye. A searing pain exploded through his bleeding body. The track lighting illuminated the hungry bones of her jaw, and she laughed, bit him again, and then paused: "You know, in the end, it's not about what's right or wrong," she said. "Some promises are true and some are false." She let her face change, full for a moment, before going to rot again. "But consequences will kill you."

# Pneumopericardium

## (*Air Around the Heart*)

Cory lay in the hospital bed trying to breathe. He pressed the button on the rail and raised the backrest, searching for the best angle for moving air. Beside him sat his mother, her face washed blue by the TV's rays.

"Mom, Mom," he said, waking her from her dozing.

"Yes honey?"

"When did the doctor say I could have another breathing treatment?"

"You just had one, sweetie. He said three hours, minimum."

"Can you ask him again?"

"It's two in the morning, honey. He's gone."

"What about the nurse," he said. "Maybe just some saline."

His mother grimaced and waved to the nursing station.

When the nurse came over he asked if he could take a treatment without any medicine in it, just take the salty mist down into his lungs. The nurse nodded and brought him the blue plastic pipe with the long segmented tube.

"I understand it's just a placebo," he said.

"I don't think I knew that word when I was in sixth grade," she said.

"I'm in seventh," he said. "They teach us Latin."

The nurse smiled and offered to stay a while after the treatment so his mother could get some sleep. Cory wished his mother did that more often, got her rest so in the morning she could run errands and stuff. She shouldn't try to stay up with him, not when he was sleeping three out of forty-eight hours.

Still, he knew she was just trying to help, and tried to appreciate that.

Because his other visitors despised him. They were always hovering just beyond the edges of the room, past the curtains pulled along the window, behind the TV, in the very walls. Their crooked faces peeked out, their melty membranous wings flapped and slithered and intertwined. Their eyes looked layered, like scales upon scales of endless black, and their tongues shot out tined tips beneath horns rising jagged and sharp.

*Devils*, they called themselves in their whispers. Some were male, some female, all risen from a spiraled void he glimpsed beyond the wall. And Cory

147

could feel their hearts were full of hatred.

"We're waiting for you, you little bastard," said the balding, gray faced one (they were all gray-faced, yet each was proud of their appearance, despite being hideous). "We're waiting with more pain than you can imagine."

The female beside him slathered through her fangs, shaking her mane of curly hair so hard scales shed from her vicious, void-ridden eyes. "Just wait 'til we get a hold of you," she hissed. "Just wait 'til we dig into your flesh!"

The whole shadowy crowd of them laughed at this as they fluttered in and out of the wall. Their bodies rolled and churned, and their clawed hands stretched outward, as if they would pull him into their infinite ranks.

~*~

The next morning his mother returned, said she had been in the chapel, praying for him. "Do you know what it's like to be a spirit?" she asked. "When you're a spirit you can whoosh all around and be with anyone you love, anytime, and when you're done you can rest in the arms of Jesus."

He nodded while his mother paused to kiss the back of his hand. As she did, one of the devils leaned out of the wall and said, "There is no Heaven, only Hell. Tell your mother that."

"Mom," he said, "I'm thirsty."

"I brought you some orange juice from Mickey-D's," she said.

He thanked her, had a few sips and went back to trying to breathe.

~*~

In the evening his father came by on his way home from work. He was dressed in a suit and rubber boots for the slushy weather. He stood in a puddle, stroking his trim beard as he spoke. "Any improvement?" he asked.

"Not yet," Cory rasped.

"The doctors say this sort of thing improves on its own. In the majority of cases, they said. Not bad to be in the majority, eh?"

"I guess so," he said.

"I know so, I know it will be fine. You're remembering to thank the doctors when they come around right? It's important to remember your P's and Q's."

"I always do."

"Always? Make sure it's always. I told your mother to remember that, too. 'Make sure he doesn't start thinking he's special,' I said."

Cory nodded at his father, needing to cough phlegm but not wanting to while the old man was still leaning over his legs.

"That a' boy," he said. "Remember, we're all up against something, we're all running a race. I mean, look at nature." He paused to flick a spot of dandruff off his lapel. "The weak wolf can't keep up with the rest of the pack, so when they chase down a deer, he eats last, if he eats at all. When he starts starving, he gets weaker. Pretty soon he's left behind and doesn't survive. That's nature's way of culling the weak.

"Anyway, that's why it's important for you to focus on getting better. If you put your mind to it, you can still make the pack."

Cory stared past his father at the wall, where gray faces swirled amid the white. "It's not really getting better yet," said Cory. "But I hope it will."

"Yes, hope," said his father. "Hope indeed."

This time Cory couldn't help himself and started coughing really hard. His father pounded his back until he brought up a plug of phlegm.

"Thank you, Dad," he said.

"You're welcome. Do you want me to buy you anything?" he asked on his way out.

"If you want," said Cory.

"Be back tomorrow," his father said with a wink.

The devils standing behind him all winked too, waving their clawed hands as the old man walked away. "Don't forget to say thank you," they hissed.

~*~

The next morning his mother woke him up by placing her clammy hand in his. He could feel the edges of her silver crucifix being pressed into his palm and smell her coffee breath.

"Oh honey, I just had to come back. Not just to be here when the doctor came. I had to be with *you*."

She kissed his hand and pressed her cheek against his knuckles.

Cory let out what little breath he had, wishing he had the strength to pull away.

"No, rest, honey, don't strain yourself," she said. "I'm always asking you not to strain yourself. I told you not to try to keep up with those other boys, running in the field like that. Especially when you knew you were allergic and had already come down with a virus. When you get better I want you to promise me you'll stop trying to keep up. You're not like those other boys. You're special." She smiled at him as she let go of his hand and stroked his damp forehead. She managed to push his hair in his eyes, where it stuck from the sweat, blocking his vision. He raised his own hand and brushed it away, but she kept stroking, mussing it again, and smiling.

Finally, he rocked forward with a coughing fit which turned into a gagging attempt to vomit. It curled his body into a stomach-wracking spiral, and when the nurse ran in with the kidney shaped pan, he produced a teaspoon of yellow bile.

After that he felt momentary relief, catching a lungful of air from the burst of adrenalin. In that moment he took in the nurse's smile, the oxygen-rich pleasure of her clean, white teeth and red lipstick. He imagined kissing her, but not just because he'd thought of that with girls lately, no, it was because it would act like the adrenalin, be a touch of something... different...

Another coughing spell wracked his chest. Afterward he felt around on his neck where escaped air bubbles had trapped themselves in lumpy cavities. They crackled when he touched them, and gave the strangest sensation, as if he were being strangled gently.

"I'm here, honey, I'm here," sobbed his mother. "I'm so sorry honey."

"It's still swollen pretty bad?" he rasped.

"Yes, pretty bad," she said.

"Yes, honey," echoed the gray devil leaning out of the wall. "It's pretty bad honey. Honey, honey, honey, pukey, pukey, pukey, yellow little prick!"

Some of the devils laughed at this, some just nodded. The gray baldy stood sharpening his fangs against a comrade's in gross parodies of kisses. Beside them a lean devil with a cloven chin spat a lump of gray spittle on his mother's crucifix. "Now that's what I call special," he guffawed. The curly-haired girly devil laughed and planted a real French kiss on the fiend with the cloven-chin, then turned to Cory and said, "You've never kissed a girl, you little prick, and don't think you'll kiss me. I'll tear your fucking limbs off so slowly you'll blaspheme the earth for the whore she is..."

By then he was flailing his arms and tearing at his I.V. The nurse called for the doctor and the security guard to help restrain him. He could hear his mother in the background crying about the dosage of the theophylline while the doctor barked to have her removed.

When he awoke later he heard himself as if in the third-person, as if he were just coming back into his mind: "Is bellum the Latin word for war?" he asked the nurse.

"I have no idea," she answered.

He felt himself coming into focus a little more. He enjoyed having the nurse this close to him, her hair and eyes, her red lips. "I'm sorry," he said. "I must have been ranting from the medicine."

The nurse smiled. "Yes, I've heard you do it before. I've heard you talk about devils."

A shiver shot down Cory's spine. As he looked at her, her face became narrow, a flash of her tooth sharp in the shadow of her mouth. "You know," she continued, "I don't know anything about Latin, but as an undergrad I took a little Greek. Have you ever heard of Stygiophobia?"

Cory shook his head, looking for the sharp tooth in the darkness between her lips. He couldn't see it, though he knew that it was there.

"Stygiophobia is the fear of Hell," she said. "It stems from the Greek word Stygios, meaning Hell, where the river Styx flows. Anyway, when you're better you might want to talk to somebody."

"Thank you," Cory said. "Maybe I will."

The nurse smiled again, stood up, and stepped toward the door. When she turned around her face was all torn lips, scarlet skin, and malice. "Of course you're never getting better," she hissed through a mouth clustered with fangs. "Not unless you do what you know you must."

~*~

That next evening his father arrived with a new video game console. "They had a line for these things at the Walmart," he said. "It wasn't cheap, but your birthday's coming up. The big one-three."

Cory could only nod his thanks because his chest was super tight.

His father hung up his hat, coat, and scarf in the closet, placed the box with his present beside the bed and turned to the TV. A devil hovered there, one hand between his legs, the other giving everyone the finger.

"Oh, looks like you prefer to have it off. Maybe it's better to hook this up when you get home."

This time Cory couldn't even nod. His shallow breaths sank into a mush of wheezy pain. He had to squeeze the gray-green plugs of mucous out with the sore muscles in his throat. Some of them had blood now and the doctor said they'd have to watch that.

"What are all these tissues?" his father asked as he leaned over Cory's bed.

"Expectoration?" he rasped.

His father knit his eyebrows. "You know, Cory, it's important to be clean, even when you're sick," he said.

His father washed his hands, then began picking up the tissues one at a time. "You can't expect the nurse to do all this for you."

"I don't," Cory choked.

His father continued picking them up, found the kidney shaped tray with a couple of the thicker, bloodier plugs. "This is just too much, Cory. You can't just leave this stuff around. It's disgusting."

"The doctor said we were going to have to watch it," he said, nodding toward an empty sample jar.

His father snickered. "If he gave this to you, why didn't you use it?"

"I was going to."

"Cory, don't argue. I'm trying to get you to take responsibility here. Now I'm going to have to ask the nurse to stop what she's doing and come in and dump your bloody snot into the sample jar."

"Mom did it herself yesterday."

His father's mouth straightened. "Well I don't know how clean your mother is!" he barked. "I didn't divorce her for nothing! I tried damnit, I goddamn tried!"

~*~

The next morning his mother arrived with a cafeteria tray full of Egg McMuffins, hash browns, and her plastic rosary. "How did you sleep?" she asked.

Cory took the pencil and paper the nurse left him and wrote *I didn't*.

"Oh honey, I'm so sorry," she said. "I just needed some time in the chapel. But I came right back, first thing, and I brought you McDonald's."

*Thanks*, he wrote.

Already his mother's eyes were glassy, knuckles clutching a shawl that made her look twenty years older. She ran her hand over the bruises which had formed over his trapped air pockets. "I've been praying for you," she said.

Cory nodded, pointed to the video game box beside his bed. The nurse had offered to hook it up but again he had declined.

"Oh my God," his mother quipped. "I just can't believe your father. He's always buying you things because he doesn't know how to express himself —complete Yankee shutdown. It's terrible because he's really a Cancer with Mercury rising, so he should be very sensitive. I just can't be around somebody fighting with himself like that."

She was pulling on his hand as he went into a coughing spasm. The devils were dancing on his stomach, curly girly and baldy arm-in-arm belting out a melody: "*Oh a wolf and a kitty I saw dancing in a ring, woe is me did the little goat sing...*" They stomped their hooves while their comrades sang along, thousands of them clapping their hands inside the wall's endless expanse. The stomping caused him to heave, and he threw up bile all over the McMuffin wrappers. His mother shot one hand out to hold his forehead while snatching her rosary away with the other.

_-*-_

Late the next afternoon, his thirteenth birthday, his mother was still clutching her shawl by his bedside. The doctor had ordered two rounds of x-rays and now there was talk of a pericardiocentesis because of fluid building in the pericardial sack. His father arrived just as he was being wheeled in, placed his cake carefully on the night stand, and demanded to know the purpose of the procedure, the percentage chance of success.

Cory heard the doctor sigh, then say, "Will you people get out of the way and let me do my job?" A devil crouched on his shoulder as he said this, holding his fingers behind the doctor's head as if he had horns.

His mother cried and cried, saying, "Bob, our baby, Bob, our baby..."

Cory felt like an avalanche of gray sludge collapsed on his chest. He tried pushing back at its flood of faces, limbs, teeth and horns. But his blows proved useless as the sludge burned through his chest, and the devils tore, chewed, and ripped their way toward his heart.

"Damnit!" said the doctor, then ordered the nurse to turn the monitor around, they were doing it right there.

That's when Cory felt strength pour into his arms as the devils pulled him upright in bed. "There they are," hissed the gray baldy in his ear.

He saw his father in front of him, staring and slack-jawed, one hand nervously straightening his tie. Beside him stood his mother, her shawl on the floor, rosary quivering in her left hand.

"What are you waiting for, you little shit," whispered the curly girly. Cory could feel her damp hair brushing his cheek, smell her rancid, boiling breath. "Give them a push, Cory, give them to us!"

"Yes, Cory," said the lanky-boned devil. "Push them inside and we'll do the rest. It's them for you. Do you want to get chewed and chewed and chewed forever? It's their fault anyway! Fuck them, Cory! Kill them, and we will set you free! Offer them, and we will bring them back to Stygia with us!"

He watched as multitudes of hands reached out of the wall, tugging at his father's sleeves and his mother's hair. They were rioting and howling and jumping, a grand, cavernous spiral of jeering faces. "Offer them, offer them, offer them to us," they chanted. Cory felt along his thigh, beneath his blanket. There was cold steel in his hand, with a blade at the end. A scalpel, they had brought it to him, they had brought it to him for this...

~*~

But in that moment, Cory remembered that one night when his father was going off on him, that one night when he mentioned being locked in the dirt-floored basement when he was a kid. His grandmother had locked him in the filthy hole after taking the money he'd earned from his paper route. "For college," she'd said, though he never saw it again. His father blabbered on then, switching to how his mother was impossible because she'd been touched all over by her uncle, touched all the time when she never knew it was coming. The only place he'd ever left her alone was in church...

~*~

"Fuck your forever!" Cory cried. He leapt off the bed, knocking the doctor aside, along with the syringe-wielding nurse. He dove into the wall, turning the scalpel against those who had given it to him. The devils let out a collective scream, an unearthly wail as he slashed and slashed. At first he felt exhilarated as he hacked through their gibbering, drooling crowds. But after a few minutes it felt like he was cutting into water, a river of flesh that reformed after every slice. His attack faltered, and he felt an incineration of teeth scalding him with their bites, a boiling river of claws whittling his bones to the marrow.

154

~*~

He awoke in the pediatric ward, coughed once and felt clear. He took another breath expecting pain. There was none. He sipped the juice from his tray, quenched his thirst and looked out the window. A freezing rain was falling, a storm encased in ice, and yet he felt oxygen and strength pouring into his limbs.

"Am I free?" he said aloud.

The nurse walked in and raised her eyebrows. "The doctor says you're being released tomorrow," she said. "All your tests look good."

~*~

The next day his mother helped him get his coat on. She said they'd kept track on the calendar and it was her week this week, they were going back to her apartment. "Your father left this for you," she said.

It was an envelope with twenty dollars and a note: *This is cab fare. I'm sure you can handle the bus, but I don't want to hear about it from your mother. Bring the change next week when you come to my house. It should be in the range of three-sixty to three-seventy-five.*

His mother kept trying to lead him by the hand as they left the pediatric ward and wended their way out to the lobby. "Don't strain yourself," she said as they got on the escalator.

Outside they caught a cab back to her apartment and unloaded his things in the walk-in closet that served as his room.

"It's chilly in here," she said, clearing a path through mounds of dirty clothes to check the thermostat. Cory already saw it read forty-two because the gas had been turned off. Without a word his mother dug an electric heater out of her bedroom and planted it in the hallway between her room and his. "At least the hot water's electric, too," she said.

"Yeah, I'm gonna take my medicine and take a bath," he said.

Cory rounded the corner into the bathroom, locked the door behind him and ran the water. He took the razor from the medicine cabinet, flushed his father's note down the toilet and stepped into the bath. Twenty minutes later he lay bleeding in the hot water, noting how much less painful it was than what had happened in the hospital. Pins and needles took over the entirety of his flesh, then his mind, then nothingness, sweet nothingness.

~*~

He awoke to his mother pounding on the door. "Oh Jesus, Cory, it's been over an hour! I'm calling the police Cory, open the door!"

Cory stood and vomited pink water all over the bathmat. He stepped out of the tub and wiped the steam off the mirror. In it he saw his wrists, the slashes almost fully healed. Another gush of pink water poured from his mouth, and when he was through he saw that his wrists had become completely scar-free.

"Damnit!" he said, opening the door for his mother.

The small woman stumbled in, saw the bloody water, and grabbed at Cory's wrists. "How could you!" she cried. "Oh why has God given me a Scorpio! Oh how could you do this to me?"

"But Mom, I'm fine," he said.

His mother blinked, looked at his suddenly scar-free wrists.

"But I thought you locked yourself in, I thought…"

"You think a lot of things," said Cory. "But what you really ought to think about is getting a fuckin' job."

He pushed past her and into his tiny bedroom, where he read and watched TV the rest of the night. He skipped school the rest of the week. *Something just went wrong*, he told himself. *He'd try again at his father's. Yes, his father had the tools to unequivocally get the job done.*

~*~

The following Saturday he rode the bus out to the housing development. His old man was waiting for him in his bedroom. "I set it up for you," he said, "did some rearranging."

Cory saw a neatly made bed and desk lined with text books. Beside it stood a small table with a TV, his video game console and a portrait of a man with a cowboy hat, glasses, and thick mustache.

"You're lucky I got your game back from the hospital," he said. "Your mother put it in the charity bin. That woman doesn't know the value of a dollar. To think I practically spent the night at Walmart to get that thing."

"Who's the guy in the hat?" Cory asked.

"That's Teddy Roosevelt," said his father. "He had weak lungs, too, except he did something about it. He became a boxer and a soldier and went on to become president."

"Boxer huh?" Cory turned to his father and took a play jab at his belly.

"Watch it now, son. Don't go pretending you're something you're not. You're going to have to put your time in first."

"Really? I thought boxers had to be fast…" He threw out an uppercut, pulling it just before it connected with his father's chin.

His father stepped back, spun him around by the wrist, applying enough pressure to make it painful. "That's about enough, Cory," he whispered. "Now I have to go into the office for a while. I suggest you start your make-up work because I know you didn't do any at your mother's. Show me what you did when I come back and you just might get to play some games."

~*~

As soon as his father left he went upstairs to the gun closet, found the key atop the window molding, and opened it up. He took out the Beretta, snapped in the clip, and went out behind the garage. *I'm glad it didn't work in the bathroom*, he thought. *Now at least I can be outside.* Cory took a deep breath, filled his lungs with air and studied the shadows in the scraggly grove of pines. "I can't stand you anymore," he said. He closed his eyes, held the pistol sideways to his head and pulled the trigger.

~*~

When his father returned he was waiting by the garage door. The old man hopped out of his jeep, locked it with his remote and almost walked into his son.

"Cory, what are you doing out here? It's cold."

Cory hit him with a right hook, knocking him to the ground, then kicked him under his ribs. The old man rose, fury in his bruised brow. "What the hell, Cory? You think that's funny? You think I won't put you right back in the hospital?"

"If only."

"If only. Huh? We'll see about 'if only'," said his father, rolling up the sleeves and making fists.

That's when Cory drew the steak knife.

"And what do you intend to do with that?" his father asked.

"Make sure," he said, choking out his words. "Make sure one more time."

Cory dashed behind the garage and into the grove of pines. There he worked quickly, because he knew the old man wasn't far behind. He plunged the knife into his chest, sawed through bone and lung tissue until with his left hand he took hold of his heart.

"Damnit son," his father cried behind him. "Don't think these antics will gain any sympathy from me! Don't you think it'll get any easier around here!"

"I don't," Cory whispered as he studied the still beating organ suspended before his eyes. Skewed vessels stuck out among the dark bubbles frothing in his pericardial sack. And it was within these that he saw them— flying, gnawing, slashing with claws and fangs. He saw the skinny and the gray baldy and the girly with her eyes full of hate. He saw all of them there, forever, forever gnashing and jeering, glutting themselves on the voids in the air around his heart.

# Torn from The Devil's Chest

*"When I do count the clock that tells the time,*
*And see the brave day sunk in hideous night"*

—William Shakespeare, Sonnet XII

She smiled for the camera, held her father close when it flashed. They posed for one more shot while she was still in her cap and gown, pulling her mother in with them. The woman looked ten years older than her fifty years, blinking against the fatigue from her night shift. When she managed to tuck a grin into her caked makeup and gray locks, the camera flashed again. Lyla embraced both of her parents, and kissed her mother on the cheek.

"I won't be too late," she said. She didn't wait for an answer before slipping behind the bleachers and through the broken fence.

St. Andrew's on Bell Hill had a parking lot on one side and a cemetery on the other. Lyla cut through the tombstones and picked up the dirt road that wound down the grassy slope. Clusters of dead maples and bent evergreens stood among the older graves, and she welcomed the shade from the June sun.

Although she'd turned eighteen halfway through her senior year, she didn't really feel free until she'd taken hold of her diploma that morning. Now, with an acceptance letter from the state university, a deposit on an apartment, and a waitressing job lined up, she felt like she was finally beginning her life. She looked to her right and saw an old headstone crowned with a gaunt cherub. The name under the monument was so rain-worn, it had become a mere impression. She giggled, placed her cap on the cherub's head, wrapped her gown around its shoulders, and stuffed her diploma into the back pocket of her jeans. Yes, she was truly beginning her life now—her *own* life.

"Boo."

Lyla started. She looked over her shoulder, saw only pine boughs wavering in the breeze. Her heart thumped, she looked left toward the field, then back among slanted, seventeenth century stones.

That was where he stood—tall, side-parted blonde hair, sunglasses. He took a step forward, polo shirt and creased shorts understating his athletic physique.

159

"Jed Archer," he said, extending his hand. "Sorry, didn't mean to scare you."

"Oh, no, you didn't scare me," she said. She shook his hand and brushed back her hair. "I just didn't expect to run into anyone around here."

"That's okay," he said. "I admit I saw you sneak out the back of the graduation ceremony."

"Oh," she giggled. "You too?"

"Me? No, I graduated a few years back. I was just there representing F.S., the SUNY chapter."

"What's that?"

"F.S., it stands for Fair Step."

"I don't understand," she said.

He smiled and moved closer. Sunlight flecked his tan muscles with gold. *Real smooth complexion*, she thought, *without looking fake.*

"Fair Step is a kind of student organization," he said. "We host guest lectures, have discussion groups, that kind of thing. Mostly psychology topics. We're not sponsored by the school or anything, it's more like a club."

"Oh, I see. I was thinking of majoring in Sociology."

"Another subject of interest for us. That's why I wanted to talk before you ran off."

They both smiled. For a moment she thought she should be scolding herself. A strange man coming to her school then following her ought to be a red flag. Approaching her alone in a cemetery should have made it even worse. And yet he seemed so easygoing—he had an odd thrill about him, so unlike the longhaired rocker types she'd dated in high school. Her dad always said she brought those boys home because she was mad at him about something. This sun-dappled man was so opposite all that, and so magazine photogenic she nearly blushed at the frivolousness of her budding desire.

"Okay," she said. "Can we walk while we talk?"

"Of course," he said.

They trailed down a dirt road that consisted of a pair of tire tracks with grass billowed in the middle. Jed explained that F.S. also engaged in some volunteer work—veterans and at-risk youth. Nothing too heavy, just helping with orientation, if they were returning to school or work. They had dinner parties, occasional field trips.

"Well, my place is this way," he said when they reached Western Avenue. "I look forward to seeing you in the fall."

~*~

Ten minutes later, they were kissing on his tiny porch. She pushed herself against him, urging him to bring her inside, which he did. The one-bedroom apartment was as neat and clean as his attire. When he took off his glasses and shirt, his muscles rippled beneath his ribs. She caressed his shoulders as he pulled her against him. His body felt firm and warm, and his unhurried kisses like a stream of liquid velvet. A hazy beauty to their necking made her not want to stop.

Which she didn't. She wasn't a virgin, but normally would have been at least a little coy with the belt buckle. Not this day—she kissed her way down and opened his jeans with her mouth. There his flesh felt even warmer. She didn't hold back as her kisses became something else. *Her own life*, she thought as she met the gaze of his gray-blue eyes. She worked until she brought him near the edge, then slid up, mounted him, and rode him steadily. She could barely tell he was wearing a condom. *Have to check the brand*, she mused. She grinned at the thought, and her eyebrows tensed with the rise of their simultaneous shudder.

~*~

Pleasantly out of breath, they drowsed on the carpet. After a while, he went to the kitchenette and poured her some orange juice. He wiped off the glass so it was perfectly dry and clean, then brought it to her and said, "See you in the fall."

She had an odd feeling then—glad, because she didn't want obligations, and yet also like somehow the way he spoke, he wasn't blowing her off. Beneath the surface there appeared to be something else, something in his stance, the way he moved to the window and stood looking out. Like he was standing at attention.

~*~

The busy weeks that followed helped her forget that strange afternoon. She had told her father she wouldn't be late and hadn't been, but that was the last time she was the dutiful dependent. By her last night at home, her parents were more like roommates. The next night in her own place felt eerie and dark, as if she were the only person in existence. She ended up sleeping in the middle of the floor, with every light on in every room.

Her first month of back-to-back double shifts proved harder than expected. Her friend Viv trained her the best she could. She encouraged her, saying things like, "You got through Bell Hill, you can get through this."

Waitressing didn't come easy to Lyla. She disliked all the placing and pouring, all the crud stuck to the tables that had to be turned over mint-fresh in a matter of minutes. Fortunately, *Lochran's Grill* also had a bar in need of bartenders. The chemistry of the drinks, the rhythm of sliding the glasses, and the instantaneous tips kept her going. Legally she was too young to actually serve, but they worked around it by making her technically a 'hostess'. Additionally, the manager went out of his way to let her know she wasn't expected to tolerate any disrespect among the clientele.

Not that she was discouraged to flaunt flesh. What she lacked in height, she made up for in curves. Blonde hair naturally streaked with red was unusual. It wasn't long before she had 'regulars' among the city's ample supply of disillusioned middle-aged men.

Sunday nights Viv came in with her boyfriend Cliff, sometimes with extra friends in tow. A few bikers occasionally stopped in on those nights too.

She might have been inclined to lock up a little early and do tequila shots with them, but her 'wild summer after graduation' dreams were dashed by the sheer roughness of her schedule, as well as an effort to save money for the fall. During daylight, she slept fitfully. She sometimes dreamed of that wistful afternoon she'd walked away from the private school campus feeling she was embarking on a long and wondrous journey.

Then the alarm would go off and she would head into Albany on the bus line and before being an hour conscious, had a nose full of sour beer smell and a counter-rag in her hand.

"Hey, I got you this job because it was supposed to be on the fun side," said Viv. "You know, fun side for crap work."

"Still work," she answered.

Viv shrugged. She had Cliff on her arm, though he was turned away, oblivious and talking to his friend. Viv adjusted the horn-rim glasses that contrasted her dyed-black hair and otherwise tattooed, tanned, and leather-clad figure, as if Lyla were more puzzling than she was.

"I guess it's fun sometimes," said Lyla. "Just lots of hours for little gain, ya know?"

A thunder of drums interrupted them. The jukebox squealed with a heavy metal lead guitar line that sounded like victims wailing in a burning plane crash. A longhaired dude pivoted on his left foot, crushed his leather jacket against the bar, and waved for another whiskey.

"That guy's been drinking all night," said Viv.

"He doesn't seem that drunk, though. Just the music, damn."

"Look at all those rings. Like gypsy meets Dracula. Creep-city."

"Not that bad," said Lyla. "Nice hair, just kinda, I don't know, loose."

Lyla walked to his end of the bar, poured him a double bourbon, leaned in close and shouted, "If you're gonna play metal, gotta turn it down," she said.

The guy chuckled into his goatee, might have said, *Thanks for the whiskey.*

Lyla pinched the remote, the bars wound down, and the plane-crash got under control. She glimpsed the album cover on the screen, a pale face with a two-tined fork stabbed through its eyes: *Manglechain.* She'd heard of them from some of her high-school exes, but they were obscurer and heavier than the sort of radio stuff most of them had liked.

She was just pouring the dude another shot as a thank-you-for-not-bitching, when Jimbo appeared. The ex-frat boy worked as a bouncer at the place next door. Though two years out of SUNY, he still hung out with the younger bros at Lochran's.

"Hey captain," he said to Dracula dude. "I think you owe her an apology."

"Thanks for the shot," the dude said to Lyla.

"No problem," said Lyla. "Sorry about the jukebox."

"No worries. Name's Mal," he said.

"Lyla," said Lyla. His handshake was strangely business-like for a guy with a fist full of silver skulls and corpse-dragons.

"Hey captain," said Jimbo. "I'm fucking talking to you. Three people walked out when you played that shit. That's three tips out the door."

"Huh, still kinda noisy in here," said Mal.

"Jimbo, give it rest," said Lyla. "It's under control."

"I'm about to give this hippy fuck a rest," said Jimbo.

Lyla slipped to the end of the bar. "Should I get Ken?" she asked.

"I already called him," said Viv.

Lyla had never called Kenneth Lochran before and was glad Viv took care of it. Nephew to the owner, he served as manager and de facto bouncer, when he wasn't at one of their other restaurants. She was told he preferred to be called the second there was trouble, though he tended to act pissy on the phone and rarely showed up in time to stop it.

"Jimbo won't do anything will he?" asked Lyla. "Dude's too skinny, right?"

"Since when did he care? And no, not that skinny."

When they looked back, Mal still hadn't answered him. Jimbo turned bright red. Being totally ignored enraged him like no other insult.

"Oh no, here it comes," said Viv. She tried to get to them, but it was too late.

Jimbo took the smaller man by the neck, braced him in a crushing chokehold, and spun him around. He carried Mal to the door while his laughing frat brothers followed. Lyla had seen some fights in the bar, but she had a bad feeling about this one.

Just before he was thrust out, Mal clasped the doorframe. He pushed against the outer door with his legs and they all tumbled backwards. Jimbo was too big to go all the way down, but his grip loosened.

Mal spun, gasping for air. His eyes looked dark and lucid. His fists went up, as did Jimbo's, and the two of them erupted into rapid-fire pummeling. The big man kept shouting, "Is that all you got? Is that all you got?" He beat the smaller man into the corner, as chairs and tables flew to the side. Long blood-smeared hair was everywhere. Viv was right, despite his skinniness, Mal punched like a machine gun. He didn't even try for the face as he hammered at the big man's stomach.

Lyla didn't know much about brawling, but it seemed like a bad strategy. In less than a minute, Mal was laid out on his back, coughing through bloody lips and quivering.

"Dumb hippy fuck," said Jimbo.

He clinked glasses with his friends with a swagger and chuckle. Even as the blue police car lights shown through the window, he gave the smaller man another kick.

"Hey Lyla, one more pitcher," he called.

"Jim, you're done," said Lyla.

He frowned as if he would argue, but then looked down at his stomach. The blood on his shirt hadn't all come from his opponent. The rings had ripped through the cotton and sliced into his flesh. It looked like he'd been chewed on by an animal.

"Guess we'll call it a night," he said.

_*_

Over the next few weeks, Ken made sure either he or one of the other Lochrans was in the bar after eleven. Lyla heard rumors they were going to put her back on waiting tables, but they never did. Instead, Viv brought more of Cliff's friends along to the bar. She said Lyla had to put the crap that happened behind her and get back to enjoying her summer. She went on about how they should do a day trip together, so-and-so was so cool, and Lyla really had to meet him.

They finally took a ride to Old Forge by the end of July. She had to admit, Viv hadn't set her up with such a bad guy. Terry was pre-law at Skidmore and played violin. They swam at a little beach by the town. He was lanky and handsome in the water, and not coming on too strong. He got up and fiddled with the bluegrass band later at the brewpub, and she fell asleep on his shoulder on the ride back to Albany.

Viv dropped them off by her place because he lived nearby. He walked Lyla home, she kissed him, but she didn't invite him inside.

There was something odd about the way they looked at each other. He stood pale in the streetlight's glow. The overcast, starless night deepened the shadows, and his eyes looked sunken, a portent of age interrupting youth.

"I can feel it too," he said.

She nodded. "I do like you," she said.

"But something's not right," he said.

"Maybe not. You can still call me, though, if you want," she said.

"No," he said. "It's weird, it's... it's *you*, something's not right."

Lyla saw him shiver despite the heat. He turned and walked quickly away. She should have been mad at what he said, but she felt it was true. He was everything she wanted to like. Seeing him that day made her think of when she had walked away from graduation, getting ready to begin her life, and do things for herself. An eerie shadow of a thought began to rise inside her skull. Had she taken a wrong turn that day? A ridiculous idea, what difference did it make what direction she walked after graduation, even if it was in a cemetery?

She went back to her apartment, slept and did not dream. In the morning she heard the sounds of late summer, cicadas vibrating in the high grass. She signed up to work extra shifts. When Viv came to the bar, Lyla made small talk and excused not wanting to hangout by just saying she had to work a lot. She was saving for college, she said.

~*~

September came and she realized how excited and glad she was. She used her extra money to buy clothes, got all of her books ahead of time, and went over everything she needed for orientation. This was still *her* time, she thought. Summer wasn't the wet and wild cliché she expected, but that wasn't all bad. She found herself thinking about where school would take her, a career, and maybe enough money to move to a bigger city.

The day before orientation, her father called her to wish her luck. She'd avoided her parents most of August, and decided she'd call back and see if they minded a visit. *Maybe just dinner*, she thought, *and she could pick up a few things.*

No one answered the phone, so she just stopped by. She let herself in with her key and found her father in his home office. She never felt comfortable seeing him there. He dressed in a suit even though he didn't have a job. He emailed people he called 'prospective employers' and talked to them on the phone. He acted like some kind of thinning-haired executive, even though it was sheer masturbation. His only real business was cashing his wife's paychecks.

"Oh, hi honey, how are you?" he said when she tapped on his door. "Rick, let me call you back. My daughter's here. Right, thanks."

"Hi Dad."

"Hi sweetie. I saved your mail," he said, lifting a stack from the outbox he kept on his desk.

"Thanks," she said, taking the stack.

"On the verge of a consulting position with a firm in Phoenix," he said.

"That's nice," she said, flipping through her mail.

"Are you all ready to start school? You know, I can't tell you how very proud of you I am. You're on the right track. A college education is so important. It makes you so well rounded. It certainly did for me. And I'm sure the preparation you got at Bell Hill will pay-off."

"What's this?" asked Lyla.

She held a full-sized white envelope. It had a window with her name and address, but no postmark. A photo in black and white of a group of women wearing bonnets appeared on its surface. Most of them were young and wore matching prairie dresses. Though the skirts were long, the tops were as form-fitting as corsets. The women had straight-mouthed expressions and piercing eyes. The photo's grainy texture looked artificial, as if added to intensify the somber allure.

"That's weird," she said, opening it and pulling out the letter.

"Yeah, you know, that wasn't delivered by regular mail. A well-dressed young man brought it to the door and said it was for you. You're not getting mixed up in a cult, are you?"

"Dad, what are you talking about? No way! I just, I don't know, weird."

She studied the paragraphs describing *Daughters of the Wall*, a faith-based community living in Brooklyn. The letter was somewhat casual, talking about having the same values and eating communal meals, living as a family and sharing expenses. It was unlike the photo, which she glanced at again then turned over to avoid the women's eyes, which were as sharp and penetrating as spears.

"I'm not sure what this is," she said. "Did the guy who dropped it off have blonde hair, kind of neat and preppy?"

"Yes, that was him."

"Okay, yeah, he's just part of some sociology club at the university. It's no big deal, probably just a study or something."

"All right honey, just be careful. I have to get back to work. Just don't get mixed up in anything over your head."

*Yeah right*, she thought. *Don't you either, like a job.*

"Don't worry Dad, I won't"

~*~

On the first day of classes, she ran into Jed at the student union. He looked as disgusted at the cheese slices corroding under lamps at the "Pizza Shoppe" as she was.

"Wanna dash over to my place for something from the fridge?"

She nodded and made the short walk over to the apartment where she'd last seen him. He made them a pair of tuna sandwiches and they talked requirements and electives. He seemed comfortable and relaxed, parroting a professor they both had for geology and making her giggle over her coffee.

Lyla thought she'd have to put her hand over his and say *no* because she didn't want a repeat of what had happened. Not at that moment, anyway, not on the first day of class.

But he didn't try anything. He got up, donned his tan blazer and said, "Well, we'd better get going."

"Right, okay," she said, following him out.

"By the way, did you get the literature I dropped off?"

"The creepy girls with the bonnets?"

"They're a fascinating intentional community," he said.

"Oh, well, yes. Are you studying them or something?"

"Actually, F.S. has invited one of them to speak here on campus next month, the fourteenth. Can I count on seeing you there?"

"I'll think about it," she said.

~*~

That afternoon she blew off her geology lab and ended up at Lochran's having a beer. She felt uneasy, like she didn't want to see Jed again, even though part of her did want to see him again. Not that day, but on the weekend, or when they could do something between what they'd just done for lunch and what they'd done on graduation day.

"Boo."

Lyla started. For a moment her face flushed and was she about to berate Jed for following her. When she turned, she found herself facing someone else. It was that Mal guy who'd been in the fight with Jimbo.

"Oh, you startled me. It's Mal, right?"

"Mal it is," he said. "Sorry, I didn't mean to scare you. I'll buy you another beer."

She should have said no, she had chapters to read. Instead she took a deep swallow when the bartender brought them a pair of pints.

As he slid closer, she noticed his long, black hair smelled nice, like fresh rain. His leather, rings, and tight black t-shirt were a bit much, but he carried himself with a certain confidence. It reminded her of the fight, the way he'd been so calm, yet in Jimbo's face at the same time. His slim but strong looking muscles flexed as he reached for his wallet. He didn't have any more bruises, and seemed no worse for the wear.

"So you don't work here anymore?"

"No, well, school started for me, my first semester, so I thought I'd focus on that."

"Just school, no work, huh? That means you have weekends off?"

"Technically, I guess. I'll probably use them for studying."

"Well if you can break away some Saturday, maybe we could go for a hike."

She chuckled and sipped her beer.

"What?" he asked.

"You just don't strike me as the hiker type."

"Oh I love hiking," he said. "There's some good, old country up here. Kills full of slate and rapids. We could go up on the escarpment, get lost."

"Well I don't know about the 'getting lost' part, but maybe some Saturday we could get outside."

~*~

That night she kept it to two beers and went back to her apartment to read her chapters. Viv and Cliff were in the next room, she had to pound on the wall to get them to turn down their music. When she heard the sounds it had been covering up, she asked them to turn it back up again. Near midnight, Viv came out in this red and black lingerie thing. One torn shoulder strap hung down, revealing the rosebush tattoo entwining her left breast.

"Whoops, am I leaking?"

Lyla shook her head. "You're always leaking."

"Sorry, it's Cliff's birthday. Been a happy one so far." She lit a cigarette and opened the kitchen window. "So, I saw you talking to Dracula-guy today."

"His name's Mal."

"Oh, his name's Mal," she mimicked. "So did he ask you out?"

"He wants to go hiking on the escarpment."

"Huh, he doesn't look like a hiker."

"That's what I said."

"Well, he's probably all right. Just be careful. I read they found this dead calf up there, like, that somebody killed. Paper said it looked like it was supposed to be a sacrifice, like teenagers trying to worship the devil or something."

~*~

Saturday she woke up early and focused on her books. In her *Phenomena in Psychology* class, she read an essay on Stockholm Syndrome, *Lock*

*Unlock*, about two families held at gunpoint by a fugitive church arsonist. Years after he was arrested and convicted, they attempted to break their attacker out of prison. The eight-year-old daughter was quoted as having said, "And we lit our own house on fire, in solly-darity with the bad man who was really just a child of God."

That was when she shut down her computer and picked up her phone. She texted Mal she was done studying. She'd be ready in an hour if he wanted to come pick her up.

~*~

They parked his pickup at the base of the waterfall and headed along the stream. "Here, split this homebrew with me," he said, handing her a brown bottle. "Just one, we have a hike ahead of us."

She took it and sipped. "Is home-brewing always an excuse to double the alcohol content?" she asked.

"Only double?" he answered. He flexed his forearms and squeezed the bottleneck as he chugged a third of the bottle in one gulp—so much for worrying about stamina.

They emptied the rest by the time they made it to the tree line. Her head swam a bit as she turned toward the dirt road.

Mal took gentle hold of her elbow and shook his head. "Let's stay off the track," he said.

She felt strange letting him steer her, as if in doing so she were being led to some secret hollow within the ash, oak, and pine. The steepness made her knees burn, and several times she stumbled, leaving all her weight in his grip. He just pressed on, taking hold of a sapling or a branch, not turning or speaking. In the shadows of the late autumn afternoon he looked like a shadow himself—leather and black jeans, all slim and silent, but for the crunching of the dead leaves.

When they reached the top they sat beside the strain of rapids that fed the waterfall. "We're almost there," he said.

She met the black eyes that peered between his long locks of hair.

A part of her tugged away from him, but what made her mad was that it wasn't for the reason it should have been. It wasn't because she should have been back at her apartment studying. It was because she wanted to run back to Jed's apartment, be there with the door locked. She wanted to be there waiting

170

for him, making him a tuna sandwich and telling him she was so in love, *so* in love. It was a feeling she didn't like. It was a feeling she thought not real, even with its strong pull. And yet the only way to resist its tug was to go further with the one in front of her. Though she hated it, the only way she could get Jeb out of her mind was to pull Mal toward her and kiss him. She did this and didn't stop. She tore and tugged at him and brought him down. She rode him beside the stream as he lay back in the leaves. She threw herself upon him, tearing at his hair and digging her knees into the soil. Her screams mixed with the blasting roar of the rapids.

It was Mal who stopped before they reached their height. "Enough for now," he said. "We must go further in."

"Please, don't let go of me, please," she said.

"Take my hand," he said. "We cannot be late."

~*~

They hiked for almost an hour. Her legs ached from the climb and from the interruption of their tryst. They passed a small, low-ceilinged cabin with one boarded-over window. The door was missing and the interior was dark beyond dark.

"Go there, by the oak," he said, then disappeared inside.

"Wait, what are you doing, where are you going?"

She heard a thump, a scream, and then a screech.

"Mal! Where are you? What are you doing?"

"Go!" boomed a thunderous voice.

She found herself running, her thighs damp with urine. She realized then that she hadn't put her jeans back on from when they had been by the stream. Her vision filled with a vertigo of dead branches and burnt brown leaves. She stopped when she reached a dim clearing and saw others around her, young women standing in a ring, in various stages of undress. There were men as well, most of them also young. They appeared entranced, eyes rolled upward. Some of them were chanting, others staring in front of them at an altar made out of a giant rotten stump. The trees that stood around it were white and dead. The shadows of buzzards caste from a wan setting sun played across its surface.

"He is coming soon," said the brunette beside her. When she smiled, Lyla saw gaps and cavities, though she was otherwise smooth-featured. *From one of the trailer parks nearby*, she thought, *or used-to-be farms*. The girl knelt, as did the others in the ring. She picked up a sharpened piece of dead wood, stood again, and held it like a knife. The others picked up sharpened sticks as well. Some of the men's were long as lances, and some of the women tied theirs around their waists and wrapped them with briars so they stood out like thorned phalluses.

"I don't understand, what's going on?" Lyla asked with a trembling voice.

To her right stood a man, broad shouldered, with badly cropped hair and a checkered shirt. "Tis the sacrifice," he said in that nasally, half-southern accent of the Western Catskills.

"You mean like, a calf?"

The man smiled. "Why, that'd be mean," he said. "Less yer gonna eat it."

Her heart began hammering in her chest. She wanted to want to break away. Instead, she was mad at herself, mad her fear was not that they would harm her, but they might harm her before she touched *him* again.

When she turned back to the stump, a figure stood behind it. Its eyes opened, and she recognized them as Mal's, though he was no longer wholly human. His head had grown a pair of dark horns that pierced the light of the setting sun. His body looked distorted, grown to nearly twice its original size, thick with angled muscles, and ribbed with trails of steely hair.

"Hail Dispater!" he cried in a voice that rang with a deep and corrosive rattle. "Hail the Enemy, and what prize He hath brought for rending!"

A pair of men appeared from behind one of the dead oaks. They carried a third man, naked and semi-conscious, and laid him across the stump. The horned figure took a step closer and she saw he was goat-headed, arms and chest covered in coarse hair, and he had muscular, human legs terminating in hooves. He was Mal, but not Mal. His eyes lit with rings of flame, and she smelled a reek of sweat at once sweet and desiccated.

"Let us glorify this night of sacrifice," he said as he bound the naked man's wrists and ankles to the base of the stump. When he was finished, his limbs looked like extensions of its roots. "Here the blade awaits," he said, drawing an acutely curved sickle. He swung it downward, contacting the stump inches from the man's neck.

The blade quivered with the impact, and before it was still, those standing in the ring fell upon each other, ravishing each other's bodies with feverish hunger. They broke off into clumps of two, three, and four. The odor of a second soup of sweat rose in the air, while a chorus of low moans rippled through the shadows. Lyla felt dizzy as the last blink of sunlight receded across the churning crescent of bare breasts, arched spines, and flushed veins.

"Come to me."

Lyla looked back and saw the dim silhouette of the goat-man standing over her. Nearly seven feet tall, his eyes had narrowed from flames to glowing embers. She felt a scour of wiry hair as he pulled her backwards. His snout brushed her shoulder blades, she felt his square, stony teeth and serpentine tongue. Despite her disgust, she found herself crouching on her hands and knees, curling her spine inward, her hips upward, and cackling at her own wantonness.

He rumbled against her like thunder, an immense weight that delightfully crushed her. Her thighs strained and stretched, and the vertigo that had made her dizzy became rhythmic in its spinning. She joined the others' chanting, joined when she could, when she wasn't turning and licking him like the trunk of an oak with hard, sweet bark.

Finally, she fell forward and pressed her breasts into the soil. She dug in hard, clawing roots and worms, breathing dirt. The rhythm quickened as the odor of the others mixed with the musk of animals. She saw the silhouettes of antlers and the shapes of wings in the moonlight as she shook and quaked.

She let out a peel of laughter as her whole body vibrated with their rutting's awful force. Trickles of blood ran from her fingers, nose, and mouth. A heat rose within her as if reflected from the ring of naked bodies writhing around them. The goat man, too, grew hotter as his pace got faster and faster, and their rhythm became an interplay between control and frenzy.

At the height of their strain, she braced her bones against the rocks and roots beneath her. Her loins drank in his scalding skin like boiling water poured in a bloody wound. The salty burn of pleasure exploded inside her, turning her laughter to shrieks. The goat man's thrusts felt hot and hard as pig iron, while his seed erupted like an icy stream that made her twist and collapse into the lacerated loam. In that moment, a thought emerged in her dizzied mind. She remembered reading a book about witches when she was writing a paper on *The Scarlet Letter*. At the time she smirked at passages about old women in New England sneaking off into the woods to couple with the Devil. Now here she was doing it for real—like taking a drug she'd been warned about because it would make her so high and willing to give up everything for its feeling.

_*_

"Rise," he said.

Her body still quivered. His giant arm pulled her upward. She barely stood, knock-kneed and tingling. She wanted to vomit from the dizziness. In the darkness she saw the others moving about. Had she been unconscious? A fire burned before the altar. The man lying across it was breathing in fits and starts, quietly sobbing.

The other naked figures gathered more wood for the fire, shambling about, their chanting fallen to distorted whispers. There was an aggression to it, a craving as if to finish something off, to put a final nail in an unclean house.

"Mal?" she stuttered as she followed the beast's hooves and stinking legs to the altar.

He led her in silence, then turned and spoke over the whispers of his acolytes. "Behold this man," he said. "He will be sacrificed."

"I… I don't understand, I feel… I feel dizzy," she said.

"You are strong," he said. "I have made you stronger."

He pressed the sickle into her palm, its wooden handle worn and warm.

"Who *are* you?" she asked.

"The Devil," he said.

"What?" she asked.

"Lucifer Fallen Star," he said. "He lives in me; I am one who can become Him."

"But why, why this?"

"You do not yet understand, but understand this—the world is changing. Soon everything you know will be rent asunder. You have great potential, Lyla Banes. You must choose your side, and if you choose well, you will have a place among us."

She blinked, steadying herself. Starlight twinkled above them now, and the fire offered an earthy heat unlike the frenzied fire of their coupling. The others closed in, tightening their circle around the altar, and around Lyla and this being who called himself the Devil.

"What would you have me do?" she asked. The words passing through her lips felt dreamlike. The vertigo was still upon her, albeit a slower throbbing in the base of her stomach.

"You must destroy him," said the goat-man. "He is deserving of this fate. Look into his eyes, look into your own heart."

Lyla glanced down at the twisted body on the stump. He had stopped straining to get a good breath and then his breaths became shallow and rapid. The rest of his pale, naked body was still. His eyes were slits. By the firelight they looked gray, a pair of smoke colored hollows in his skull. If there was a soul within, she thought, it was obscured.

She noticed tattoos on his arms, tribal. His triceps and biceps looked gym-built, and with the shaved head, she thought he resembled a cop or a soldier. They might have made him look that way, might have prepared him for this. As they gazed at one another, his slitted eyes did not blink.

*He is deserving*, the goat man had said. She thought of how she was just a student, a graduate of a small Catholic school, now in her first year of college. Articles on the death penalty flashed in her mind like the book on witches had earlier. Debates in the past that seemed absurd—it wasn't that the worst didn't deserve to die, she had said, it was that she didn't trust those who would judge them.

She raised the sickle. Such absurdities really didn't matter. What mattered were the roots and soil below, and the stars above, and the flaming eyes holding secrets which to her must be imbued. *He is deserving!* She swung once. *He is deserving!* She swung again. *He is deserving, deserving, deserving!*

~*~

Lyla awoke blanketed in wet leaves, naked and shivering. Her teeth chattered, chipping at her tongue as she tried to speak: "C-c-clothes... I need my clothes."

"There," said Mal, pointing at the root of a large oak. Her jeans and flannel sat atop it, folded neatly beside her backpack. She crawled over and began to dress. "Here," he said, handing her another label-less bottle of his home brew. "For the hike down."

Her skin flushed as she took a few gulps. Her shivering stopped, but her teeth kept chattering all the way to his truck.

"You all right?" he asked as they pulled out of the lot.

"What happened last night?" she asked.

"Stayed on the mountain," he said.

She remembered everything, and yet other than both being soaked, their bodies showed no signs of what they'd done. The cuts on her fingers had somehow healed. Her thighs were sore, but no more than they would have been

175

from any hike.

They rode in silence the rest of the way to her apartment. She hopped out and was already swinging the door shut when he stopped her. "Don't forget this," he said, handing over her backpack.

"Thanks," she said. "Listen Mal, last night, we said things. We said and did things that I... I don't understand."

"We'll talk next time," he said, shutting the door and pulling away from the curb.

*Next time*, she thought. *After all that, he assumed there would be a next time.* She wondered if she'd been drugged. The bottle that morning had been beer, but the night before? She'd hallucinated before in her life when she was very sick with a fever. The creep must have dosed her with something that made it happen again. So no, there wouldn't be a next time. Paying her rent and trying to get through her first semester of school was proving stressful enough without impromptu weekend acid trips.

She went into her room, peeled off her wet clothes and began to unpack. When she reached in her backpack, she shrieked. The sickle lay inside, its blade wiped clean.

~*~

That week she didn't return anybody's calls. She forced herself to study for hours and hours, and was able at times to take her mind off what had happened. She told herself it still couldn't have been real. She would have heard something about it, seen something on the news. No way something like that could have been secret. By Friday she was almost feeling better again. She told herself she'd learned her lesson. This was what carving her own path was really about, and that feeling she'd had on graduation day was hers to claim again. Experiences like this were necessary tolls for freedom, and she would be wiser in her purchases from then on.

Satisfied with how her first psychology exam went, she decided to meet Viv at Lochran's. If Mal showed up, she would ignore him and he'd hopefully get the message. As for Jed, well, he didn't really go to bars, and the attraction she had to admit she still had for him could be at least partially drowned in beer. Either way, if there was trouble, she could always invite Jimbo over from next door as a last resort.

"Hey kiddo," said Viv as she walked in. "Don't you look perky!"

"What's that supposed to mean?"

"I mean you got some color."

"Don't know how. I've been studying all week."

"Oh, well then maybe it's just an extended afterglow." Her roommate giggled behind her black cat glasses. She sipped her Jack and Coke through a straw and ordered them some fries to share.

"I don't know what you're talking about," said Lyla, then added a beer to their order.

"Oh come on, you stayed out all night last Saturday. I saw your jeans on the floor all covered with leaves. Looks like somebody got back to nature." She giggled again and gulped from the glass this time.

"Yeah well, let's just say next time I go fall camping, I'm bringing a sleeping bag for one." She took a long swallow from her pint, tried not to think of Mal or Jed, then took another.

"Aw, Ly, no way he can be *that* bad. I mean he's weird, but he's cute. Hey, why do you keep looking at the door?"

Lyla turned back to her friend—it was true, she had been watching the entrance, still afraid Mal might reappear. She tried the fries this time, picked some from the basket and dipped them in ketchup.

"Besides," said Viv as she munched, "I wouldn't recommend going up there alone, not after that dude got killed."

"What?"

"It was on the news, that body they found up there last weekend, coroner ruled it a homicide."

Lyla dropped the fries, ketchup staining her blouse. "What do you mean? What body?"

"It's been all over the news."

"But I read the news! I went online! I read the news!"

"Okay, okay, hey, you read the news. You got a lot on your mind, you probably didn't notice. Bad stuff happens all the time, right? Only this one was kind of strange, I mean, not that this guy was any saint. You always hear about awful things psychos do to women, but this guy, he was like, an ex-cop who'd done time for sexual assault, had messed with his wife and some high school kid. Real scary, though apparently not as scary as whoever got him."

Lyla palmed her phone in her pocket, glanced again at the door. "Is Jimbo working next door tonight?"

"Jimbo? No... you didn't hear? He's got some kind of infection, he's sick. I guess it's a big deal, he's in the hospital, his parents flew in and everything. Ken even said there's a rumor he blames your new boyfriend for it."

"Viv, stop, he's not my boyfriend."

"Now you're making me really jealous. You know, I think I'd prefer a friends-with-benefits thing these days, too. Cliff gets so clingy sometimes."

Lyla felt a chill. She closed her eyes and saw black leaves, the stump, and bones. "Viv, I have to go. I have to go now."

"Wait, there's still tons of fries, you can't leave them all for me. And you didn't finish your beer."

"It matters not," said Lyla. "For whether therefore ye eat, or drink, or whatsoever ye do, do all to the glory of God."

"What the hell was that?" said Viv.

"I… I don't know. I don't feel well. I have to go."

~*~

She went back to her apartment, crashed all night and into the next day. She missed her Geology class. When she finally did get herself out the door into the rainswept October day, she felt crazy wearing dark sunglasses with her poncho. She sat at the back of the room in all the rest of the classes and only checked her phone to delete messages.

Seventeen new texts, the screen read, but that had only been this morning. She'd had another thirty or so since the weekend before, yet she didn't remember ever seeing them: *They will throw them into the fiery furnace, where there will be weeping and gnashing of teeth*, and *But the cowardly, the unbelieving, the vile, the murderers, the sexually immoral, those who practice magic arts, the idolaters and all liars—their place will be in the fiery lake of burning sulfur. This is the second death.* They appeared to be Bible quotes, mostly about fire, punishment, and perversion. There were also some about gluttony, like what she had said at the bar. As if she had read the words and memorized them, and yet how could something be committed to memory and forgotten at the same time?

And though she hadn't read the gospels much since her time at Bell Hill, there were some passages that struck her as odd. At first she thought maybe they had come from Revelations. When she was a kid she remembered sitting around with friends at slumber parties, staying up with a flashlight and scaring each other sleepless with the visions of that brain-plagued hermit of Patmos. As she read the texts, the language was even more intense, literally making her skin crawl. Something in them made her childhood heebie-jeebies look like a case of strep compared to anthrax: *Those of the brittle star took his shining head and brought it earthward to be buried. Verily, the emissaries of the all-renewing fire fell upon them with many terrible cuts, until their bodies were all one bleeding wound, and they cried out for mercy, and they released His most hallowed vessel.*

~*~

When she returned home that night, she found the door open. Viv wasn't home but there was someone waiting for her in the kitchen: "Give me your things," said Jed. "And sit down."

"What are you doing here?" she asked.

"Making you chicken soup. Vivian kindly let me in and showed me the cookware." He grinned ironically, indicating their sole pot being stirred with their lone serving spoon.

The soup did smell good though, and with Viv out—second night in a row without Cliff around—the apartment felt so quiet and still.

"I'm making you soup," said Jed. "And you're getting some more rest. It's common to bite off more than you can chew when you kick off your first semester. You know, with the first round of real exams coming up, this is when a lot of freshmen fall off their studies, get mixed up in destructive behavior."

She chuckled. "Self-destruction's a broad category. Care to be more specific doc?" She belied her sarcasm by hungrily spooning the soup. She detected a hum in the background, behind their words, and saw a small white machine resting on the floor, neither heater nor air conditioner.

"Air purifier," he said, following her eyes. "I brought it over. I want you to be comfortable. Much of success is creating an environment for success. Many think hard work is about strain, about wracking your body and soul. Yet we feel there is more to it, that to take yourself further on the path of success, as well as redemption, you need to consider all the tools available. Not technology versus nature, so much as the proper placement of each."

"Who's we?"

"The F.S. of course."

~*~

"I've been trying to call your roommate."

"How's that workin' out for ya?"

"Not like it should. That's why I'm coming to you."

"Yeah, in a parking lot after work, which isn't friggin' creepy or anything."

Vivian stood in the center of the circle the streetlight made on the pavement. Mal stood opposite, decked in his leather and rings. The way he looked at her, something in his glare, made her want to bolt for her car. He looked vulpine, an animal on the hunt. He stepped closer to her and she smelled a metallic odor she couldn't quite place… copper? What was it that smelled like that?

"I have to talk with her," he said. "She could be in danger."

"Yeah, and when she runs into you again, she will be in mortal fucking peril."

The man ignored her words, his expression remaining intent. There was something different about him—his shoulders seemed broader, his torso set to pounce, his hands about to take hold of her arms and rip them off her body.

Vivian thumbed her car key, prepared to strike. *Try it if you want, creep,* she thought, *but it's gonna cost you.*

"I hold no quarrel with you," he said. "I'm here because Lyla is in danger."

When he stepped forward, he took her by the elbow. Surprisingly, she relaxed a little. The grip was light, and the urgency in his eyes struck her as sincere.

"Well I guess I hold no quarrel with you either, Sire. If we were at a Renaissance fair, I might ask you to pin my scarf to your nuts. But I'm tired and I'm going home, so if you could just creep on back to Castle Drunkula…"

"Do not mock me!"

She stumbled back as he roared. Flames erupted from his eyes with a sickly brightness. Horns stabbed up and out from his forehead, splattering her cheek with hot blood.

Vivian screamed and slashed at his face. He squeezed her elbow harder and shook, causing her to drop the keychain.

"You must take me to her," he bellowed.

"Get off me," she cried, kicking him in the stomach. He absorbed the blow, but let go of her arm. In that second she bolted, sprinting to Western Avenue and ducking into a taxi.

~*~

Lyla's phone buzzed in her pocket. She pulled it out and saw a missed call from Viv glowing on its screen. It snapped her out of the trance she'd been in as she walked through the cemetery with Jed.

"I thought you turned that off," he said.

"Must have forgot," she said, gazing into the inky darkness. They weren't far from where they'd first met, and yet in an area she'd never known existed. The stones here were small, many broken and chipped. He'd used his pen light to illuminate the worn characters: *John and Anna Stimes, b. Dec 1, 1865 d. Dec. 1, 1865.*

"A time when humans were accepting of their fates," he had said. "As they shall be again."

The October night chilled her fingers as she gripped her phone. She felt a wave of nausea in the pit of her stomach. The reek of rotten soil assaulted her nostrils, as if she could smell the dead desiccating in their tiny coffins. She had followed him here because it had felt safe, had entered the shadows with a feeling that the quiet was palpable and peaceful. However, that peace transformed, becoming as stifling as a shroud pulled over her head. She wanted to get away from this place, she wanted to stop listening to the strange things Jed was saying, and yet she didn't dare tear away from him.

"Call her back," he said. "It could be an emergency."

As he spoke, he began walking back toward the road. She called Viv, and her friend answered in a panic, something about the creepy guy from the bar, "He's looking for you," she said. "*I'm* looking for you, I need to find you!"

"Calm down," Lyla said.

"I can't, I don't even have my car, I ran, I'm in a taxi."

"Tell her to meet us at my place," said Jed.

"Meet us at my friend Jed's," she said, and gave the address.

This finally calmed her down, and when they finished the short walk back, they found Vivian waiting on the porch railing, crying into her eye shadow, tears running in black rivers down her cheeks.

"That guy Mal from the bar," she said. "He followed me. He… he grabbed me."

"Let's go inside," said Jed. "We can call the police from there."

Once inside he said she should have something to eat first. He turned on the lights and the heat and the television. He brought her a hot water bottle,

181

made everyone hot toddies, and handed Viv a hydrocodone.

"A venal sin," he said, "given the circumstances."

Viv giggled and said she felt better. Calling the police could wait. He hadn't exactly assaulted her, she said. "Just what a creep. Lyla, you *cannot* see him again. He's crazy. If he ever comes near our apartment, I *will* call the cops."

"Maybe you could get Cliff to take you home for a few nights?"

"I've actually been avoiding him lately," she said. "Can't deal with the chem-student-by-day, rebel-by-night thing anymore. Not the way he does it. I doubt he'll ever make a real pharmacist, and the last time he stood up to a dude on my behalf, he talked big then got his teeth knocked out. And that guy was half the size of current creepy-dude."

"I think you should both stay here tonight," said Jed. "Take my bed, it's a queen. I'll take the couch."

Lyla had drunk enough of her hot toddy not to protest. The hydrocodone kicked in for Viv and they retired to the bedroom where they finished one more cocktail in bed while watching some singing show. Jed said he didn't want any more to drink, had to read a few chapters. Lyla thought it odd as she glimpsed him at the desk. The book before him had a leather cover and silk bookmark, like a bible. He looked up periodically, murmuring to himself with his eyes closed, as if in prayer.

Four hours later she woke to find him standing over their bed. The TV glowed gray, cut from all channels and offering little light. Viv still lay beside her, had lost her t-shirt somehow, and was naked except for her thong, with her arm thrown over Lyla.

"Jed," she said. "What's going on?"

He reached down, turned Viv's shoulder and traced a cross on her chest. His finger made a line down her sternum, back up and over, brushing each nipple.

"In nomine Jarwhalum," he said.

"What?" she said.

"Shhhhhh," he said, turning and heading back out to the couch.

~*~

The next morning, he was up and out the door before they awoke. Viv came out of the shower while Lyla was still in bed. The room filled with steam as warm water dripped from her bare skin.

"Since when do you air dry?" asked Lyla.

Viv giggled. "What does it matter?"

Lyla rolled out of bed and pulled on her jeans. They *were* roommates, and they'd passed through the common area plenty of times unclothed. This was different though, the way Viv padded around their host's bedroom, barefoot and goose-bumped, casting sly glances and opening closet doors.

"What are you doing?" she asked.

"Looking for something to wear," she said. "I can't wear those clothes again. They reek of Lochran's, buffalo sauce, and drunks. Whoa, get a load of this."

Viv turned and held up a black, ankle-length skirt. It had a frilled edge and pattern of crosshatched threads, that prairie-meets-pilgrim style she had seen before.

"Why's he have skirts in his closet?" Lyla wondered aloud.

"Don't know," said Viv. "But I don't have time to stop home and change, so it's good luck for me."

~*~

That afternoon she ran into Jed outside her psych class. "Oh, yes, the skirt belongs to my sister," he said. "I'm glad she found it." At first Lyla was uneasy about the way he just followed her down the stairs and across the campus. He went on about how it was high time she came to a meeting and met the F.S. members. "Chad and Anton are really nice. They actually live near you guys, so they agreed to keep an eye out."

She was about to stop in her tracks, tell him she didn't want them to 'keep an eye out', or him either.

He turned off before she could, said, "Meeting's Thursday, if you can make it. Call me this weekend either way."

She watched as he strode away, sweater tied over his shoulders, books tucked into his arm. He looked so easygoing, same as on that first day. She caught her words in her throat. Maybe she was overthinking it. The nausea she'd been feeling and the bad night on the escarpment. She needed to go home and study, eat something simple and get back into her routine.

When she got back Viv was there, taking a night off from the restaurant, she said. She wasn't wearing the skirt anymore, but Lyla couldn't remember the last time she'd seen her in faded jeans and a sweatshirt. They made pasta then sat at the kitchen table, studying. An hour in Lyla rubbed her eyes in the lamplight, "Cup of tea?" she asked.

Vivian didn't respond. Lyla couldn't remember the last time she'd seen her roommate reading. Ostensibly an English major, she always joked how not reading helped her understand irony. She relied heavily on Internet summaries and always crammed for tests. Tonight she poured over a photocopied article without moving or blinking. Lyla literally watched the bags swell into being beneath her roommate's eyes. A crooked smile spread across her face, and a pool of saliva formed in the corner of her mouth.

"Viv, are you all right?"

Viv started as if she had been woken up. "Oh sorry, it's just this article," she said. "Jed gave it to me. It's so interesting, like, the personal story of this girl Mary, and how she found this teacher, and how she was being abused in this small town, and thought it would help to like, go to the city and do something for herself. But then all she found was addiction, and when the teacher came, it was just in the nick of time. He taught her selflessness just in time!"

"Can I see that?" Lyla asked.

Viv slid the article across the table. Crooked shadows from the hasty copy job lined the margins. Debris spattered black speckles through the text and over the inset photograph. It reminded her of the texture in the photo of the women in the bonnets. The woman in this picture wore the same clothing, though her head was uncovered and her hands clasped in front of her, palm to palm in prayer. *Surprised by Redemption*, read the title. *Mary McKinley was drowning in a haze of cocaine and methamphetamines, at the mercy of poverty and disease—until it was revealed He had other plans.*

Tap-tap. "You ladies doing okay?" Tap-tap. Tap-tap-tap.

The sounds were coming from the front door. She moved from the kitchen to the old house's rickety foyer, saw a young man peering through the slanted glass. "Hi, I'm Chad," he said when she opened the door.

"So I guess he's Anton," she said, nodding at the second man. She could see why they'd made Chad the spokesman. He was slim, with short blonde hair and a friendly smile, whereas Anton was hunched, with very pale skin and cropped black hair. He wore what appeared to be permanent five-o'clock shadow and his muscles pressed into his veins like his body was under constant pressure.

"Yes," said Chad. "We're with the F.S. Jed asked us to check-in on you."

"I know," she said.

The way Chad said F.S. sounded official, as if he were referring to some kind of government agency instead of some corny campus sociology club. She wanted to shake her head and laugh at these door-to-door salesmen, a couple of dudes who couldn't quite make it as telemarketers. Yet that feeling from the cemetery returned, that gravity that had kept her from tearing away from Jed.

"You guys can come in for a while if you want," she said.

They hung out for about an hour. Chad declined a beer, saying not while he was on duty. Anton didn't even come in the kitchen, just hovered in the foyer, staring alternately at the walls and ceiling. He frequently scratched at his chest, and it was strange because she caught Chad doing it once, too, between sips of tea.

When they said goodnight, Viv followed them out the front door onto the porch. "Thanks you guys," she said. "I really appreciate you coming around, and I'll see you at the meeting."

"What meeting?" asked Lyla when they were back inside.

"The F.S. meeting, you know, Thursday? We promised we'd go, remember?"

~*~

That Thursday night they met in a coffee shop, off campus. Lyla had been dreading it, but aside from the way these guys dressed in their clone-like collared shirts and dark slacks, it wasn't so bad. They handed out an article on PTSD, and talked about a volunteer event they were conducting at a soup kitchen.

"And don't forget," said Jed at the end, "we'll be hosting our speaker this Saturday. Sister Liza Tupper will be speaking at Halford Hall, Room 108. She will have with her several representatives from the intentional community, *Daughters of the Wall*. Let's make sure all Fair Steppers are there, and let's remember to invite any friends and family, so we can have a great turnout for this important event."

~*~

That Friday night the harvest moon shone through Jed's bedroom window. Vivian insisted she keep the black skirt on, and bunched it up around her knees as she scissored her legs around Jed's thighs. The three of them made a crescent on his bed, Lyla sprawled across the pillows as he licked between her legs. Jed lay in the middle, in rhythm with both of them at once, and Vivian was willowing to and fro, arms stretching with the rise of her moans. Afterward Lyla held her friend's hand while Jed stood her up, pressed her against the wall, and had her once more from behind.

"To possess all and see such possession reflected by total acceptance," he said.

His voice was steady, quiet as was possible without being a whisper. "Yes, Sister Vivian, you must kiss me there, and give more even as you take more," he said.

By morning they were exhausted and unslept, yet remained awake as he showered and dressed.

~*~

Though Halford Hall had a brick and ivy exterior circa 1912, the interior had been gutted and refurbished. The first floor sported a dozen blue-carpeted "conference rooms" that were hardly more than a warren of sheetrock booths beneath a mezzanine strewn with plastic tables. The upper floors still had the original full-sized classrooms, but for some reason F.S. had signed up for one of the windowless booths numbered 108, with its podium on the floor and its half-dozen rows of folding chairs.

The Sisters from the Brooklyn community entered the building the same time as Lyla and her friends. They stood outside the locked door with their rolled posters tucked under their arms until the custodian came and unlocked it, then filed in as if they were students themselves.

The sight of them in person struck twice as hard as the photo. Their black dresses clung to bodies so emaciated, their ribs pressed lines into the fabric. Fattened breasts protruded above, mocking their shrunken skin. It wasn't so much their size as the way they were swollen. Lyla had only ever seen pregnant women with such strained looking glands.

Their lips looked dry and chapped, trickles of blood cobwebbing the corners of their mouths. They couldn't help but chew their lips, their teeth enlarged and pressing outward like their breasts.

As they trooped inside and picked out their seats, Lyla notice Chad and Anton split off and follow the Sisters to the front of the room. They took the rolled posters from the women and began hanging them on the wall behind.

The one she assumed was Sister Tupper tapped the microphone and said, "Are all of us in? Let us begin."

"Ready when you are," said Edwin Price. The know-it-all from her psych class was sitting in front as always, beaming his snarky grin. He kept his legal pad on his lap, cover page lined with questions written neatly in cursive.

"Good, well, let us turn our attention to the butter churn. Sister Bethany, if you would?"

The second bonneted Sister lifted a black rod that looked like a half-sized pool cue. She pointed it at a detailed cross-section drawing of a hand-operated butter churn. Lyla couldn't guess the century, but it certainly didn't have a GE logo. That's when she took in the other posters they had hung in a row behind the podium—a brick baker's oven, a loom, and a washboard. Any one of these crafts would have been charming in its own right on the wall of an antique shop or museum. In tandem, there was something stifling about them, something that brought a strange word to Lyla's mind: re-education.

She found her eyes fixed on the last poster on the right, midwives bent between the legs of a woman giving birth. Towels, cast iron tub, crucifix on the wall, and another figure, a man in a suit and conical hat. In his hands he held what looked like a giant pair of calipers with wingnuts that adjusted serrated clamps. *Doctor in attendance!* read the caption.

"Excuse me," said Edwin. "I know you're leading up to something with this butter churn thing, but are we connecting this to the sociological implications of a technologically retrogressive community living in the heart of New York City any time soon?"

Sister Tupper's black eyes narrowed. "Some of our machines are old. Others, quite new. Now, as I was saying, you must focus your heart and mind as you stir the cream, you must avoid singing, and conversation."

As she listened, Lyla felt a chill in the room. Chad and Anton altered between hovering around the Sisters and marching between the rows of chairs. Anton looked hunched, constantly coughing and clearing his throat. Lyla could smell his spit. Both he and Chad scratched at their chests through their collared shirts. One bulb must have been dead in the paneled ceiling lights, which made the room dim and the posters look yellowish and as old as the acts they were depicting.

Jed sat beside Lyla, hands clasped on his lap. Viv sat on her other side, holding Cliff's hand more out of control than affection. She nodded continuously as Sister Tupper spoke, treating each word about the paddle and crank as a divine revelation.

"Hey, come on Viv, enough," whispered Cliff. "Let's get out of here, let's go somewhere and talk."

"Spawn of Adam, speak not!" snapped Sister Tupper, glaring at Cliff where he sat.

"Give me a break," he said with a chuckle.

In response, Anton sprinted up the aisle and stood over him. His saliva and sweat reeked. A reddish stain shown on his shirt, its shape a crooked cross carved into his chest. He clenched his fists by his sides as if at any second he would raise them and strike.

"We hope you will contain your insolence," said Sister Tupper. "Our presentation is brief, but our love for Him is eternal, and we would like for all of you to share in it."

"Perhaps that's a good segue," said Edwin. He picked up his pad and read off a question: "Do you see any irony in breaking away from a culture you accused in your article as possessing 'swarm intelligence', only to replicate a family structure many would dub gender-oppressive?"

"Oh my, why, I never thought of that," said Sister Tupper. "Thou art bright, my child. His light truly shines down upon thee."

"Heh, well, certainly shines on my GPA. But you didn't answer my question."

Sister Tupper took the pointer from Sister Bethany. Chad stepped aside as she moved in front of Edwin's seat. "Oh, well, my little brain's just trying to think of an answer," she said as she raised the pointer toward the ceiling. "Perhaps His divine light will offer *me* a revelation as well. Oh wait, I've got it!"

Sister Tupper bashed the pointer over Edwin's head. His glasses flew from his face, and his cheekbone cracked when she hit him again with the back blow. He snuffled blood as he fell to the floor. She put her knee on his back, drew the string out of her bonnet and wrapped it around his neck.

The girl sitting beside him screamed, leapt from her folding chair, and ran for the door.

That's when Lyla saw Chad standing in front of it. He'd locked it with a key and held a sledgehammer in his right hand.

A half-dozen other students clambered for the emergency exit. Sister Tupper released the bonnet string, picked up the bloody pointer, and moved toward them. Sister Bethany and Anton fell in alongside. They didn't stop the students from running through the exit, but slipped out after them, slamming the door behind. Lyla heard screams coming from the parking lot, a high-pitched whine amid cries of *No, please no! What is that? Please! No!*

Cliff had also leapt up and pulled Viv against him. He'd drawn a lock-blade pocketknife from his jeans and was inching toward the exit. "You're gonna let us both out of here," he said. "Come near me, and I'll cut you! I'll do it!"

"It should only take Anton a few minutes," said Jed. He stood and stepped to the podium, as if everything happening around them was just a matter of course. "Is the mic still on? Oh, good," he said. "As you can see, not everyone has quite accepted our message. I'm afraid we didn't have the resources to train all of you ahead of time. Once we *do* get outside, I would like those of you still among us to move to the van in an orderly fashion."

A thump sounded against the emergency exit, followed by a scream and more thumps. Cliff moved backwards, pulling Viv with him.

"You'll only complicate things," said Jed as Cliff kicked the bar and opened the door.

A bloody student stumbled back inside. Anton ran in after him, and Lyla saw that the wound on his chest had opened, and a stone figure protruded from it. The figure had blank eyes, carved ringlets of hair, and gray arms stretching out of daggered sleeves. It clawed at the bloodied young man as he collapsed to the carpet.

"What the hell?" said Cliff.

He didn't have time to slash before Anton jumped back up. His chest made a ripping sound as the torso turned and its stone hands clamped onto Cliff's arms.

They were like two men locked in a ludicrous and deadly dance. The figure clawed, Cliff's mouth erupted with blood, and his arms smacked against the walls, painting the sheetrock red.

"Always knew he didn't have it in him," said Vivian. She shook her head, but didn't look back at her dying lover as she passed through the exit.

~*~

Lyla's hands felt icy and she was shaking. *They don't believe I'll fight them*, she thought. *They think it's because I'm afraid.* And she knew they were at least partly right. She had let Chad coax her through the emergency exit to where they had parked a van. She saw bloodstains on the concrete, but no signs of the sisters or the other students. Chad seated her on a steel bench in the van's cargo space beside Viv. They sat in two rows, and she was directly opposite Anton. The angel statue had receded back into his ribs so that it looked like he wore some kind of bizarre 3-D t-shirt. He sneezed and coughed and hiccupped handfuls of blood and saliva as the statue nestled back into his body.

It had squirmed back inside, but its empty eyes remained fixed on Lyla. *Bastards*, she thought.

The vehicle felt like a rolling prison as they pulled out of the lot. Jed had kept her a virtual captive for weeks, she realized, and yet it was as if she were hypnotized. Maybe he'd finally forced a new move because he'd seen cracks in the spell. He'd traded hypnosis for full incarceration at the moment of his choosing.

Their first stop was her apartment. "Collect your belongings," he said. "They will be gifted to your new sisters upon arrival." Chad and Anton helped her. She noticed Viv had already packed her things, and that Jed wore an approving smile as he helped her out with the suitcases and boxes.

Once the van was loaded, they moved east on 90 into Massachusetts, then south on 91 through Connecticut. Somewhere in the after-midnight darkness, they stopped in a town south of Hartford, at an old church where they met another van along with some aged sedans, forming a convoy.

At first Lyla had faded in and out of consciousness, trying to bide her time, save her strength. After the stop, Anton began humming and babbling. His chin went into a nod, dribbling saliva onto the face in his chest. In response, the stone angel reached up and pushed his head away, slapped his cheek with his palm. The blow made him drool more, the reek of bile mixing with the spit.

"B-b-b-b-bombs," he mumbled. "B-b-bombs away!"

Lyla yanked her feet back as he retched pink liquid on the floor.

"Isn't this fun?" said Viv. "It's like we're on a field trip."

Lyla looked away. Anton kept retching.

"Oh, oh, here we go again," he choked as he leaned forward over Lyla's lap.

Lyla kicked reflexively, her hiking boot contacting the angel's face. It let out a hollow scream and leapt out of Anton's chest. Its hands clawed at her calf and its chin lengthened outward, stretching into a beak-like jaw, like an eagle with teeth. It struck first at her leg, then at her head, tearing out a piece of Lyla's hair. She pushed back with both legs, straining to keep it from chewing down to her face.

"That's enough," barked Chad. He pulled a syringe from his pocket and stabbed Anton in the arm. Within seconds his strength sapped and he collapsed in a puddle of pink drool, the angel torso crumpled on top of him.

Lyla lay back, panting and holding a clump of her hair in her hands. She almost said thank you, but caught her words on her tongue.

"You shouldn't provoke him," said Chad. "You've made me waste resources. A record will be made of this when we reach the sanctuary."

This time she couldn't hold back: "I'm not going to the sanctuary. Next stop I'm walking away. If you don't try to stop me, I won't call anybody, and you can get your own asses busted."

Chad grimaced. "You're lucky Jed likes you," he said, and tapped a text into his phone.

The van pulled over. Jed came around, opened the back doors. He whispered a few minutes with Chad, then to Lyla said, "Come with me."

He brought her to the front passenger seat where he said she could sit for now. The sun was rising over a block of square houses. Perfectly trimmed lawns that resembled chess squares ran to the corner where there stood another steepled, white-rectangle of a church. "I love Connecticut," said Jed. "Don't you?"

They picked up 95 and sailed down into the city just before rush hour. She recognized the Triborough Bridge and the BQE, but once off they were on a warped grid of mottled concrete streets whose names she didn't recognize. At first they were passing a mix of rotted brick buildings and warehouses, sprinkled with a few brownstones. Soon they passed into a district that was almost all warehouses and factories.

They pulled up beside one of the latter, an old mattress factory not quite restored. Half the five-story factory's windows were inset with steel plates, while the doorway itself was made of new glass and opened onto a hardwood-floored lobby.

"Come with me," said Jed, leading Lyla to a freight elevator. "The others will unpack. There are things we must discuss now, and there is someone I would like you to meet."

They got off on the fifth floor. He led her down a hall walled with a mix of sheetrock and exposed brick. She could hear saws running further down, work being done. They arrived at a steel door that hung ajar and he pointed inside. "Your bed is made," he said. "You have a closet for storage, and your own bathroom."

Lyla poked her head into the narrow room. The bed was a shelf set into the far window with a mattress on it. The closet was a second alcove covered with a curtain. What he called the bathroom consisted of a toilet and a sink covered by a sheet.

"So this is my cell?"

"Now Lyla," said Jed. "I know you know better than that. That's why I chose you." He paused, removed his glasses and rubbed them as if they were dirty. "I brought you here before they corrupted you. Your friend Vivian, for example, is coming along nicely, even better than expected. But she has so much to learn about acceptance. You have so much more potential, if you could only see it. The ambition I saw in you, the look on your face when you were walking through the cemetery the day you graduated."

"Where are my things? You're a kidnapper *and* a thief?"

"Please, stop it," he said. He was struggling to keep calm now. When he put his glasses back on, she noticed the slightest sweat shone on his forehead. "Your things will be brought to you, for the ceremony. Your Rite of Seclusion begins tonight. I suggest you follow the cues you are given. So much could be yours."

"So much could be mine, sure, like the right to take a squat with my feet sticking out of a bed sheet."

"No," Jed barked. For a moment he glared, the veins in his neck pulsing with rage, then he regained control and spoke: "No, rather, after the rite, you will have earned the privilege to be my wife."

~*~

*At least it has a window*, she thought as she sat on the bed. She was able to unlock the bottom pain and slide up the glass, though a set of narrow bars prevented climbing in or out. From the alcove where her bed was inset, she gazed out across the city. The Brooklyn skyline glowed hazily against Manhattan's, the light of a minor moon against the stars of the Milky Way. She found her phone among her things when they brought them up and dumped them in a pile by the closet. They'd cut off her calling and Internet somehow, but the clock still worked and she could play solitaire on it.

The first woman to come to the door was elderly and pressed an electrolarynx to her throat as she spoke: "Don't lay nothin' special on me," she buzzed. "I'm not long for this world, and I hain't no husband in the sanctuary neither."

"Take what you want," she said. "They're gonna take it anyway."

"Yer 'sposed to choose," she buzzed, but then dug through the clothes and books and finally snatched up a chocolate bar and a hair dryer.

*Damn*, she thought. He had said that during the Rite of Seclusion she had to be as Christ and give up all her worldly possessions. He had also said the Rite was seven days. If she had somehow kept the dryer, she might have been able to at least start a fire. She thought of something then, looked through her bags until she found it and re-wrapped it in a separate set of clothes.

~*~

A second woman came the next morning. She said she was one of Chad's wives. She took a belt and some blouses, said she could use the material sewing. Did Lyla sew? No, she answered, thinking of the phrase 'one of Chad's wives'.

She saw the purpose in Jed's method then, and after the next night passed, she heard the expected third knock on the door. "Come in," she said, not without irony as she waited for her guest to slide back the outside bolt.

"Good evening," said the young bonneted woman as she stepped inside. "My name is Prue."

"Short for Prudence?" asked Lyla.

"No, just Prue. My parents liked it, and Jed says it's okay to respect them that way."

"Well as long as Jed says it's okay," said Lyla.

The humor was lost on Prue, who just nodded. "Oh yes, he is my husband, after all. I am his first wife, though I am not *the* first wife, I mean family-wise. That's going to be *you*."

Whereas the other two women had each appeared worn and weathered in their own way, the elderly woman barely clinging to life, taking the chocolate as if it were the last sweet on Earth, and Chad's wife being desperate for something as simple as clothing, for children perhaps, Prue seemed different. Her round blue eyes shone clear beneath her snug bonnet, her hands were humbly folded before her, and yet her long dress clung to her form belying its humility. She had the body of a magazine model, and couldn't be much older than Lyla. Jed was fetishizing them even as he acquired them.

"If you prove to be eager," said Prue, "you will do well. I might be able to help you with this, I mean, in my fashion."

"Well, that's nice I guess," said Lyla. "I mean I appreciate it. All I have left to give you is this bag of my old clothes. You probably don't have much use for it here, but that's all I've got, and Jed said I had to give you something."

"It's just fine, Sister-Wife. I thank you for your gift." Prue picked up the bag and gave a shallow bow. "May you have many blessings in the eyes of the Lord," she said as she closed and locked the door.

~*~

The next day no one came. Someone entered early, left her a plate of eggs and toast, then left again. *They weren't kidding when they said seclusion,* she thought as she watched the sun climb higher and then lower again. A cloud of smog always appeared in the morning, then again in the evening, but some nights she could still see stars.

It was on the sixth night he came for her. She peered through the window into the shadowed streets and saw him standing in the alley. The shadows were deeper there from the raised rail platform and the tangle of skeletal fire escapes that clung to the buildings. She made out a tall figure with horns rising from its head. When a train passed, a flash of sparks illuminated his body, naked, hairy, and hoofed. When the shadows returned, they reduced him to a blurred silhouette. She watched as he took hold of the fire escape and scuttled up.

When he emerged on the roof of a nearby building, he looked human again, Malcolm from the bar, rings glinting beneath his smile.

"Lyla, I'm here, I came for you," he called.

She slid the window open, took hold of the bars and peered between. "You came for me?"

"Yes," he said. "You must see them for who they are now."

"I feel like I don't know who anybody is."

"You know who I am." A reddish light rose in his eyes. She felt the heat and draw of the night on the mountain and had to look away.

"I know what you made me," she said.

"What I made you is stronger. Courageous. Now we must be courageous together."

"What's that supposed to mean, you're rescuing me?"

"Yes, well, we're leaving together if that's what you mean. Lyla, listen to me, F.S. has something here in their compound. A series of artifacts. If we retrieve them, we can expose Jedidiah Archer and his organization. If we can bring them to my contacts, we can trade them. We will acquire the weapons we need, F.S. will weaken, and we will grow stronger."

She slammed her fist against the row of iron bars. Pain exploded in her knuckles. She pounded again. "I don't care, I'm sick of them, I'm sick of you, what you've done, what you've all done!"

"Lyla, stand back," Mal answered.

Lyla slipped to the side just in time to dodge the object Mal hurled through the bars with precision accuracy. The pistol spun across the floor and stopped just before thumping against the door.

"Be ready. We will mount our assault tomorrow. Be ready, and you can join us in the midst of battle."

~*~

Lyla waited an hour in case her captors had heard. When no one came to the door, she slid off the bed and picked up the gun. *Seclusion has its advantages*, she thought. Despite resenting his tactics, the sight of his glowing eyes had revived something in her. She considered the odd attraction she felt for Mal and realized it was an energy within him that intensified her desire. A kind of dizziness came over her, and yet in spite of it, she still wanted this intensity within herself. Between this realization and the fact she trusted the horned man was an ally against Jed Archer and his F.S. maniacs, she steeled herself to their shared cause.

She waited by the door until the first rays of morning's smog-ridden light shone through the window's bars. She used the time to figure out the pistol, eject and reinsert the magazine, discover the safety and make sure it was off. When she heard the sound of the deadbolt sliding back, she pressed herself against the wall.

The old woman whom she'd given her hairdryer to stepped in with her eggs and toast. When Lyla pointed the pistol at her head and put her finger to her lips, the old woman dropped the electrolarynx.

"What's the matter?" asked the man escorting her. When he stepped inside and turned his crew-cutted head, Lyla fired.

The bullet tore a crevasse in his skull. His scream was cut short, and for a moment, he sank to his knees. Lyla pushed into the hallway. When she spun around to slam the door, the man's body was already back on its feet. The torso of a bald angel rose from between his ribs. Its forehead wrinkled with rage as it charged, the dead man's head dangling behind and leaking clumps of brains.

Lyla slammed the door, banged it again and again against the angel's face. The statue bit, snarled, and clawed, while the man's body hung to the side, convulsing. She kept hammering until she knocked them both back. With her last glimpse, she saw the weeping woman and the torn man collapsed together. The statue was rising out of their heap, its enraged eyes glaring as it reached toward Lyla's throat.

She slammed the door once more, slid the bolt, and sprinted down the hall. The freight elevator was open, but she didn't dare close herself inside. Instead she pushed into the stairwell, leaping downward two and three steps at a time. She was already winded, her heart pounding in her chest. Sweat stung her eyes, and the gun felt slippery in her hand.

When she hit the second floor, a hinge squeaked as a door opened below her. She heard hushed voices and the shuffle of fabric. The smell of candles wafted upward, and she ducked through the exit door into the hallway. Before she rounded the corner, she stopped herself. *Most of them haven't seen you*, she thought. Better off walking slowly, acting natural in her prairie-pilgrim getup, and hoping she didn't have bloodstains on her cheeks.

She reached under her skirt, tucked the pistol into her bloomers just as a woman came around and almost crashed into her.

"Oh, oh my, what are you doing here?" she asked.

Lyla's hand was already going for the pistol when the woman smiled and took her arm. "Are you Sister Banes? I'm Sister Gannon, one of the midwives. I thought you were in seclusion. Well, we must not question Him. The nursery's this way."

The woman guided Lyla down the hall and through a curtained archway. Wooden cribs lined the walls of a long brick chamber. Cage-like bars rose from their edges, and side tables strewn with empty bowls and steel syringes stood beside them. A gaggle of bonneted women floated from crib to crib, as a black-robed man walked among them. He wore a medieval doctor's mask, its beak casting a blade of a shadow across the women's bloodstained aprons.

"Here," said Sister Gannon, handing her a syringe. "Start with the ones the doctor marked for deletion. Then you can stir the vat for a while." She pointed to a cauldron at the far end of the room. Brownish pink steam rolled from its surface, along with the stench of feces and vinegar.

Lyla choked against the stench as she pushed the woman away. The doctor turned, his mask's beak pointed at her heart. She lifted the pistol and fired. Sister Gannon screamed, and she fired at her, too.

She ran before she knew whether the shots hit home. She made a right, then a left into another hallway where most of the doors hung ajar. She heard a commotion behind her, but also outside. A gunshot sounded, then another, then a crack-crack-crack. She went through one of the doors into an empty room. She could tell it was on the side of the building opposite her seclusion cell by the position of the window. It faced the street, where she saw a sedan parked across the sidewalk. Its doors were open, and she saw a man with an automatic rifle crouched by the driver's seat, firing across the hood.

Someone was firing back at him from the building's entrance, though she couldn't see who. Sirens sounded, police cars were screeching in, and she recognized the man with the machine gun as the one who stood beside her that night on the escarpment. He alternated his shots, firing in two directions as the police blocked off the street.

Chad appeared, striding across the sidewalk from the building's entrance. His arms hung slack as a statue pushed out of his chest holding a stone sword. Another man ran beside him, spine curved impossibly backwards. He cried in agony as the angel statue rode his body. It shrieked like an eagle as it smashed through a car window and yanked a woman out of the passenger seat.

The man with the machine gun took a bullet in his back. Dark blood flooded his checkered shirt. That's when he looked up at the window. His crazed black eyes stared up at her, his smile as slack-jawed and ecstatic as it had been on that night of fire and flesh.

Lyla spun away, back into the hall. She looked back the way she came and saw the doctor and the midwives coming toward her. He held a syringe before his black robe, its tip pointed toward her. "Apostate!" the midwives shrieked. "Seize her!" They were carrying swords, and she could smell the reek of the cauldron's filth.

She ran and reached a dead end with a locked metal door. The door itself was old and rusted, but the deadbolt was new. She took a few steps back, tried not to turn her head as she fired the pistol at the lock. She fired until grip was hot in her hand, until the trigger clicked empty. Flipping it over, she bashed off the bolt.

The women behind her shrieked and began to stampede. She leapt onto the landing, spun around and re-locked the door with a sliding bolt on the other side. Through the metal she could hear them pounding and wailing. "Deceiver," they cried. "Come back! Come back for your redemption!"

Lyla descended the stairwell until the walls became windowless stacks of stone. She smelled the basement's musty air, and followed a curved passage that sloped downward. The ceiling was high, but the passage very narrow. Her eyes blinked as they adjusted to the low light.

Amid the must, she detected the smell of timber and charcoal, and gradually saw an orange glow flickering on the walls. *Torchlight*, she thought. She considered turning back, but there was no way out. *Maybe there would be another exit*, she thought as she pressed forward.

The tunnel made a final steep slope that led to a rectangular chamber spreading outward to the left and right. In the opposite wall she saw a pair of large double doors. Sconces with lit torches hung on either side of them. A table with a book and a bowl of water stood to her left. *Like the narthex in her church*, she thought. The doors hung slightly ajar, and she could hear moaning from inside.

*If it's a church, there may be another way out, behind the altar maybe.* She took a deep breath and slipped inside.

Smoke from a ring of braziers filled her lungs, causing her to cough. She shielded her eyes, blinking against the burn and moved forward. She could make out something ahead of her, at the opposite end, shrouded in the grayish clouds that billowed down the aisle between the pews.

The moaning grew louder and louder as she reached the front, and there she saw its source: a figure nailed to a cross, a figure covered in feathers. Blood ran out of gaping wounds in its legs and chest. Fluid gurgled in its throat as it tilted back a head that looked half-human, half-eagle.

Beside it stood a man and a woman, their faces buried in its wounds. They stood on wooden daises, the woman moaning and sucking at the arteries in its legs, while the man suckled beneath its ribs.

The figure's eyes opened. "Welcome, Lyla," it said. "You've shown great initiative, coming here on your own."

Feathers hung matted from its pockmarked face, puss oozing where quills tore out of the skin.

"W-what... who... who are you?"

"My name is not for you," said the crucified figure. "Let us say I am just an old soldier, an old knight in His legion. They drink from me, I give them strength. Jedidiah, the groom whom you have scorned, has taken his fill from me and become Sainted."

Lyla raised the pistol, aiming between its narrow, avian eyes. "How do I get out of here? I'll kill you!"

"You cannot kill me," it said. "The .45 is empty, and Plutysium is hard to come by."

As it spoke, Lyla looked at the paintings that adorned the wall behind the cross. Near a dozen she could see, with more trailing upward into the darkness beyond the sconces' light. Some appeared to be traditional iconography —nativity, passion, ascension.

Those in the center depicted something else—Christ standing on a forested shore beside wind-whipped waves. He was holding a round object, wrapped in a cloth, before an empty cross.

An armored angel stood beside him, holding a lion on a chain. It was like no lion she had ever seen, the three eyes in its forehead glaring hungrily at Christ's body.

In another he hung on the cross, mouth open as if crying out to a figure that stood below him. This figure wore a dark robe, its conical hood pulled back from an overlarge globe of a head that glowed pearlescent white. The paint's pigment carried its own inner light, flecks from a brooding, mocking, and alien metal.

Lyla started when she realized this figure appeared in all the paintings. Even in the traditional nativity scenes, the blank bulging head hovered in the background. In one of them, the figure stood on the same forested shore, holding the head in its hands. Armored angels knelt around it in prayer, while Christ's corpse lay bleeding in the tide.

"That is *The Recovery*," gurgled the thing on the cross. "Its nature will be revealed when the time is right. Do you not know He has a plan for you? Do you not know He has a plan for each and every one of us? Go into the vestry, Lyla. Look at the security monitor. The demon-spawn are all but slain. Trapped, with our brothers and sisters on one side, and the police on the other. Their attack will fail, you will be recaptured. It is better to submit to us, it is better to submit. It is better to submit to us, it is better to submit…"

The eaglehead's speech had become a chant, the warped warbling of a great, sick songbird. She heard the suction of the couple's lips as they drank of its fluids. She felt dizzy, and stumbled back against the pews.

*He will come for you*, said a voice within her. *He will come for you and take you back into His bosom.*

Lyla felt a scream peel from her throat as she leapt to her feet. "Never!"

she cried, hurtling the empty pistol at the thing's face. Sprinting up the steps, she tore one of the burning torches from the wall and plunged it into its scab-encrusted wing.

The eaglehead wailed in pain, and the man and the woman pulled away and fell off the daises. When they rose to their feet, partially formed angels wriggled in their chests. Half chiseled faces and twisted, fetal arms reached outward.

Lyla recognized Vivian as she stumbled toward her. She hesitated, sweeping the torch back and forth. "No, no, get away!"

Vivian's torso dangled backwards, spine broken. Her tongue lolled in her mouth as she tried to form words: "K-killlll… k-k-kill me…"

Lyla steeled herself to plunge the torch into her friend, but before she could, a crackle of gunfire sounded in the doorway. The double doors crashed down and a shadow stepped forward, a seven-foot silhouette of a man with a goat's head. She recognized Mal as he strode down the aisle, firing a submachine gun.

Vivian's body crumpled to the floor, the angel shattered like broken cement. The volley of bullets had ripped through her neck and knocked her head crooked. What was left of her face wore a relieved, glassy-eyed expression.

The remains of the man lay in a heap beside her. His aborted, calcified worm of an angel lay ejected from his chest and in a heap of semi-formed armor.

Mal reached the altar and kicked over the cross. He dropped the gun and drew a two-handed sword from a black scabbard that hung across his back. "Galondelius nomen tuum, et hodie mortu eternuru venirum!" He growled the words as he drove the sword downward. The blade was wide enough that even driven from the tip, it separated the head from the body.

Mal turned to Lyla: "That painting, hurry!"

He pointed at the one in the center, where the omnipresent figure held his head in his hands. The eyes of the bowing men glared at her maliciously as she removed the painting from its wall mount. Mal handed her a leather case with a thick strap, and they were headed for the vestry, when a clamor erupted among the pews.

She turned and saw Jed Archer striding toward them. It was Jed, but his slacks and collar had been traded for a suit of plate mail armor. He held a sword in his hand and a shield on his arm. A cross with an eye carved into its center adorned his shield, with a matching image sewn in silver on his tunic.

"Turn and face His wrath," he cried. He glared out of the riveted steel helmet that contoured his face. When Mal pivoted, brandishing the two-handed sword, Jed dropped the visor and charged.

The goat-man was nearly twice the armored man's size, but their crashing failed to knock either off his feet. Mal swung savagely, some blows contacting with the flat of the blade, some with the edge.

Jed raised his shield, absorbing the impact. He screeched in pain, the sound inhuman, not unlike sounds made by the thing that had been on the cross. Still, he held strong and countered with calculating side swings. The smaller sword cut true. Three strikes, and the beast's abdomen puckered with wounds, dark clots and bare sinews appearing under his ribs.

Mal threw out his elbow, bashing the side of Jed's helmet and knocking him across the pews. Wood splintered as he brought the gargantuan two-handed blade down again and again. The armored man dodged the attacks, but was getting slower with each turn. Mal heaved the sword high to make the final blow.

Before it fell, Jed vanished with a quick roll into the shadows, and the goat man's sword cut into nothing but broken planks. He began kicking and smashing the wood all around him, searching for his opponent.

He made as if to turn back to Lyla, and instead found Jed moved into the aisle, sword already swinging. The armored man slashed the beast's thigh, and put another wound in his belly. He braced himself then sprang off the pews, striking with sword, shield, his entire body, like a shell fired from a tank.

The collision shattered the two-handed sword. The beast fell to all fours and fled toward the altar. Lyla saw the submachine gun where it had spun across the floor and picked it up. Jed was striding toward them, bloody sword in hand.

She heard, "You wouldn't dare!" before she squeezed the trigger and let loose a burst of bullets. When the dust cleared, she could see Jed crouched behind his shield. Blood ran through the seams of his armor, turning the plates red. He was wounded, but again stood and continued toward them.

"You can't kill him with that," said Mal as he crossed the altar and took her arm. "You'll slow him down, but he won't die. Damn it, my sword!" Mal bowed his head, the goat horns sharp shadows in the torchlight. He hesitated as if he might run back, then squeezed her hand and handed her two fresh clips. "Use them if he gains on us. We have to get out of here."

Lyla thumbed the switch, sprang the magazine, and reloaded. She watched as the armored man advanced toward them. She had the oddest feeling as she crossed the altar that she had just said *I do* in the most gruesome of weddings. She'd chosen the Devil, and the knight who was following them had objected a little too late, and intended to never hold his peace.

She fired another burst at Jed's helmet as Mal guided them through the dim vestry and through a side door. They burst into the alleyway's light, and she followed him to the edge of the sidewalk, gun in hand, painting slung over her shoulder. The smell of sulfur and burnt gasoline assaulted her nose. To her left she saw NYPD cruisers parked at odd angles. Mal's old pickup truck lay on its side across the sidewalk, the passenger side blackened and burning. The body of the guy who'd stood beside her on the mount was splayed over the sewer cap, torso pocked with gunshot wounds.

An ambulance was loading covered bodies into the back. She saw women in braids and prairie dresses milling about, red-faced and silent. Chad stood among them in a long, bulky trench coat talking to the police.

"Over here," said Mal, bringing her to a second alley, behind a dumpster.

She noticed his body had changed. The horns had shrunken, and were hard to pick out among his tousled locks of hair. He had returned to his original height, and his torso was crisscrossed with slash wounds. "Come on," he said. "We have to win this. We have to win if I'm going to keep my strength."

She watched as he pushed aside a row of plastic trashcans and uncovered a fat-tired, low-seated Harley Davidson. Rolling it right, he squawked the starter and twisted the throttle. She leapt on the back and crammed against him on the single seat.

Jed appeared in his bloody armor, just as they rounded the corner. She let loose another burst from the submachine gun. A wave of sparks exploded through the cloud of exhaust, and she tightened her hold on Mal as their speed increased.

Swinging around Throop Avenue and behind the hospital, they nearly crashed into an NYPD tactical van speeding against the traffic. It spun out across the yellow line, the officers in back clambered out and shouldered their rifles.

Mal made a hard left with the bike, an inelegant hop over the curb, stopping just shy of the brick wall.

"Damn it, keep shooting!"

She read in his frustration he thought her slow to unload on the cops, though they were seconds from firing themselves. Still she couldn't banish the man laid across the altar from her mind, the one they'd hacked to death with the sickle. *And yet it wasn't even there where this started*, she thought. She knew now it had been no accident Mal had come into the bar after Jed had chosen her on graduation day. Mal had come to use her against his enemy.

"Damn it, Lyla, shoot," he cried. He twisted around on the seat, pushed her arms and the gun up simultaneously, pointing the muzzle at the police.

As if in response, a burst of bullets from the tactical team's rifles tore through his chest. Despite the wound, he managed to pull away from the wall. He swung the bike around in the opposite direction, hit the throttle so it felt like they were in an aircraft accelerating down a runway.

His screams melded with the roar of the engine. The police were firing on full automatic, trying to stop his charge. They were hitting him, but like Jed, he wasn't dying. And yet he listed to the side, the motorcycle tilting low. Lyla braced herself to be dragged across the pavement, but he regained balance and made for Broadway.

A pair of cops braced against a streetlight pole and took aim. *This is what's worse*, she thought. Worse than what Jed had done to her physically and mentally, worse than Mal's brutal and seductive rituals. It was the way they wanted all of her. More than toleration, than alliance of convenience, they wanted to force her to choose sides.

She tightened her grip around Mal's stomach and swept the submachine gun in an arc. The spray hit the pair by the streetlight below the knees. She couldn't hear their screams above the engine, just read their pain in how they squirmed and thrashed.

In the last seconds of her sweep, the gun jammed. She pulled it against her, tucking it through the strap that held the painting.

Mal was back in front of the old factory, heading straight at the crisscross of police cruisers parked across the avenue. Most of the officers here were attending the ambulance and clustered by the lobby dealing with Chad.

She heard only a few shots as Mal made a hard right and wove his way to Broadway. He throttled it once more, up the steel stairs to the raised train track. The engine ground to a halt on the landing, tank leaking gasoline like it was blood.

"Come on," he said, taking the submachine gun from Lyla and running for the vertical turnstile. Taking the bar in both hands, he cranked until the steel fractured. When they burst through the other side, his feat of inhuman strength left him collapsed with a very human looking fatigue. "Got to get up top... get east… lose them and make for the church."

Lyla helped him to his feet, adjusted the painting on her shoulder, and retook the gun. "Show me how to undo the jam," she said.

"There's only one more clip," he said. "Nevermind it for now and come on."

As they moved along the track, she peered over the metal fence at the street below. An eerie silence had fallen, sidewalks and stores devoid of human traffic. A dozen or so men remained in front of the building. They clustered around Jed where he stood in his bloody armor. He was speaking with a cop who was looking down at the sidewalk. The man was nodding, as if in obedience, as a procession of cruisers followed the ambulance away to the south. The setting sun cast a fiery amber light, and Lyla raised her hand to her eyes and squinted. That's when Jed looked up, the visor of his helmet lifted. He stood a foot taller than the men around him, his eyes meeting hers as he pulled a heavy gray cloak over his shoulders. The men around him were twitching, their limbs contorting, skin stretching and throbbing. They trooped forward, coughing and staring, pregnant with angels. In some she could see wide-eyed faces and feathered wings pressing bloody imprints into their shirts.

Along their flanks strode other men, these in black fatigues carrying heavy machine guns. The barrels extended from hydraulic harnesses strapped to their arms. The group of them marched forward together, Jed following in back, gliding toward her, an inexorable weight in his predatory eyes.

"Gotta move," said Mal.

They turned and scrambled on, barely avoiding the rails as they leapt up to the adjacent platform and over the fence. They landed on the awning of a long-closed restaurant. Her limbs splayed as they slipped down its sloped surface and fell again into a weed-choked lot.

"My ankle," she said as she limped to her feet and followed him to the chain link fence.

"Gotta move," he said.

He was already ripping at the metal, tearing a hole. She noticed it took more effort this time than when he'd broken through the platform entrance. He was winded, face haggard, horns shrunken. The sun's amber light made him look sickly. As they passed through the shredded fence, she had the feeling she was being watched through the windows of the dilapidated townhouses lining the street. She almost tripped over a rooster's carcass as they ran east. They passed crumbling bricks, boarded-over windows, and plastic bags clustered in courtyards like a giant beast's hardened snot.

She glanced back and saw Jed and his men pressing after them. *They must want at least one of us alive*, she thought, knowing those with guns had to be within range.

*Damn, the submachine gun*, she thought, realizing she must have lost it when they leapt off the track.

"Come on," urged Mal, though his own pace had slowed and he seemed increasingly winded.

"Where are we going?" she asked.

"You don't understand," he answered. "We only have one chance." They pushed another block east, under the sweep of another raised track and onto a curbless sidewalk. Here the brick buildings gave way to slenderer architecture, frames with sagging siding and rotting tarpaper.

"What's wrong with you?" she asked. "Why can't we fight them?"

"I need strength," he said. Even as he spoke he was trying to catch his breath. He leaned on her in the shadows. Dark circles had formed under his eyes, and she could see his skull through his skin.

"Just tell me where we're going," she said.

"There," he said.

She looked where he was pointing, saw a pair of spires looming in the dusky light. The autumn darkness deepened as they made for the old cathedral. The building's stained glass windows were dark, and as they stepped through the cracked door, they found none of the candles in the nave were lit.

"This way," said a voice.

Lyla blinked as her eyes adjusted. She was looking at an older man in a monk's robe. The hood was down, and a rosary hung from his belt. He nodded in the direction he was pointing, a side stairway. "Go on," he said, closing the door and barring it.

At first she stumbled on the steps as they ascended into blackness. When they reached the second landing, a Madonna appeared in an alcove. In her hands she held a charred lump of tallow candle, as if cradling fire instead of a child.

"Go on, hurry," said the monk, pushing her on.

When they reached the top, they made a right down a narrow hallway. Running in a crouch, she saw the tips of the stained glass windows. She smelled an odd odor, not quite gasoline, something she couldn't quite place. A dim blur from distant streetlights lit their way to a door. There Mal paused, leaning against the dark plaster and wheezing as the monk took a key from the pocket of his robe and opened it.

Once inside, he moved to a small desk, found a glass lamp and lit the wick.

Kerosene, she thought. That's what she had smelled.

"I'm thankful you made it," said the monk. "Both of you."

He cranked the lamp's wick with his fingers. The increased light illuminated his face.

"I'm Father Dodson," he said, grinning beneath his wispy-haired scalp. "I wish I could welcome you in better circumstances."

Lyla found his smile a mix of parental and insane. For a moment he sat silent beside the lamp that filled the room with an almost cozy golden glow. She wanted this to be some after-chat at a charitable function her parents forced her to before letting her find her friends on Christmas Eve. She wanted it to be some silly meeting her father asked of her when she brought home some boy who might take her to the homecoming dance.

As if in sympathy to her thoughts, Father Dodson handed her a dented plastic bottle of spring water.

"To business then," he said. He turned to Mal, who had one pale hand pressed against the wall, his sweat and blood-stained hair hanging in his face. "Do you have the painting?"

Inhaling a crackling breath, he rallied his strength and snatched the case from Lyla's shoulder. "In there," he said.

The monk nodded. Unbuckling the clasp, he drew it forth. He wore a look on his face only ten percent fascination. The rest was an immense sadness that filled the room like a wraith. Lyla took a gulp of the spring water. She realized she had been incredibly thirsty, but the relief was mitigated by the kerosene fumes, and the strange angles of the room itself. *A nook that was not supposed to be here,* she realized—tucked above the nave, one wall bending away from the other in a nauseating curve due to the vaulted ceiling below. *An attic hole for a deranged bat,* she thought.

The monk ran his fingers over the surface of the oil painting as if it were the portrait of a lover whose blood he wished to drink.

"That will be all then," he said. "I require nothing more of you."

"Are you mad?" asked Mal. "The weapons! Where are they?"

Father Dodson did not look up. Though Lyla could only see the back of the canvass, she could tell his eyes were fixated on the orbed head of the being

206

who stood in the middle—the being to which the armored angels had bowed down.

"The weapons are in the duffle," he said.

Mal slid the bag out from under the desk and unzipped it. Rifle muzzles glinted in the lamplight.

"Two Kalashnikovs and a grenade? This wasn't our deal. You promised Plutysium, a zweihander, and a halberd from a desecrated tomb!"

"Oh dear," said the monk. "And here I thought any old weaponry would do. Then again, under what obligation was I? Alas, what is it those young corporate people call it, *bait and switch*? Yes, you took the bait, and I switched."

Mal's eyes flared red. Horns rose upward, and Lyla saw a glimmer of his former strength begin to rise. "You will keep your word, old man! You will fulfill our bargain!"

"Or what?" Dodson spat back. "As we speak, His minions are making their way here, to Saint Dominic's. They could easily have already stormed the front doors, but they conduct their due diligence, lest I had gained more allies of your ilk. If they knew I had no more use for Heaven or Hell, they would be trooping up the stairs already."

"You showed me the sword, you said the sword for the painting!"

"Quit being childish. The sword is long sold, the painting is here and mine. Didn't you pay any attention to all those bad movies about selling your soul? When you sell your soul, you don't win."

"They sold their souls," said Lyla. "They're winning."

"Ah, Aphrodite speaks," said the monk. "Aren't you a worthy prize of a bloodheart, as they would say."

"A what?"

"It is what they call your kind. Those whom you say have sold their souls. In a sense you are correct, if you are talking about Fair Step. Its leader, Jedidiah Archer, is one of many who are organizing for His return. They seek His favor, and they fancy themselves little despots self-made in His image. If what you say is true, and they sold their souls, you might say they at least sold it for a high price, unlike this other with whom you've thrown in your lot."

Mal was glaring at him as he spoke, crouched as if to pounce, his muscles taut beneath the bristling black hair that squirmed as it grew along his shoulders and arms. Lyla felt a pang of his power, yet he still looked haggard, his sweat having a sickly reek that mixed with the kerosene.

"You must give us more, monk. It is not a question I'm putting to you."

"Save what strength you have left for the angels, hellspawn. Or don't. It's nothing to me now."

The monk clutched the lamp, pulled it toward him and cradled it beneath his arm. Black smoke curled across his bald scalp, and Lyla saw tears trickling from his eyes.

"Just tell us how we get out of here," she said.

"Out? Out you say? There is no out. I have dedicated thirty years of my life to the Dominican Order. I thought I was following in Christ's footsteps, becoming closer to the Lord. Nothing could be further from the truth."

"A back or side exit, tell us where it is and we'll let you live."

"Dear child, do you know what the Pearl is? The Pearl of Great Price? The Pearl is His head, child, and its price is all the world. The Pearl is the Earth! Ha, ha, ha—it is the Earth! The Pearl is the Earth!"

Mal's fist shot out, bloodying the monk's eye. He threw another punch, smashing his mouth. "This is your last chance. Make good on your promise. Give us a weapon."

"You speak as if you have a real choice, hellspawn, however, you do not —you have only to face death at the hands of your enemies, or remain here with me. There is nothing else left for you."

"We're the ones who gave *you* a choice, Dodson," said Mal. "Your last one."

The monk laughed, the words running out as if his lips were an open wound. "Would you like to know something about choices?" he asked. "Let me tell you, for I used to be a counselor. The depressed, the drug addicted, raped, beaten, and bruised, I used to tell them they had a choice, that they could choose healing. But do you know what my patients taught me?" Here the monk's eyes rolled up and he began nodding, like some deranged schoolmaster who himself had been naughty in class. "They taught me there is a difference between choosing from without and choosing from within. Yes, even these pathetic creatures had this to teach us, though they lived most of their lives on their knees." The monk paused again to offer the blood-drinking smile he'd shown when he fondled the painting. "For when we choose from without, we make the best of options handed to us, a leaking lifeboat or a freezing sea. When choosing from within, however, the options are of our own invention, yes, they are dreams composed on a limitless canvas. A rare mix of luck and skill one requires to make choices from within. I thought at the time they are too often acts that are only imagined, only occasionally realized. Now I know the nature of freedom is but a final affliction, to know what it means to truly choose, and yet due to the conditions of this sickened world, never be allowed to do so."

Lyla shivered at the monk's words as a hammering sounded on the locked doors below. She thought of the moment she walked behind the bleachers, clutching her diploma. The moment she hung her cap and gown on the grave and knew what it was to truly choose. And now she realized it was a gift the world wished to steal back.

She reached for Brother Dodson's throat. She reached for it faster than Mal could strike him, but not before he let go of the kerosene lamp, smashing its glass and sending a streak of flames across the wooden floor.

"Blood of the damned!" cried Mal. He stood, heaving in the flames. His horns stretched outward and blood dripped from his square toothed maw. Though wounded, he had managed to transform. His clawed hands shook as he ripped the door off its hinges. He took hold of Lyla, threw her through the flames, and she tumbled down the stairs onto the first landing.

She forced herself to her feet, hair singed and body streaked with burns that might have been much worse. Below her the church's doors burst open, and two armored men stepped inside.

The first she recognized as Jed Archer. His armor bore the marks of blood and gunfire, the wounds inflicted on him in the factory's chapel. The second figure stood even taller, wore no helmet on his fair face, and had wax-smooth beige skin and glowing blue eyes. Though his lips were thin as some pretty Hollywood hero, his smile was terrible, wrought with wrath and vengeance. He lifted a sword longer than Lyla was tall and whispered, "Come to me, my child."

Before she could answer, Mal leapt down out of the smoke and flames. He rammed the two men, knocking them to the floor. Lyla took her chance and fled through the open doors, only to be thrown back by one of the guards with the rifle-harnesses.

Behind him, on the sidewalk, stood the rest of the troop. Statues had torn out of their chests, and their former torsos hung twisted and weeping with pain. The blank-eyed stone faces were parodies of the visage on the being she had just seen at the bottom of the stairs, and Lyla felt dizzy with despair, like a figure in a painting about to be hoisted onto a cross.

"Kneel and be bound," said the man in the gun harness.

"Never," she cried. She struck him with a right hook, expecting to be shot in return.

Instead when he fired it was not at her, but at the beast staggering onto the street. Mal was dragging Jed in a headlock, his feet kicking for lack of breath. The taller angel raced out after them, swinging his sword, cutting a wound across Mal's already scorched back.

A burst of tracer rounds exploded from the guard's gun barrel. It turned on a gimbal attached to the harness, following its target, drilling him to the ground. With his assailant weakened, Jed twisted out of the headlock and bashed the beast's head with his shield. Like a troop of hunters, the angels and their minions fell upon him, slicing, firing, and bashing.

Still the goat-man fought back, raking the tall angel's face with his claws, sending a stream of blue blood down his silver breastplate.

The angel did not flinch. "You shall yield," he said. He raised his sword, as if he would slice high, then in a flash flipped it over and drove it downward through Mal's hoofed foot. Sparks flew as he drove it into sidewalk. Mal shrieked in pain as he tried to tear himself away.

The group moved closer, gazing down at their pinned prey. The machine gunner fired two more bursts, hitting each of Mal's arms. Jed drew a dagger from his belt, circled around, and took hold of Mal's head. He lifted the wounded man's chin, as if he would draw the blade across his throat.

"No!" Lyla cried charging into them. She reached for Jed's dagger, but he effortlessly spun away. She heard the tall angel laugh as he smacked her back with the flat of his sword, knocking the wind out of her. Though she stumbled breathless, she used the last of her strength to grab at the gunner's harness. They fell in a heap onto the beast's bloodied body. Mal clawed at him with the last of his strength, opening the man's throat.

Though she couldn't pull off the harness, she managed to pop the gun out of its gimbal. She'd never seen a weapon like this. It fit her forearm, with the stick and trigger protruding from the top. She glimpsed the tall angel's frown just before she fired, full automatic, fired and fired as Mal got to his feet, tore himself off the sword, and pulled her down the alley beside the burning church.

~*~

"It's no use," he said. "They'll recover. You've only stunned them."

They were standing in the window of an empty third floor apartment. The block was all abandoned buildings, the windows wearing rotten boards. In the morning light they'd seen one drunken vagrant lying on a stoop, sleeping maybe, or maybe dead. They had made their way to the tallest of the buildings, found that its door had been removed and replaced with mortared cinder blocks.

Before his form had faded completely to his human body, Mal had climbed the side of the building, window by window, with Lyla clinging to his back. Like a giant, goat-headed spider, he had ascended, ripped away the window's wooden plank, and carried them inside.

They had rested, lost consciousness for unknown hours. Now they stood clinging and shivering in the cold November morning, a sheet from an old mattress hanging where the plank had been.

"What's the plan?" Lyla asked.

"Plan?" said Mal. "There is no plan. Run if you can. When they come for me, I will surrender."

Their breath steamed in the frosty air. He coughed, body wracked with the deep wheeze in his chest. He had been naked when he returned to his human form, and now wore a ragged blanket, soaked with blood from his wounds. They weren't healing as they had when he transformed into the beast. She thought of when she had seen him in the bar, with all of his rings, the night he had fought Jimbo and ripped open his stomach. He'd had swagger even in his human form then. The figure before her now—collapsed to its knees, teeth chattering, and leaning against the wall—looked a shadow of what he had been.

"I don't get it," she said. "We have to fight, we're supposed to fight. You brought me to that mountain. You... you... indoctrinated me! Made me commit murder!"

"The sacrifice, he was a half-angel," said Mal. "The sickle was small but it was Plutysium, and we used it to kill a half-angel and a murderer."

"Oh yes, he was a *half-angel*," she parroted. "And you're the Devil!"

"But I'm not."

"Yeah, yeah, but he enters you, whatever."

"But he doesn't. Not anymore. I was possessed by a demon. A powerful one, but just a demon. I mean, don't get me wrong. I really was building my power. I really was practicing a craft. When I found Archer and challenged him, I'd started building up my own cult, and then I found you, you were a great move."

"Great move?"

"Yeah, a chance to move up."

"So let me get this straight—you're not the Devil. *You're a Devil wannabe?"*

Mal looked at the floor.

"Where are you really from?"

"Pennsylvania," he said, not looking up. "I moved to New York City, worked in a restaurant for a while, then as a security guard."

"Fuck," she said. She was cold, her stomach empty. She lifted the curtain and peeked outside again. The streets were still empty save trash and the unconscious vagrant. She clutched the gun to her chest. *Did she hear something?* Hushed engines, the machinations of a column of vehicles approaching. She thought for a moment of guerrilla warfare, things she used to see on the news, civilians fighting against armies. She felt the cold steel of the weapon in her hand, and the sense that something immense was coming for her.

"The world really is changing," said Mal. "That part was true, and that's why I'm surrendering."

*Wannabe devil to successful coward*, she thought. When she turned to where he sat shivering, coughing, and bleeding, she realized he really had no choice. "Do what you gotta do," she said. She checked her ammunition. From what she could tell, by the size of the bullet when she removed the clip, she might have thirty or forty rounds. The spare clip snapped to the side made it double. She still had to keep running, conserve her supplies until she had time to figure out what she could do.

Lyla crossed into the other room, picked up the empty painting-case along with the grenade, the only weapon she'd snatched from the duffle. She was considering what she would do if Mal asked her to kill him before she fled when a roar of engines sounded in the street. They were loud and close this time. She ran to the window and looked out on a column of vans and SUVs. They parked in front of her building, and several dozen Fair-Steppers emerged onto the sidewalk. Beneath their long suit jackets and dress shirts swam blank-eyed statues, their stone swords and axes sawing through fabric stained with their host's blood.

Beside her Mal lifted himself up, tore away the curtain before she could stop him. "Up here," he cried as his chest erupted in a coughing fit. "Third floor, 3A, on the right."

Lyla struck his head with the harness-gun's barrel, knocking him back to the floor. "You fool, what are you doing?"

"What are you doing?" he retorted. "I helped you get a head-start on them and you're wasting it. Now go!"

Furious as she was, she had to admit that in a way he was right. She hadn't wanted to believe the cathedral had been their last chance, but he had already known, because he knew what he really was.

She struck him again with the gun and he lost consciousness. Turning to the window she hollered out: "I have a grenade! You come in here, I'll use it! There'll be nothing left! Nothing!"

The troop of statue-chested men halted on the sidewalk. Jed Archer stepped out from behind one of the SUVs with three tall, golden haired men beside him. She could tell by the contours of the cloaks they all wore armor. Jed came forward, his helmet tucked under his right arm, and stopped beneath her window. He smiled up at her like some kind of nightmarish Romeo. Had the armor not been real, she could have a good laugh at them, a quartet of Renaissance Fair escapees, except for the slight uniformity to their movements, their martial stances.

Jed spoke: "Lyla Banes, your failure is imminent. Stop running from us, for you are ours."

"Go to hell, I'll do it!"

"Hell, as you've discovered, is not all they've cracked it up to be. Disillusioned or not, we will not let you stay there."

"I'll never go with you! I never wanted you!"

"There was a time when you did want me, and I still want you. You will become one of us, like it or not. But don't rely on my word alone. Listen to the advice of another man in your life."

Jed Archer raised his right hand, as if introducing an actor on a stage. In response a man exited the back of a black van. He had neither armor nor deformity. At first she didn't recognize him, looking down at the dusky bald spot that crowned his head. When he looked up, he seemed older and grayer than he should have been, yet his eyes held such a crazed energy and light she hardly realized it was her father.

"Ly, it's me," he said. "It's me sweetie, they brought me here to talk to you!"

"What? What the hell are you doing here?"

"I have a job, Lyla! I'm working for Mr. Archer." His face grew brighter yet more contorted as he stepped forward. "I am Mr. Archer's personal secretary. A rank if you will, a professional position with Fair Step."

"Where's mom? I want to talk to mom."

"You don't understand. Your mother's very happy, very supportive of me."

"Heh. Always has been."

"Do not mock us, Lyla. You see, I brought her with me. I brought her to Mr. Archer's headquarters. She's resting in the infirmary. The doctor takes good care of her there, and I can help take care of you now, too. I can be at your wedding. First a graduation, now a wedding!"

Her father began giggling, shifting on his feet. The longhaired angels came alongside him, slipped their arms beneath his and turned him back toward the SUV. When they turned back to her, their perfect lips straightened. Their eyes, once glowing blue, changed to a dead gray to match the clouds. Sharpened, steel nails protruded from the gauntleted hands that curled around the grips of their swords, and a shadow fell over them as their cloaks fell from their shoulders and they spread white feathered wings.

"Your time is nigh, Lyla," said Jed Archer. "Come to me now. Put down the grenade and come to me."

Lyla's shivers turned to hiccups and sighing convulsions in her chest. They mixed with Mal's wheezes and her father's distant cackles. As she stood in the window, she tried to force her gaze away from the cruel faces rising toward her. She looked for the horizon, saw an endless expanse of filthy rooftops and gray clouds. Some blocks were burning, others had empty pockets of shattered rubble, like the city had lost its rotten teeth. Behind it all, stood Manhattan's skyscrapers, slender giants in the smog. They stood like soldiers behind the soldiers, like the armament of Heaven behind the cruel apparitions that rose before her.

"Come along peacefully, Lyla," said Archer as the angel swooped up and reached for her with its gauntleted hand.

Lyla pulled the pin and threw the grenade.

A second angel swooped in, caught the explosive, closing its wings just as the flames burst. A sharp pain pierced Lyla's ears, and she lost her balance. The first angel's hand took hold of her neck, choking her as they plunged downward. For a split second she took in air when it let go, then felt the wind gush back out when she was tossed across the sidewalk.

~*~

When she came to, the reek of charred flesh filled her nose. A pained sighing sounded, and she saw the burnt angel's body writhing beside her. His long limbs were darkened with blue blood. Pale, splintered bones shown in his cheek, and his arms flailed about his comrade, who was crouching over him. This angel had brought her down and was the one emitting the sickly sighs.

He turned to her, drew a long dagger, and strode to where she lay. "Thou art damned! I shall skin you while you yet breathe!"

"No," said Jed, reaching up and staying his hand. "We have an agreement. She is mine."

"The bloodheart has insulted us," hissed the angel.

"Ananiel will survive," said Archer. "Go to him and leave us, for she is mine."

~*~

They drove west, toward the city, picked up Broadway, then turned south toward the F.S. building. Lyla sat in the passenger seat of the SUV, wearing a white robe over her naked skin. Her bloodied clothes and the broken harness gun lay across the back seat. Jed was driving, one hand on the wheel, the other on her knee.

"Isn't this romantic?" he said. "It reminds me of our ride through Connecticut."

Lyla didn't answer. Her head and side ached, a concussion, she thought, and at least one broken rib.

"I'm glad you've started making good decisions," Jed continued. "That's what it comes down to in the end, isn't it? And that's what Fair Step is all about."

"Ow," she said, drawing a painful breath.

"Don't worry, you'll feel better. You've met our doctor. He'll have you right in no time. Anyway, that's unfortunate about Malcolm—a nice boy from Pennsylvania, intelligent. He gave in to short term pleasures, made some bad decisions, and is paying the price. He too, will need some time in the infirmary. Perhaps a very long time. For now, there is nothing for him but to pay the price of sin."

"I'm like him," Lyla said.

"Well," said Jed with a chuckle. "At least we're talking now."

"Only difference is I don't regret it. And he gave up."

"My child, you do not understand," said Jed.

"I'm not your child," said Lyla.

"Oh but you are," said Jed. "For you shall be forced to surrender as he

215

who fancied himself my equal was forced to surrender. He is mine, and you are mine. Don't you see? The Pearl is ours, this world and all that's in it is becoming ours." Jed's eyes widened as he stared through the windshield. His hand tightened its squeeze on Lyla's thigh. "You are but a small yet not unremarkable jewel, torn from the Devil's chest. I shall treasure you, and keep you among my relics."

Lyla looked away as they crunched over broken concrete and shattered glass. *She would not be his bauble*, she told herself. She fought back tears, thinking of what she had learned since graduation. Far less about Psychology and Sociology than about weapons she never thought she'd touch in her life.

What reading she had done haunted her. *Maybe there was something useful about Stockholm Syndrome*, she thought. *Maybe it too, had a place in the hideous painting in which she was now the central figure.*

"Jed, I'm sorry," she said. "I'm confused, is all. This isn't what I expected when I got out of school. It's not what I was prepared for."

"Indeed," he said, raising his eyebrows. "It is true the changes are rapid. Had we more time, I would have given you a few days for reflection. Nevertheless, am I to understand your heart is not fully hardened?"

"No, it's just, I'm no child, I wish… I wish only to be your wife."

The SUV pulled up in front of the factory building. Its glass façade had been shattered during the gun battle, and a pair of sentries in trench coats and slacks stood by the metal grates they'd temporarily erected in its place.

Jed turned off the engine and took her hands in his. "I hope it is true, I hope you have had a change of heart. You know, at first I had a mind I would marry you to Malcolm. I would have married you to him once he was fully repentant and working in my service among the very least of my vassals. Sixty to eighty hours a week laboring at various tasks. Pleasing my liegemen, angels, and half-angels at their whim. And babies, of course, just think—your entire impoverished, very repentant family living in a basement room of this very building. And all because you thought it was *cool* to side with the Devil. Would you have liked that?"

Lyla shook her head.

"Of course not. And so, you have one more chance to be my bride. You will be the least among my wives, answering to them and answering to me. I believe the Lord has smiled upon you, in this change of heart. Now, let the guards bring you upstairs. You will clean up, and prepare for tonight's ceremony."

~*~

Lyla sat on the bed beside the room's barred window. A steady rain fell on the city, blurring its lights, drowning its rooftops in mist and shadow. *The one useful thing about Stockholm Syndrome*, she thought, *was the ability to feign it.*

A knock sounded on the door. She stood up, walked across the room. "Come in," she said, and waited while three new bolts were unlocked. The door opened to reveal Prue, standing with the bag of clothes Lyla had given her.

"I'm sorry, I'm returning your gift. It is no longer customary, as you are no longer First Wife."

"Thank you," said Lyla. She tried to meet Prue's eyes, but the young woman would only look down.

"I am to be First Wife now," she said. "Since you were kind to me, I promise I shall try to be kind in return."

"You've already been as kind as I could ask," said Lyla.

Prue looked up, smiling slightly. "I have but brought you a bag of your own clothes."

"It is all I need," said Lyla.

"Lyla, I'm sorry about this. I'm not sure myself, I mean, often I am not sure this is bearable. No, wait, I didn't mean it that way, I just, it's just... hard to explain."

"There is no need."

"After the ceremony," she said. "When he comes for you, he may be not as he is with others. It is better to be compliant, it will keep him... calmer."

"He can be any way he likes," said Lyla. "Now if you please, you may go."

~*~

Lyla hunched over the plastic bag full of her clothes. After what happened she assumed they put a camera in her cell, so she took off her robe and pulled out some shirts and jeans like she just wanted to wear something normal again. She was careful with her fingers, feeling around toward the bottom until she found the sweatshirt and the thing wrapped within it.

Keeping it cradled in her arms, inside a clump of clothes, she moved over to her bed. She threw the clump against the wall and curled up a moment, as if in despair. When she righted herself, she folded everything up to give an air of resignation to obedience.

Deftly as possible, she pulled the sickle out of the sweatshirt and slipped it beneath her pillow. Plutysium, Mal had called it. She had kept the weapon and secreted it in Prue's gift, betting on the clothes lying unused. Now it had been returned, and the blade that had slain the half-angel on the mountain would next taste her captor's blood. She thought of the desperate fight she and Mal made on their failed run. *I won't get out this time either,* she realized. *They'll come for me and kill me or worse. But not before I see Jed Archer a corpse on this bed.*

As the cloud-hidden sun began to set, she lay down and pretended to sleep. Beneath the pillow her fingers ran across the sickle's curved blade. She had moved out of her parents' house and gone to school in order to make her own way, only to find the lessons thrown back at her were beyond imagining. She had replaced essays with fire, books with blood. Still, as she touched the weapon, she relished a feeling that had finally returned—that this was her *own* time, a time to do something for *herself.* If what she had read was true, and nothing stood but for time's "scythe to mow," she had her own insight to add— that vengeance was indignity's balm, and even unto death held fast its bond.

# About the Author

Carl R. Moore lives in upstate New York with his wife Sarah and two daughters, Maddy and Izzy. His fiction has appeared in Thuglit, Macabre Cadaver, and numerous other magazines and anthologies. When he's not writing or working the night shift, he enjoys listening to heavy metal, plucking steel-string guitar, and walking miles through the woods.

CPSIA information can be obtained
at www.ICGtesting.com
Printed in the USA
BVHW03s2133290818
526022BV00001B/23/P

9 781941 706596